Rev. Dr. Mario DeSean Booker

First Edition

Written by Mario DeSean Booker, Ph.D.
Edited by FaLessia Booker, The Editing Expert. www.falessiabooker.com
Published by: Punny Girl Books
ISBN: 979-8-9999707-4-9

Cover image is AI-generated.

i

Dedication

For every soul who stood at church doors wondering if grace extended far enough to include them.

You traded the club for the sanctuary, only to discover that stained glass can cut deeper than broken bottles. Your past became ammunition in the hands of those who forgot their own journeys through darkness. You believed God's promises of new creation, then watched religious gatekeepers demand receipts for your transformation.

But Acts 10:15 declares truth that shatters every human hierarchy: *"What God hath cleansed, that call not thou common."*

Not what the mothers' board approved. Not what the deacon's council sanctioned. What **God** has cleansed.

Your conversion wasn't committee-approved. Your salvation didn't require pastoral endorsement. Your transformation wasn't contingent on making comfortable people comfortable.

God called you. God claimed you. God cleansed you.

Nobody—absolutely nobody—has authority to call common what He's declared clean.

Your past doesn't disqualify your purpose. Your designer shoes don't diminish your devotion. Your complexity doesn't contradict your calling.

You belong—not because they finally understand you, but because God never stopped calling you His own.

What God hath cleansed, that call not thou common.

Acknowledgments

First, to my Almighty Father—the Author of every story worth telling, the Redeemer of every broken narrative. This book exists because You never stopped writing redemption into my own chapters.

To my wife, FaLessia—my editor, my anchor, my voice of reason during the late-night wrestling matches with characters who refused to cooperate. You kept me focused when plot lines tangled and deadlines loomed. More than that, you listened to every wild idea, every theological question, every moment of doubt about whether this story needed to be told. It did. And you knew it before I did. And no the character in my book is not based on you. Just love your name!

To my family at Hope Outreach Ministries—you taught me what authentic church looks like when grace isn't theoretical and acceptance isn't conditional. You showed me that sanctuaries can heal instead of wound.

To the Booker family—thank you for enduring the creative chaos, for tolerating my absence during those late nights when Trange's voice demanded to be heard, and for supporting a calling that sometimes looks like obsession. Your patience made this possible.

And to every reader who journeyed through the first book of the Tried in Fire series—you gave these characters life beyond my imagination. Your messages, your tears, your testimonies about seeing yourselves in these pages mean more than I can articulate. You reminded me why these stories matter. This is for all of you.

Prologue: When Sanctuaries Become Battlefields

The mahogany doors of Greater Mount Calvary Cathedral swung open with the weight of centuries, revealing a sanctuary where stained glass windows filtered morning light into jeweled patterns across polished pews. The air hung thick with the scent of altar flowers and sanctified secrets—the kind that festered in holy places where human nature wrestled with divine calling.

Trange' Moreau paused at the threshold, her Louboutin heels clicking against marble that had witnessed more confessions than absolutions. She'd conquered boardrooms across three continents, commanded respect from Fortune 500 executives, and built an empire from nothing but ambition and designer armor. Yet standing before this congregation felt more treacherous than any hostile takeover she'd ever navigated.

Lord, if You really called me here, You better have reinforcements ready.

The burgundy Valentino dress that hugged her curves like liquid silk had cost more than most church members earned in a month—a fact that registered immediately on every disapproving face that turned toward her entrance. *Let them stare.* She'd learned long ago that presence was power, and power demanded acknowledgment whether wrapped in couture or covered in condemnation.

But today felt different. Today, something sacred pulsed beneath her cultivated confidence, whispering promises about new beginnings and divine purpose that her analytical mind couldn't quite dismiss. The transformation that had begun in Shaniece's living room during those late-night prayer sessions continued evolving, reshaping not just her schedule but her soul.

As she moved down the center aisle—because Trange' Moreau had never entered anywhere except center stage—she felt the familiar electricity of commanded attention. Men's eyes tracked her movement with appreciation their wives would make them pay for later. Women's gazes dissected everything from her makeup to her handbag, cataloging evidence of worldliness that didn't belong in sacred spaces.

Mother Bernice Williams sat in the third pew like a fortress of righteousness, her silver hair pinned into submission beneath a hat that screamed both tradition and territorial authority. Sixty-three years of faithful service had earned her the unofficial title of Church Mother Supreme, guardian of moral standards and gatekeeper of acceptability. Her lips pursed into a line thinner than communion wafers as she watched this fashion magazine reject pollute their sanctuary with secular success.

"Well, I never," Mother Bernice whispered to Mother Jones beside her, though her voice carried with practiced precision to surrounding pews. "Some folks think church is a fashion show instead of a house of worship."

Mother Jones nodded with sage disapproval, her own ensemble carefully calculated to project both prosperity and propriety—the delicate balance that separated blessed saints from brazen sinners. "Mm-hmm. That dress is tighter than bark on a tree. Who she trying to impress in the Lord's house?"

Three rows back, Deacon Martinez elbowed his neighbor with masculine appreciation that his wife would definitely address during Sunday dinner. "That woman sure knows how to make an entrance."

"Richard!" his wife hissed, her sanctified sensibilities offended by his obvious appreciation. "Eyes front, focus on Jesus."

But even Sister Martinez couldn't deny the magnetism that accompanied Trange's presence—the kind of confidence that didn't apologize for taking up space or demanding attention. It was insufferable. It was intimidating. And it absolutely did not belong in their carefully ordered spiritual ecosystem.

Young Usher Timothy Johnson approached with stuttering steps, his nineteen-year-old composure crumbling under the weight of escorting someone who looked like she'd stepped off a magazine cover. His grandmother had raised him to be respectful to all church visitors, but his teenage hormones hadn't received that memo about spiritual propriety.

"G-good morning, Sister," he managed, his voice cracking like puberty was attacking him mid-sentence. "Welcome to Greater Mount Calvary. Can I ... uh ... help you find a seat?"

Trange's smile could have powered the sound system. "Thank you, baby. Somewhere near the front would be perfect."

Timothy's face flushed crimson as he gestured toward available seating, his movements awkward enough that he nearly knocked over a memorial arrangement. Several older women exchanged knowing glances that communicated volumes about young men being led astray by Jezebel spirits masquerading in designer clothing.

As they processed down the aisle, Mother Jones rose with the determination of someone called to immediate action. Her approach carried the authority of righteous intervention, her face arranged in expressions of Christian concern that barely concealed territorial aggression.

"Excuse me, dear," Mother Jones announced with volume designed for maximum audience, "but you might be more comfortable with this." She produced a crocheted lap scarf from

3

her oversized purse, holding it toward Trange' like a shield against spiritual contamination.

The sanctuary fell silent except for the whispered rustle of programs and barely suppressed gasps. Every eye fixed on this moment of public correction, waiting to see whether the newcomer would accept guidance or reveal her true character through defiance.

Trange's smile never wavered, though something dangerous flickered behind her perfectly applied makeup. "How thoughtful. But this dress is Haute Couture—straight from Milan's fashion week. It's absolutely my Sunday best, and I'm quite comfortable, thank you."

The temperature in the sanctuary seemed to drop ten degrees. Mother Jones's face cycled through multiple shades of mortification before settling on righteous indignation that would fuel gossip circles for months.

"Well," Mother Jones huffed, her voice carrying to the rafters, "I *suppose* some people have different definitions of appropriate."

She turned on her sensible heel with enough force to rattle the pew cushions, her retreat broadcasting disapproval to anyone who might have missed the initial confrontation. Scattered murmurs rippled through the congregation like stones thrown into still water, each whispered comment creating expanding circles of judgment.

Trange' continued to her chosen seat—third row center, naturally—settling into the pew with grace that suggested she'd rather face a boardroom full of hostile executives than this sanctuary full of sanctified sisters. But something deeper than defiance kept her planted in that wooden pew. Something that whispered about divine appointments and purpose beyond human approval.

Lord, I hope You know what You're doing, she prayed silently, because these church folks are already planning my spiritual execution.

The morning sun continued streaming through stained glass windows, casting rainbow patterns across a congregation divided between curiosity and condemnation. In the choir loft, robed singers prepared to lift voices in harmony while hearts harbored discord. At the altar, fresh flowers adorned a space where grace was preached but rarely practiced when outsiders dared to seek sanctuary.

And in the third pew, a woman who'd spent decades armoring herself against rejection felt something she hadn't experienced since childhood—the vulnerable hope that maybe, finally, she'd found where she belonged.

The organ's opening notes filled the cathedral with sacred sound, but underneath the melody, battle lines were already being drawn. This wasn't just Sunday morning worship—this was the beginning of a war between divine calling and human gatekeeping, between grace and judgment, between the woman God was reshaping and the church that couldn't see past her packaging.

What happened next would determine whether Greater Mount Calvary Cathedral would become her spiritual home or her spiritual battlefield.

The music swelled, voices joined in tentative harmony, and Trange' Moreau prepared to discover whether faith could survive first contact with the faithful.

At sixty-two, Bishop Marcus Howard commanded respect through presence rather than volume. His salt-and-pepper beard framed a face that had witnessed both triumph and tragedy, while his eyes held the kind of compassion that made hardened sinners weep and cynical saints remember why they'd first answered the altar call. When he opened his Bible, the sanctuary fell silent with anticipation born of countless Sundays when his words had pierced hearts and changed lives.

"Church," Bishop Howard began, his voice carrying the authority of someone who'd earned his title through service rather than politics, "I want to talk to you today about forgiveness. Real forgiveness. The kind that costs everything and changes everything."

He opened to Ephesians 4:32, his finger tracing words that seemed written specifically for this moment. *"Be kind and compassionate to one another, forgiving each other, just as in Christ God forgave you."*

Trange' felt the words strike her chest like arrows finding their target. Every syllable seemed crafted for her ears, addressing wounds she'd carried and walls she'd built, speaking to places in her heart that still bled from judgments both deserved and undeserved.

"But let me take you to Luke chapter 6, verse 37," Bishop Howard continued, his voice gaining momentum like thunder rolling across summer skies. *"Judge not, and you will not be judged. Condemn not, and you will not be condemned. Forgive, and you will be forgiven."*

Judge not. The words echoed through chambers of her memory where voices still whispered accusations—foster families who'd labeled her "difficult," teachers who'd written her off as "troubled," business associates who'd dismissed her as "too ambitious," lovers who'd reduced her to "high maintenance."

Even the women in this very sanctuary who'd sized her up and found her wanting before she'd spoken a single word.

Her throat tightened as Bishop Howard's sermon gained power, his voice painting pictures of divine mercy that transcended human limitations. She thought about where she'd been— boardrooms filled with cutthroat competition, penthouse parties where souls were currency, relationships where love was leverage. The old Trange' would have been anywhere else on a Sunday morning, probably nursing a hangover while planning her next conquest.

But something had shifted in her spirit. Those late-night prayer sessions with Shaniece had awakened hunger for something her success couldn't satisfy. The God who'd seemed distant and disapproving suddenly felt present and pursuing, offering transformation that money couldn't buy and status couldn't secure.

"I lift up mine eyes unto the hills, from whence cometh my help," Bishop Howard declared, his voice rising with conviction. "My help cometh from the Lord, which made Heaven and earth!"

Tears began gathering in Trange's eyes like storm clouds promising cleansing rain. A whisper escaped her lips— "Hallelujah"—so soft she barely recognized her own voice.

"Hallelujah," she repeated, louder this time, the word carrying weight she'd never given it before.

Something electric moved through her spirit, something that had nothing to do with performance or pretense. Before rational thought could intervene, she was on her feet, her voice lifting in praise that surprised even her with its authenticity.

"HALLELUJAH! HALLELUJAH!"

The congregation erupted. Sister Williams began shouting from the fifth pew. Deacon Martinez raised holy hands while his wife forgot her earlier criticism and caught the spirit herself. The sanctuary transformed into a celebration of divine presence that transcended denominational protocol and social propriety.

But even in her moment of surrender, Trange' caught the disapproving stares, the whispered criticisms that cut through spiritual atmosphere like knives through silk.

"She don't need to be jumping up like that in that dress," Mother Jones hissed to her neighbor.

"Some people just do things for attention," another voice added with righteous disdain.

"All them parts just moving and jumping around in church ain't right," Mother Bernice declared loud enough to shame a saint.

But Trange' couldn't stop herself. Something had broken loose in her spirit—years of protective armor cracking under divine pressure, walls crumbling before love she'd never experienced. She could have been anywhere in the world. Paris, Milan, Dubai—destinations where her passport held regular stamps and her presence commanded automatic respect. But she wanted to be here, in this house of the Lord, despite the judgment radiating from sanctified sisters who'd appointed themselves as gatekeepers of grace.

When Bishop Howard announced he was opening the doors of the church, Trange' didn't hesitate. His words ignited something deeper than decision—this was divine compulsion, spiritual magnetism that pulled her from the safety of her pew toward an altar that promised transformation.

She felt the Holy Spirit moving on her in ways she'd never experienced. There had been moments before when God's presence seemed tangible—quiet times when she'd sensed something greater than herself, business deals when divine favor seemed evident, crisis moments when protection felt supernatural. But this was different. This was the precipice of rebirth, the threshold between who she'd been and who God intended her to become.

Bishop Howard's hand, warm with anointing oil, pressed against her forehead with gentle authority. His eyes held the kind of compassion that made pretense impossible and walls unnecessary.

"Do you give your life to God?" he asked, his voice thick with emotion that suggested he recognized the magnitude of this moment.

"Absolutely," Trange' replied, the word erupting from depths she didn't know existed. "Yes, Sir. Yes, Lord. YES!"

The church exploded in celebration. Voices lifted in harmonies that seemed to reach Heaven itself. Hands clapped rhythms that matched heartbeats quickened by divine encounter. Even the disapproving mothers rose to their feet, though their body language radiated reluctant participation rather than genuine joy.

Bishop Howard stepped back, tears streaming down his face as he raised trembling hands toward Heaven. "Glory to God! GLORY TO GOD!" He turned to address the congregation with authority that silenced even the musicians. "Church, I want to introduce you to our newest sister. Welcome Sister Trange' Moreau to the family of God!"

Peace flooded through Trange' like warm honey, sweetness she'd never tasted despite sampling life's finest offerings. For the first time in decades, she felt unconditionally loved, completely accepted, divinely welcomed. The twisted expressions from certain church mothers couldn't diminish this joy, couldn't taint this sacred moment of belonging.

Bishop Howard began singing—"Let the church say amen"— his voice cracking with emotion as the congregation joined in celebration that shook the cathedral's foundations.

But then something shifted.

Bishop Howard's eyes glazed over, not with Holy Ghost anointing but with something alarming. His expression transformed from spiritual ecstasy to physical distress, his face contorting as his hand pressed against his chest.

"Bishop?" someone called from the front pew.

He staggered backward, his other hand reaching for the pulpit that suddenly seemed miles away. Ushers rushed forward as he collapsed, his body hitting the altar with a sound that silenced every voice in the sanctuary.

"OH MY GOD, BISHOP!" Church Nurse Patricia Williams rushed toward the altar, her medical training overriding shock. Her hands found his wrist, then his neck, searching for vital signs that weren't there.

"Someone call an ambulance!" Her voice carried panic that infected the entire congregation. **"He doesn't have a pulse! Get them here NOW!"**

Chaos erupted. Screams echoed off cathedral walls. Members scattered like startled birds while others pressed forward trying to help. The celebration of new life had transformed into potential vigil for death, joy replaced by terror in the span of heartbeats.

Trange' stepped backward, horror freezing her in place. This couldn't be happening. Not now. Not during her moment of divine encounter.

But then Mother Bernice Williams rose from her pew like an avenging angel, her voice cutting through chaos with accusation sharp enough to draw blood.

"I KNEW IT!" she declared, her finger pointing directly at Trange' with righteous fury. "This heathen, this harlot—**SHE KILLED OUR PASTOR!** The moment this Jezebel stepped foot in God's house, the devil followed her in!"

Gasps echoed through the sanctuary like shock waves. Every eye turned toward Trange' ', who stood frozen at the altar where moments before she'd experienced divine acceptance. Ambulance sirens screamed in the distance while whispers spread through the congregation like wildfire.

"Coincidence? I think not!"

"Never seen anything like this!"

"What kind of spirit did she bring in here?"

Trange' remained motionless, her designer dress now feeling like scarlet letter, her moment of spiritual triumph transformed into public accusation. Members scattered toward exits while others formed prayer circles, but she stood alone in the center of chaos, isolated by suspicion and condemned by timing she couldn't control.

Confusion flooded her mind. Betrayal pierced her heart. The welcome she'd felt moments before evaporated like morning mist, replaced by the familiar sting of rejection dressed in religious language.

So this is my first day as a Christian, huh? she thought, tears mixing with makeup as her new beginning threatened to become another ending.

The sanctuary that had promised sanctuary had become a battlefield, and Trange' Moreau found herself standing at ground zero, wondering if faith could survive its first encounter with the faithful.

Chapter 1: Grief and Conspiracy

FaLessia Shaw cradled her third cup of coffee, watching steam rise in the soft morning light filtering through her office windows. The calendar on her desk read Wednesday, October 9th—three days since Sunday's catastrophe had transformed a celebration into chaos, since the sanctuary witnessed both spiritual birth and physical death.

Her office reflected her personality—efficient but warm. Framed photos of her nonprofit's success stories lined one wall, while her master's degrees hung beside them. The mahogany desk that had belonged to her father held stacks of church business, but this morning, none of it captured her focus.

The hospital. Sunday evening. She kept returning there in her mind, unable to escape the loop of memory.

Flashback: Sunday Evening - The Hospital Horror

FaLessia had followed the ambulance to Ochsner Medical Center, prayers tumbling from her lips in fragments. Half the congregation had already assembled in the waiting room—some praying, others gossiping, creating a chaotic mixture of spiritual warfare and social spectacle.

First Lady Clarice Howard had been unreachable, spending Sunday afternoon with her sister in Baton Rouge. FaLessia made the call that shattered Clarice's world.

"What do you mean *collapsed*? Marcus was fine this morning!"

Clarice made the ninety-minute drive in sixty-five minutes, arriving like a force of nature—Sunday best rumpled, mascara already streaking, hair escaped from its careful arrangement.

FaLessia caught her as grief threatened to buckle her knees. "Where is he? I need to see him NOW!"

Two hours stretched into four. The night deepened while hope thinned. Congregation members drifted between waiting room and chapel, their vigil sustained by vending machine coffee and desperate faith.

Dr. Rajesh Kumar emerged, his expression carrying the news no physician wanted to deliver.

"Mrs. Howard, I'm so very sorry. Your husband suffered a massive myocardial infarction. The damage was too extensive. We did everything we could."

Clarice's scream shattered the sterile atmosphere. She collapsed into FaLessia's arms, sobs tearing pieces from her soul.

"NO, NO, NO! NOT MARCUS! GOD, PLEASE, NO!"

The waiting room erupted—women wailing, men standing in shocked silence, prayers rising in desperate chorus. FaLessia held Clarice as the First Lady's body shook with grief that wouldn't be contained or comforted.

But even in that moment of collective mourning, FaLessia heard Mother Bernice Williams's voice cutting through the chaos, speaking to the cluster of church mothers surrounding her: "This is what happens when you let the wrong spirits into God's house."

The words struck like a slap. FaLessia's head snapped up, making eye contact with Mother Bernice across the waiting room. The older woman's expression held no apology, no recognition that such judgment amid tragedy violated every principle of Christian compassion.

Mother Eartha Jones stood beside her, nodding in agreement. But something else flickered across Mother Jones's face— something that didn't quite match her stern disapproval.

FaLessia filed the observation away, too overwhelmed by Clarice's grief to process it fully.

Wednesday Morning - Present

A knock on her office door pulled FaLessia back to the present. Church secretary Vivian Parker appeared in the doorway, her expression sympathetic.

"The joint board meeting starts in thirty minutes."

"Thank you, Vivian." FaLessia forced a smile that felt like lifting weights with facial muscles.

But she wasn't ready—not for navigating grief while managing church politics, not for protecting Bishop Howard's progressive vision from those who'd opposed it, not for supporting Trange' Moreau, the woman blamed for circumstances beyond anyone's control.

Bishop Howard had been more than her spiritual father—he'd been her actual father's closest friend, stepping in when cancer claimed David Shaw too early. When her brother Dalvin spiraled into the darkness that destroyed his marriage and landed him in federal prison, Bishop Howard had tried desperately to pull him back from that edge.

And now he's gone too.

FaLessia gathered her materials for the meeting, trying to focus on practical matters rather than the grief threatening to swallow her whole. The administrative corridor of Greater Mount Calvary Cathedral blended traditional elegance with contemporary efficiency. Polished marble floors reflected light from the chandeliers, while oil paintings of biblical scenes alternated with photographs documenting the church's seventy-five-year history.

As she passed the main boardroom, voices stopped her mid-stride. The meeting wasn't supposed to start for another twenty-five minutes, yet angry voices filtered through the heavy oak doors.

She recognized them immediately. Mother Bernice Williams and Mother Eartha Jones—the twin engines of church politics who had opposed Bishop Howard's progressive agenda at every turn.

Professional ethics warred with practical necessity. Eavesdropping violated her sense of propriety, but as a trustee with fiduciary responsibility to the church, could she ignore a potential conspiracy against the institution she'd sworn to protect?

FaLessia positioned herself just around the corner from the boardroom, close enough to hear clearly but hidden from view should anyone exit unexpectedly. She pulled out her phone, pretending to review emails in case someone discovered her, creating plausible deniability for her presence in the hallway.

The Conspiracy Unfolds

Through the partially open door, she heard Mother Bernice Williams addressing the assembled deacons and mothers. At seventy-one and rail-thin, Mother Bernice commanded rooms with the authority of someone who'd spent thirty-five years teaching high school students. She'd cultivated a carefully crafted prudishness that masked what FaLessia privately termed "hellacious determination."

Beside her sat Mother Eartha Jones—voluptuous and honey-complexioned, a naturally beautiful woman whose bone structure and carriage suggested the modeling career that Louisiana's racism had probably prevented. At sixty-eight, she still turned heads, though she cultivated a quiet reserve that fooled those who didn't know her well.

"Before the busybodies arrive," Mother Jones commanded, her voice carrying the steel beneath her usual composure, "we need to get all our business in order."

Deacon Harold Williams—Mother Bernice's brother—shifted uncomfortably in his chair. "What business do we need to take care of without the trustees?"

FaLessia's attention sharpened. They were deliberately excluding the trustees from preliminary discussions—a violation of the church's collaborative governance model.

Mother Bernice fixed her younger brother with a look that had terrorized students for three decades. "Harold, our dear bishop died at the hands of some trollop dressed like she was working Bourbon Street on a Saturday night. We need to keep people like her out of God's House. And we need to be the ones to select who our next bishop is going to be."

The accusation sent anger flashing through FaLessia's chest. Trange' Moreau hadn't caused Bishop Howard's death—the man had suffered from hypertension for years, had ignored his doctor's warnings about stress, had refused to take his medication consistently. But grief and fear were transforming medical reality into spiritual scapegoating.

Mother Bernice stood dramatically, her slight frame casting a disproportionate shadow. "The trustees are always trying to run the show. But we are the deacons and the mothers—WE know the people. We understand their spiritual needs. This is OUR church, and it's time we took it back."

Her voice rose with theatrical fervor that would have been impressive if it weren't so manipulative. "We need to come together as a united front. Does anybody else agree with me?"

The room fell silent as board members exchanged glances. Then slowly, murmurs started—agreements camouflaged as spiritual concern rippling through the assembled leadership.

"Bishop Howard was a good man," Deacon Joe Willie Thompson ventured, his tone suggesting an approaching "but" that would undermine the compliment. "But some of his decisions made folks uncomfortable. Made them question whether we were holding fast to biblical standards."

"*Uncomfortable?*" Mother Jones seized the opening like a prosecutor spotting weakness in a witness. "He nearly tore this church apart with his progressive agenda. It started when he welcomed back Sister Patricia Henderson after she got pregnant out of wedlock. No public repentance, no restoration process— just immediate reinstatement to full fellowship."

FaLessia remembered that situation differently. Patricia had been a teenage girl seduced by an adult youth pastor. Bishop Howard had protected her, held the predator accountable, and refused to compound trauma with public humiliation. But apparently, that compassion had been filed away as evidence of theological compromise.

"And then that sermon," Mother Bernice added, her voice dripping with disapproval. "When he said *gay* people are welcome here. That they deserve access to Christ *just like the rest of us*. As if sexual immorality could be baptized into righteousness through pretty words about inclusion."

FaLessia's stomach churned as she listened to theology being twisted to serve prejudice. Bishop Howard had preached grace without compromising scripture—but these mothers couldn't distinguish between welcoming sinners (which Jesus commanded) and endorsing sin (which He never did).

"We sent him a letter," Mother Jones continued, her voice taking on the edge of someone recounting grievances they'd been nursing for months. "Jointly signed by both boards, outlining our disbelief and concern. We advised him we would take a vote of no confidence if he continued down this path."

"Per the church bylaws," Mother Bernice interrupted, slipping into teacher mode as she explained church governance, "it takes a majority of both the Deacon Board and the Mother Board, plus two trustees, to issue a vote of no confidence against sitting pastoral leadership."

Her voice hardened with barely concealed rage. "We would have secured one trustee—my daughter Patricia Jones would have voted with us. But FaLessia Shaw led the other trustees in supporting Bishop Howard's progressive agenda. She convinced them that 'grace' meant abandoning biblical standards."

"Although all three boards are supposedly equal under our bylaws," Mother Jones added, "the trustees hold the purse strings. They control the finances, approve all major expenditures, and ultimately have veto power over any significant church decision. That situation has enraged us for far too long."

FaLessia noted the shift in Mother Jones's tone—the word "enraged" carrying personal emotion that seemed to exceed mere theological disagreement. There was something deeper here, something more visceral than church politics usually generated.

Deacon Harold Williams tried again, his voice carrying the uncertainty of someone who knew he was about to be overruled but felt compelled to object anyway. "But that beautiful young lady on Sunday didn't do anything wrong. She was just answering an altar call, same as hundreds of people have done over the years—"

"Beautiful young lady?" Mother Jones's voice could cut glass, and FaLessia heard her chair scrape against the floor as she stood. "This is exactly the problem. The deacons are caught up in their flesh. Some scantily clad woman comes in here wearing a dress that costs more than most people's mortgage payment, and suddenly y'all don't know what a virtuous woman looks like anymore?"

Through the crack in the door, FaLessia watched Mother Jones pace, her movements agitated in a way that seemed excessive for the subject matter. Something about this particular argument was touching a nerve that went beyond the immediate situation.

Deacon Joel Hearns—a gentlemanly scholar with a PhD in theology from Emory University—rose to his feet with the dignity of someone preparing to take a stand. "Excuse me, Mother Jones. I won't allow you to question my relationship with God or suggest that my defense of basic Christian compassion somehow indicates moral compromise."

FaLessia felt a surge of hope. Hearns carried significant influence among the deacons. If he pushed back against this conspiracy, others might follow.

But Mother Jones turned to face him, and something in her expression made FaLessia lean forward, trying to see more clearly through the narrow opening.

"Let me be very clear, Deacon Hearns," Mother Jones said, her voice dropping to a tone that carried layers of meaning FaLessia couldn't quite decode. "You can't possibly have a genuine relationship with God and support unrighteousness. If that statement offends you, perhaps you should take it up with God—because that's His Word, not mine."

The words themselves were standard religious rhetoric, the kind of thing FaLessia had heard countless times. But the way Mother Jones delivered them, the way her eyes held Hearns's gaze, suggested subtext that had nothing to do with theology.

Hearns opened his mouth to respond, but something passed between them—a look that lasted perhaps two seconds but contained volumes of unspoken communication. His face changed, color rising in his cheeks, and he slowly lowered himself back into his seat without saying another word.

What was that? FaLessia's mind raced, trying to decode what she'd just witnessed. The look Mother Jones had given Hearns wasn't merely disapproval or spiritual correction. It carried intimacy, familiarity, even a hint of playfulness that seemed wildly inappropriate given the context.

Mother Jones brushed her hands together with a gesture of finality. "As you can see, there are many empty seats at this table. Anyone who finds our commitment to biblical standards too restrictive is welcome to find somewhere else to exercise their 'progressive' theology."

Hearns's wife, Mother Sandra Hearns, started to rise in her husband's defense, but she locked eyes with Mother Bernice Williams across the table. The unspoken warning was clear: *Sit down, or you'll be next.*

Mother Sandra slowly lowered herself back into her chair, but her hand found her husband's under the table, squeezing it in silent support.

This is more than church politics, FaLessia realized, watching the complex dynamics play out. There are personal relationships, hidden agendas, and power plays happening beneath the surface of theological disagreement.

"Can we all just take the temperature down a bit?" Mother Delilah Chain raised placating hands, her voice carrying the exhaustion of someone who'd mediated too many church conflicts. "Can we at least agree that we all want what's best for the church? That we want Greater Mount Calvary to return to the traditional values that made us strong?"

Murmurs of agreement rippled through the room—safer ground than the personal confrontation that had just occurred.

"We need biblical preaching," Deacon Thompson offered, his voice gaining confidence as the conversation moved back to familiar territory. "No more of this progressive Christianity that tries to make the gospel palatable to modern sensibilities."

"Amen to that!" Mother Jones declared. "And we need to restore proper Sunday attire. No more of these worldly fashions that distract from worship."

"We should implement mandatory membership classes," Deacon Williams suggested, apparently emboldened by his wife's assertiveness. "No more of Bishop Howard's open-door policy that let anyone walk in off the street without proper vetting."

"These are all excellent ideas," Mother Bernice declared, nodding approval at each suggestion. "But we need to address the immediate threat. We need to deal with Miss Triangle Moreau who brought a spirit of death with her on Sunday."

FaLessia's hands clenched around her phone. The casual accusation of spiritual murder, delivered with the same tone one might use to discuss weather patterns, revealed the depth of malice driving this conspiracy.

"I propose we draft a letter," Mother Jones suggested, settling back into her chair with the satisfied expression of someone whose plan was coming together. "We'll request—politely but firmly—that she not return to Greater Mount Calvary. We'll explain that her presence creates spiritual disruption and suggest that she might be more comfortable at a church whose ... culture ... is more aligned with her lifestyle."

The coded language wasn't subtle. "Lifestyle" was church-speak for, "we think you're sinful but we're too polite to say it directly." And "more comfortable elsewhere" meant, "we don't want your kind here."

Deacon Joel Hearns cleared his throat, and FaLessia saw him sit up straighter, apparently preparing to object despite his earlier retreat. But when he looked at Mother Jones, something flickered across both their faces that made FaLessia's breath catch.

Mother Jones's expression softened almost imperceptibly, her eyes holding his with an intimacy that had nothing to do with church governance. For just a moment, the stern church mother disappeared, replaced by something younger, more vulnerable, almost ... tender.

Hearns's response was equally revealing. His face flushed, but not with anger or embarrassment about church politics. His discomfort seemed more personal, more complicated, layered with emotions that didn't belong in a board meeting.

Oh my God.

The realization hit FaLessia like a physical blow. Mother Eartha Jones—divorced for twenty years, vocally disdainful of men in general, fierce defender of traditional morality and biblical standards—was involved with *married* Deacon Joel Hearns.

This is leverage, FaLessia thought, her strategic mind already calculating implications. *Information that could protect Trange' if these mothers escalate their attack.*

23

But even as the thought formed, something in her spirit recoiled. Using someone's personal sin as political ammunition felt like descending to their level, fighting fire with fire in ways that would leave everyone burned.

Hearns adjusted his tie and settled back into his chair without speaking, apparently deciding that silence was safer than confrontation. His wife squeezed his hand again, but her expression suggested she'd noticed the exchange too—and questions would follow later.

Mother Bernice Williams had also caught the look between Mother Jones and Deacon Hearns. The two women locked eyes in what FaLessia mentally termed an "eye-sation"—an entire conversation conducted through glances, each woman acknowledging what the other knew without speaking a word.

Mother Bernice's slight smirk: I see what you're doing. I know your secret.

Mother Jones's return gaze: Yes, you know. And you're going to keep it to yourself because you need me for this campaign.

The unspoken negotiation complete, Mother Bernice turned back to address the room. "Well then, it seems we have an agreement. We'll draft a letter to Miss Moreau requesting she find a more suitable congregation. We'll establish committees to restore traditional values, implement proper membership vetting, and begin the search for pastoral leadership who will honor our guidance rather than fight against it."

"And the trustees?" someone asked from the back of the room.

"The trustees," Mother Jones replied with cold satisfaction, "are about to discover that their financial control doesn't translate to spiritual authority. This is our church. We're the ones who've been here through generations, who've buried our mothers and fathers in the church cemetery, who've given our lives to this ministry. We're not going to let some progressive trustees destroy everything we've built just because they control the bank account."

FaLessia had heard enough. She needed to warn the other trustees, coordinate a response, and prevent this conspiracy from solidifying before they had a chance to counteract it.

She began backing away carefully, trying to maintain silence while retreating from her hiding place. But as she turned to leave, she nearly collided with Trustee Patricia Jones—Mother Eartha's daughter—who had apparently materialized from the shadows like a ghost.

"Well, Trustee Shaw," Patricia announced in a voice deliberately loud enough to carry into the boardroom, "why are you lurking in the hallways like a thief in the night?"

FaLessia froze, caught. "Pat, I was just—"

But Patricia strode past her and threw open the boardroom doors with theatrical force. "Seems like y'all have a guest who was eavesdropping on your private meeting. Come on in, FaLessia. Don't be shy."

Every eye in the room turned toward where FaLessia stood exposed in the hallway. Mother Bernice's expression mixed triumph with disapproval. Mother Jones's face was harder to read—anger, certainly, but also something that might have been relief that the confrontation was finally in the open.

"Well," Mother Jones said with icy composure, "if you wanted to participate in this conversation, you should have just come in through the front door like civilized people do."

FaLessia straightened her spine, channeling every ounce of her father's dignity and her own hard-won authority. "I'll be back for the official joint board meeting—which is scheduled to begin in twenty minutes, not now. We still have time before the meeting officially starts."

She turned and walked away with as much dignity as circumstances allowed, her mind already racing ahead to strategy and countermoves.

Behind her, she heard Mother Bernice's voice: "Well, now the trustees know what we're planning. Patricia, I thought you said FaLessia was meeting with donors this morning?"

"I thought she was," Patricia replied, her voice carrying confusion. "She must have finished early."

FaLessia didn't slow down, didn't look back. She needed to reach her office, needed to call the other trustees, needed to prevent this coup before it solidified into irreversible action.

The battle lines had been drawn.

War was coming to the sanctuary.

And FaLessia Shaw had no intention of surrendering without a fight.

Chapter 2: Strategic Warfare and Hidden Hearts

Back in her office, FaLessia grabbed her phone and immediately called April Richardson—the corporate attorney whose sharp legal mind had saved the church from several potential disasters over the years.

"Girl, where are you at?"

"Just pulling into the parking lot. Why? What's going on?"

"These demons are trying to orchestrate a coup d'état. They want to install a pastor they can control and usurp the trustees' authority over church governance."

FaLessia provided a rapid-fire summary of everything she'd overheard—the conspiracy to reverse Bishop Howard's policies, the letter targeting Trange' Moreau, the plan to seize control of pastoral succession, and the barely concealed affair between Mother Jones and Hearns that could serve as leverage if necessary.

April was quiet for a moment, processing. "So we're walking into a setup meeting where they've already decided everything, and they're just going through the motions of democratic governance?"

"Exactly. And they don't care that I overheard because they think they have the votes to override us anyway."

"Here's what we do," April said, her voice taking on the tactical precision that made her formidable in courtrooms. "I'll call the other trustees right now. Tell them not to show up for this so-called joint meeting. Let's have our own emergency session to discuss these shenanigans and develop a proper response."

"A joint session can't happen without a quorum," FaLessia said, relief flooding through her. "The bylaws require representatives from all three boards."

"Right. So we deny them quorum, which means no official decisions can be made today. That buys us time to develop a strategy and coordinate with First Lady Clarice."

FaLessia gathered her belongings quickly, already planning her exit. She stopped at Vivian Parker's desk on her way out.

"Vivian, please inform the Deacon Board and the Mother Board that they will lack the necessary quorum for today's joint meeting. The trustees will not be attending and will need to reschedule for a time when all boards can participate in good faith."

Vivian's eyes widened slightly—she'd worked at the church long enough to recognize political warfare when she saw it. "Yes ma'am. Should I suggest an alternative date?"

"Tell them the trustees will be in touch once we've reviewed our calendars. And Vivian? Everything discussed in that boardroom this morning was supposed to be private. If anyone asks what you heard or observed, you didn't hear anything. Understood?"

"Understood." Vivian nodded, her expression suggesting she'd been navigating church politics long enough to know when discretion was wisdom rather than deception.

FaLessia walked out of the building with her head high, already planning the strategy session that would protect Bishop Howard's legacy and prevent these church mothers from transforming Greater Mount Calvary into an exclusive club for people who'd already mastered the art of looking sanctified.

The battle lines had been drawn.

War was coming to the sanctuary.

And FaLessia Shaw had no intention of surrendering without a fight.

Emergency Trustee Session

Three hours later, FaLessia sat in an emergency trustee meeting convened at April Richardson's law office rather than church property. The decision to meet off-site had been strategic—no risk of eavesdropping, no church mothers "accidentally" walking past conference rooms, complete privacy to plan their countermoves.

Coffee cups multiplied across the conference table as legal pads filled with notes. Five trustees sat in various states of professional dress—some had come directly from work; others had changed after FaLessia's urgent calls pulled them from their Wednesday routines.

April Richardson commanded the head of the table, her laptop open to the church bylaws document that would govern whatever came next. At forty-three, she'd built a successful corporate law practice while maintaining pro bono representation for Greater Mount Calvary—partly from genuine faith commitment, partly because church politics provided intellectual challenges that corporate contracts rarely offered.

"We need to move quickly," April advised, her fingers flying across her keyboard as she pulled up relevant sections of the bylaws. "Bishop Howard's death creates a power vacuum. Whoever controls the narrative during this transition period shapes the church's future for the next generation."

"The bylaws require a three-month interim period before we can begin the pastoral search process," FaLessia noted, referencing the document she'd practically memorized over her years as trustee. "During that time, the trustees have increased authority over operational decisions while the boards jointly handle pastoral duties."

"Which Mother Bernice and Mother Jones clearly understand," April replied, highlighting several passages on her screen. "That's why they're moving to consolidate power now—before the bylaws give you formal authority to override them."

Trustee Marcus Webb—a retired judge whose legal expertise rivaled April's—cleared his throat with the gravity of someone about to render judgment. "We need to address this proposed letter about Sister Moreau immediately. We cannot allow the church leadership to officially exclude someone who came seeking salvation. That's not just morally wrong—it's potentially illegal."

His fingers steepled in the gesture he'd used countless times on the bench. "If they send that letter on church letterhead, using their official positions to intimidate someone from exercising their First Amendment right to worship, we're opening ourselves to civil rights litigation that could bankrupt this institution."

"Agreed," FaLessia said firmly, relief flooding through her that someone else recognized the legal danger. "Any communication to Sister Moreau must come through official channels with full trustee approval. We need to establish that immediately, before they draft something we'll spend years defending in court."

"But we need to be smart about how we frame this," April cautioned, her attorney's instinct for strategy evident in her careful word choice. "If we come across as protecting her out of personal loyalty or political alignment, it undermines our position. This has to be about governance, church law, and our fiduciary responsibility to protect the institution from legal liability."

Trustee Sandra Mitchell—a CPA who managed the church's finances with precision that bordered on obsessive—leaned forward with the practical concern that numbers people always brought to theoretical discussions. "What about the financial implications? If the Deacon and Mother Boards convince enough members that we're compromising biblical standards, we could see significant drops in tithing. People vote with their wallets."

"Then we need to control the message," April replied. "Frame this as protecting the church's integrity and Bishop Howard's legacy rather than abandoning traditional values."

"What if we propose a formal reconciliation process?" FaLessia suggested, the idea crystallizing as she spoke. "Something that brings all parties together for mediated conversation about what happened Sunday. It positions us as reasonable leaders seeking healing rather than confrontation, while preventing their witch hunt from gaining momentum."

"Brilliant," Marcus declared, already making notes on his legal pad. "It accomplishes multiple objectives simultaneously—delays their attack on Sister Moreau, demonstrates our commitment to due process, and creates a paper trail showing we acted in good faith if this ends up in litigation."

April's fingers flew across her keyboard. "I can draft a formal proposal for a Reconciliation and Healing Committee. We'll cite biblical principles of conflict resolution—Matthew 18 and all that—which makes it harder for them to object without looking spiritually deficient. And we'll structure it so that trustees have equal representation with the other boards, preventing them from stacking the committee with their allies."

"We also need to address the pastoral succession issue," Trustee David Chen interjected, his background in corporate

31

governance making him particularly sensitive to power transitions. "They want to control who we call as the next bishop. If we let them frame the search criteria around 'traditional values' and 'biblical standards,' they'll use those code words to exclude any candidate who doesn't fit their narrow theological box."

"The bylaws give the trustees final approval over pastoral candidates," April noted, pulling up another section of the document. "Even if the other boards recommend someone, we can veto the selection if we have legitimate concerns about their qualifications or fit."

FaLessia felt strategy coalescing like pieces of a puzzle sliding into place. "So our immediate action items are: draft the reconciliation committee proposal, establish trustee oversight for all communications regarding Sister Moreau, and begin developing pastoral search criteria that honor Bishop Howard's vision while being legally defensible."

"And we need to meet with First Lady Clarice," Marcus added. "The bylaws give her significant informal influence during the transition period. If she's on our side, it strengthens our position considerably."

The meeting continued for another ninety minutes, strategies emerging from the collision of legal expertise, financial pragmatism, and genuine spiritual concern. By the time they concluded, the trustees had developed a comprehensive response that would protect the church's integrity while honoring Bishop Howard's progressive legacy.

As FaLessia gathered her materials to leave, her phone buzzed with a text from Shaniece:

HEARD ABOUT SUNDAY. TRANGE' CALLED ME DEVASTATED. THANK YOU FOR STANDING WITH HER WHEN

OTHERS WERE THROWING STONES. THAT'S WHAT JESUS WOULD ACTUALLY DO.

She smiled, responding quickly:

YOUR SISTER IS STRONGER THAN SHE KNOWS. SHE'S ABOUT TO TEACH THESE CHURCH MOTHERS THAT MADAME MOREAU DOESN'T BACK DOWN FROM BULLIES—EVEN ONES CARRYING BIBLES. THIS IS GOING TO BE INTERESTING.

April walked her to the door, lowering her voice so the others couldn't hear. "FaLessia, I need to ask something sensitive. This information you have about Mother Jones and Hearns—are you certain? Because if we deploy that as leverage and we're wrong, it could destroy everything we're trying to build."

FaLessia considered the question carefully. "I'm not certain about the exact nature of their relationship. But I know what I saw—and more importantly, I know what Mother Bernice saw. There's something there that gives Mother Bernice power over Mother Jones. Whether it's an affair or something else, it's real enough that Mother Jones backed down when confronted."

"Then we keep it in reserve," April decided. "Nuclear option only—if they escalate to the point where we need to neutralize Mother Jones's influence completely. But we don't lead with it."

"Agreed. I don't want to fight their ugliness with more ugliness. We should be better than that."

April squeezed her shoulder. "We will be. But it's good to know we have options if things get worse."

Meanwhile, in the Shadows

In her comfortable Gentilly home—a 1950s ranch-style house that had belonged to her parents and now served as headquarters for her increasingly isolated existence—Mother

Bernice Williams sat at her dining room table with Mother Eartha Jones, their heads bent over documents scattered across the polished wood surface.

The dining room reflected a lifetime of church service and middle-class respectability: China cabinet displaying formal dishes that only emerged for special occasions, family photos documenting generations of Williams family members, a cross-stitched scripture sampler proclaiming "As for me and my house, we will serve the Lord." Everything orderly, everything proper, everything carefully arranged to project the image of a godly woman living a righteous life.

But the documents they were reviewing revealed a less righteous agenda.

"The letter needs to be perfect," Bernice declared, reviewing their third draft with the red pen she'd used to mark student papers for thirty-five years. "Strong enough to make our position absolutely clear, but careful enough that the trustees can't claim we violated bylaws or exposed the church to legal liability."

Eartha adjusted her reading glasses—a recent concession to aging that she resented more than she cared to admit—and studied the document with critical eyes. "What about this paragraph: 'While Greater Mount Calvary welcomes all who seek Christ, we must maintain standards of behavior and dress that honor God. Your attendance on Sunday created spiritual disruption that culminated in tragic loss. We believe it would be in everyone's best interest if you explored other congregations.'"

"Too direct," Bernice cautioned, her teacher's instinct for identifying problematic phrasing kicking in immediately. "We can't explicitly blame her for his death—that opens us to defamation lawsuits. But we can suggest correlation without claiming causation."

She pulled out her red pen and began editing with practiced efficiency. "What if we say: 'Recent events have demonstrated the importance of ensuring all new members share our commitment to traditional values and modest presentation. After prayerful consideration, leadership feels it would be in everyone's best interest if you explored congregations whose culture and expectations might be more aligned with your lifestyle and preferences.'"

Eartha read it over twice, nodding slowly. "Perfect. We're not banning her—we're expressing concern for her comfort level. We're suggesting she'd be happier elsewhere, which is technically a kindness rather than rejection."

"Exactly. We'll present this at next week's board meeting before the trustees can organize effective opposition. Strike while the iron is hot and the congregation is still traumatized."

Eartha's phone buzzed on the table between them. She glanced at the screen, and something flickered across her face— something Bernice had been watching for all evening, waiting for confirmation of suspicions that had been building for months.

"Speaking of control and propriety," Bernice said carefully, her voice casual but her eyes sharp, "I noticed something during our meeting this morning. Something between you and Deacon Hearns that seemed ... personal."

Eartha's hand stilled over her phone. Her body language shifted almost imperceptibly—shoulders tensing, breathing changing rhythm. The response was subtle enough that most people wouldn't notice, but Bernice had been reading human behavior professionally for decades.

"I don't know what you mean," Eartha replied, her voice carrying exactly the kind of studied neutrality that confirmed she knew exactly what Bernice meant.

"Don't you?" Bernice leaned back in her chair, hands folding in her lap with deceptive relaxation. "We've been friends for thirty years, Eartha. I know when you're hiding something. I know when you're playing a role versus being authentic. And that look you gave Joel Hearns this morning? That wasn't church business."

The silence between them stretched long enough that the grandfather clock in the hallway ticked through fifteen seconds before Eartha finally responded.

"Are you asking me something specific, or are you fishing for information you don't actually have?"

"I'm acknowledging what I observed," Bernice replied, her tone still friendly but containing an edge that suggested consequences if the conversation continued to be evasive. "And I'm wondering if there's something you need to talk about. Something that might affect our campaign to restore this church to biblical standards."

Eartha stood abruptly, moving to the window where she could watch evening shadows lengthening across the manicured lawn. Her silhouette against the dying light created dramatic effect that might have been intentional—Eartha had always understood the power of staging and presentation.

"Some things are better left unsaid, Bernice. That's all I'm going to say about the matter."

"Fair enough." Bernice's voice was mild, but her expression suggested she was filing this conversation away for future reference. "But be careful, sister. We're campaigning to restore traditional values and biblical morality. If we're going to advocate for those standards publicly, our private lives need to reflect them. Hypocrisy is the one sin the world won't forgive, and the one thing that will destroy our credibility faster than any trustee opposition."

"I'm handling my personal business," Eartha replied, her voice tight with barely controlled emotion. "You focus on church business, and trust that I know what I'm doing."

After Bernice departed—her exit marked by polite goodbyes that didn't quite mask the tension between them—Eartha returned to her phone and scrolled to the text message that had arrived during their conversation:

CAN WE TALK? I KNOW IT'S LATE AND DANGEROUS, BUT I CAN'T STOP THINKING ABOUT WHAT HAPPENED THIS MORNING. ABOUT US. ABOUT EVERYTHING THIS COULD COST IF WE'RE DISCOVERED. I DON'T KNOW HOW MUCH LONGER I CAN MAINTAIN THIS PRETENSE WITH SANDRA. - M

Eartha's fingers hovered over the keyboard, mind warring with heart, decades of caution battling against loneliness that had become almost unbearable.

Finally, she typed:

NOT TONIGHT. TOO DANGEROUS WITH BERNICE SUSPICIOUS. I'LL SEE YOU SUNDAY. KEEP YOUR DISTANCE UNTIL WE FIGURE THIS OUT. WE'VE BEEN CAREFUL FOR YEARS—WE CAN'T RISK EVERYTHING NOW. - E

She hit send, then immediately deleted the entire text thread from her phone. Technology left trails that could destroy reputations, end marriages, and validate every accusation their enemies might level against them.

After clearing her cache and browsing history—paranoid rituals she'd developed over the past months—Eartha moved to her bedroom and knelt beside the bed in the prayer posture she'd maintained since childhood.

But the words that came felt increasingly hollow, prayers that exposed the growing chasm between her public theology and private reality:

Lord, I don't even know what to pray anymore. I've been faithful so long—forty years since my divorce, forty years of celibacy and service and denying every desire that doesn't fit the church's expectations. But I'm so tired. So lonely. Is it wrong to want to be loved? Is it wrong to question whether the rules we've built around Your grace have become more important than the grace itself?

I know what the Bible says about adultery. I know what I'm doing is sin by every definition we teach. But Marcus sees me, Father. Really sees me. Not the church mother or the divorced woman or the perpetual volunteer. He sees Eartha—the woman I was before church politics and theological debates and maintaining appearances consumed my entire existence.

I'm sixty-eight years old. How many years do I have left? Is it so terrible to want companionship, affection, someone who makes me feel alive rather than just righteously dead?

The prayer trailed off into silence because she had no answers, only questions that grew more complicated the longer she examined them.

The First Lady Speaks

In the parsonage—the stately Victorian house that had sheltered five generations of Greater Mount Calvary's pastoral families—First Lady Clarice Howard sat in her late husband's study, surrounded by his books and papers. The room still carried his scent: Old Spice cologne mixed with the leather of ancient theological volumes and the faint smell of the pipe tobacco he'd secretly smoked despite her objections.

She'd barely slept since Sunday. Every time she closed her eyes, she saw Marcus collapsing, heard his labored breathing, felt his hand slipping from hers in those final moments before the paramedics rushed him away toward a medical miracle that never materialized.

Her phone rang, cutting through grief-soaked silence. FaLessia's name appeared on the screen—the daughter Marcus never had; the trustee he'd depended on to protect his progressive vision from conservative opposition.

"First Lady, I needed you to know what's happening before you hear it secondhand from people with agendas."

Clarice listened in growing fury as FaLessia outlined the conspiracy—the plans to reverse Marcus's progressive policies, the letter targeting Trange' Moreau, the attempts to control pastoral succession and transform Greater Mount Calvary back into the exclusive club it had been before Marcus's thirty-seven-year pastorate.

"They're trying to erase everything he worked for," Clarice said quietly when FaLessia finished. "Every policy he fought for, every person he welcomed, every bridge he built—they want to burn it all down and pretend his ministry never happened."

"Yes ma'am. The trustees are fighting back, but it's going to get ugly. I wanted you to know what we're up against."

Clarice was quiet for a long moment, staring at the photograph on Marcus's desk—their wedding day, fifty-three years ago, when she'd been a twenty-year-old dancer and he'd been a twenty-five-year-old seminarian with more idealism than sense.

"FaLessia, can I tell you something most people didn't know about Marcus and me?"

"Of course, First Lady."

"When we first met, I was a dancer. But not the church kind—I was a professional dancer in clubs across Louisiana and Mississippi. I wasn't living for God, wasn't interested in church, wasn't remotely the kind of woman a young preacher should have been pursuing."

FaLessia remained silent, sensing this was confession that had been waiting decades for the right moment.

"Marcus saw me performing at a club in Shreveport one night— he was there visiting a friend who owned the place, not there for entertainment, but he saw me anyway. And instead of judging me, condemning me, or treating me like some fallen woman who needed saving from herself, he SAW me. Really saw me. Saw the woman God was calling me to become, not just the woman circumstances had made me."

Her voice strengthened with remembered love. "He came back the next night. Not to preach at me or recruit me for his church, but just to talk. Asked about my life, my dreams, what had led me to dancing in clubs instead of pursuing the education I'd always wanted. He listened—really listened—without judgment or agenda."

"I didn't know any of this," FaLessia said softly.

"Because Marcus never told the story publicly. He protected my dignity while helping me transform into the woman I wanted to be. Paid for my education, introduced me to people who saw my potential, created space for me to grow at my own pace rather than demanding immediate perfection. That's who he was—that's what grace looked like when it wore human skin."

She moved to the window where she could see the cathedral's steeple rising above the tree line, silhouetted against the evening sky. "So if you think I'm going to sit quietly while Bernice Williams and Eartha Jones transform this church into an exclusive club for people who already look sanctified, you don't know me very well."

"First Lady—"

"No." The word came with steel that surprised them both. "Marcus spent thirty-seven years building a church that reflected Heaven's actual diversity rather than earth's comfortable segregation. He fought to create space where dancers like I was could become first ladies, where pregnant teenagers could find grace instead of condemnation, where gay people could seek God without being told their existence was an abomination."

Her voice rose with prophetic authority. "I'm not going to let Bernice and Eartha dishonor his memory by undoing everything he sacrificed for. If they want war, they'll get war. That quiet little first lady they've ignored and patronized for thirty-seven years is about to remind them that I was a warrior before I was a saint—and that grace doesn't make you weak, it makes you dangerous to systems built on exclusion."

"What do you need from me?" FaLessia asked, recognizing the shift from grieving widow to strategic general.

"Invite Sister Moreau to have coffee with me this week. I want to hear her story directly rather than filtered through gossip. I want to pray with her, encourage her, and let her know that Marcus's widow stands with her against these wolves in sheep's clothing."

"Yes ma'am. I'll reach out to her today."

"And FaLessia? Marcus always said you reminded him of your father—righteous without being rigid, principled without being prideful, strong enough to fight battles but wise enough to choose which hills are worth dying on. He was counting on you to protect his legacy and continue his vision. Don't let him down."

After the call ended, Clarice returned to Marcus's desk and pulled out fresh paper. She began writing—not the eulogy people expected, not the tearful remembrance of a grieving widow, but a battle plan for protecting everything her husband had built.

First Lady Clarice Howard was done being quiet.

She was done being patient.

She was done letting church politics trump the gospel Marcus had lived and died proclaiming.

Thursday was coming—the women's group meeting where Trange' would walk directly into the lions' den that Bernice and Eartha were preparing for her.

And battle lines were being drawn in ways none of the conspirators had anticipated.

The war for Greater Mount Calvary's soul had officially begun.

Chapter 3: Lavender and Liberation

The Lavender Rose Bistro occupied a corner building in the French Quarter where centuries-old architecture met contemporary sophistication. Exposed brick walls bore witness to generations of transformation, their surfaces textured with history that no amount of gentrification could erase. Original cypress beams—salvaged from an 1840s plantation house—crossed overhead, their hand-hewn marks preserving testimony to craftsmanship born from bondage.

Edison bulbs cast warm light across tables draped in lavender linens, creating an atmosphere that was simultaneously rustic and refined. Floor-to-ceiling windows framed cobblestone streets where a saxophonist played with Juilliard precision, his open case collecting bills from passersby who recognized excellence.

The air carried stories: lavender-infused simple syrup sweetening craft cocktails, fresh-baked beignets dusted with powdered sugar, café au lait strong enough to resurrect the dead—or at least sustain them through French Quarter nightlife that never acknowledged normal sleep schedules.

Vintage photographs lined one wall—black and white images capturing the Quarter's evolution through the jazz age, civil rights movement, and every transformation between. They weren't decoration; they were testimony, reminding patrons that beauty and brutality had always coexisted in this city.

Abstract paintings by local artists covered the remaining walls—explosions of color suggesting Mardi Gras parades or hurricanes or simply the city's soul made visible. The bar itself commanded attention: reclaimed mahogany from a demolished antebellum mansion, its surface refinished to reveal wood grain like frozen liquid gold.

Small touches throughout revealed obsessive attention to detail: fresh lavender sprigs in crystal vases, monogrammed cloth napkins, mismatched vintage China making each place setting unique, silverware heavy enough to suggest substance rather than disposability.

The lunch crowd was thinning toward the afternoon lull. A couple conducted what might have been romance or business negotiation—in New Orleans, and the distinction was often academic. A woman nursed lavender honey cake while typing on her laptop. Three tourists studied maps while their waiter patiently explained walking routes that wouldn't mark them as obvious targets.

This was where Trange' Moreau had chosen to meet Sage Beaumont—not in a corporate Starbucks where efficiency erased personality, not in her office where professional masks were mandatory, but in this space that honored authenticity and understood that healing sometimes required beauty alongside truth.

Trange' sat at her usual corner table, positioned strategically with clear sightlines to the entrance and street. Years of business negotiations had taught her that positioning mattered, that small advantages accumulated into decisive leverage.

Her burgundy Hermès blazer and matching silk trousers suggested someone fresh from a boardroom conquest rather than someone nursing sanctuary wounds. The outfit cost more than most monthly salaries—armor against a world that tried to diminish her, a statement that her worth transcended others' opinions.

But shadows beneath expertly applied makeup told different stories. The slight tremor in her hands lifting her lavender latte. Eyes scanning the room as if expecting attack. Tension in shoulders braced for impact even in a space designed for relaxation.

Three days since her public humiliation. Three days since a divine encounter had transformed into an accusation of spiritual murder. Three days of replaying every detail, questioning every decision, wondering if maybe they were right—maybe she didn't belong.

The bistro's front door opened with theatrical flair that could only announce one person.

Sage Beaumont swept through like he was walking Milan runways rather than entering a French Quarter café. His cream linen suit was tailored with precision that transcended clothing into wearable art—raw silk blend catching light differently depending on angle, cut with European sophistication that suggested continental taste rather than American business casual.

A silk scarf in lavender and gold draped around his neck with calculated casualness that had probably required fifteen minutes before a mirror. Oversized sunglasses perched on platinum blonde hair styled in deliberate disarray. Rings adorned every finger—Celtic knots, rose gold that might have been his grandmother's, chunky turquoise from Santa Fe. Each piece was a conversation starter, a memory keeper, and a small rebellion.

Italian leather loafers in cognac brown—soft as butter, hand-stitched, probably more expensive than car payments. No socks, because Sage believed life was too short to hide beautiful ankles behind cotton, and sockless shoes telegraphed European sophistication Americans were too uptight to embrace.

But energy more than ensemble commanded attention. He moved with confidence that transcended physical space, occupying rooms through presence rather than size.

"DARLING!" His voice carried across the bistro, heads turning. He air-kissed both cheeks with European flair—right, then left, hands on shoulders establishing connection, a slight pull back to assess her condition, then a second round with murmured French endearments that may or may not have been grammatically correct but sounded fabulous regardless.

"You look absolutely ravishing," he declared, settling with choreographed grace, "though I detect shadows suggesting improper sleep. We'll discuss that after I order something divine."

He flagged their server—a young man who clearly recognized him and approached with professional courtesy mixed with genuine affection.

"Hello, beautiful," Sage greeted warmly. "I need a Lavender Rosé Spritz—extra lavender because I'm feeling particularly in need of calming properties, light on the prosecco because daytime drinking requires pacing and I'm too fabulous to embarrass myself before 5 PM, and please add those adorable, candied rose petals because presentation matters almost as much as taste."

The server smiled, familiar with the elaborate ordering. "Fresh lavender sugar cubes from Marcel?"

"You absolute ANGEL!" Sage pressed a hand to his chest. "Yes, please. You're getting twenty-five percent today instead of twenty. Excellence deserves recognition."

As the server departed, Sage removed his sunglasses with a flourish, revealing eyes mixing genuine concern with strategic assessment.

Trange' shook her head, lips twitching despite everything. "You are entirely too much."

"Darling, I'm exactly enough," Sage corrected. "Too much would be showing up in my full drag show costume. This—" he gestured with pride, "—is tastefully fabulous. There's a difference."

He leaned forward, the performance giving way to authentic friendship. "Now. What's the tea, sis? And don't tell me everything's fine, because I can see the shade you're carrying like last season's Prada. Metaphorically speaking, your actual outfit is obviously current season and impeccable."

Trange's carefully maintained façade crumbled. Tears she'd been suppressing through sheer willpower finally gathered.

"Sage, it was ... " A shaky breath. "I can't even describe how horrific. I went seeking God. SEEKING GOD. And it became the most traumatic experience of my life."

The story poured out in fragments—Bishop Howard's sermon speaking directly to her wounds, his altar call pulling her forward like a magnetic force, standing there feeling his hand with that oil, hearing him ask if she was giving her life to God.

"I meant it," she whispered, wiping tears. "With everything in me. This wasn't performance or social climbing. It was real. The most spiritually genuine moment of my entire life."

"I believe you," Sage assured, his voice carrying conviction. "Anyone who knows you knows Trange' Moreau doesn't do anything halfway. When you commit, you COMMIT."

"And then he collapsed," she continued, her voice breaking. "Right there. One moment blessing me, the next moment on the floor clutching his chest. I tried to help, but people pushed me back like I was contaminated."

She grabbed another napkin, her makeup beyond saving. "But that wasn't even the worst part. This church mother—this sanctified sister who looks like she hasn't smiled since Reagan—stands up and points at me like I'm a demon incarnate. Declares I killed him. That I'm some harlot who brought death into God's house. DECLARES it, Sage. In front of everyone."

Her hands gestured wildly, composure abandoned. "Everyone staring like I'm demon possessed. Whispering. Pointing. Taking steps backward like my evil might be contagious. Like my dress was somehow responsible for a sixty-two-year-old man's heart attack."

She collapsed back. "And you know the absolute worst part? Some believed her. I could see it—they actually thought my presence caused this. That I was too worldly, too sexy, too MUCH for their precious sanctuary."

The Praise Dance

Sage's expression cycled through sympathy, fury, and vindictive satisfaction. "Oh honey, I know exactly who that was. Mother Bernice Williams and Mother Eartha Jones, right? Bernice is the slim one who eats lemons for breakfast and judges people for dessert? And Eartha could have been America's Next Top Model but chose religious condemnation as a career path?"

Trange's eyes widened. "How did you—"

"Because those heifers did the exact same thing to me," Sage declared, his voice hardening. "I was the choir director at Greater Mount Calvary for three years. THREE YEARS of dealing with their homophobic microaggressions dressed as 'spiritual concern' and 'biblical standards.'"

The server arrived with Sage's drink—a crystal glass frosted to perfection, purple liquid catching light, candied rose petals floating like edible jewelry, lavender sugar cubes waiting on a small plate.

Sage took an appreciative sip before continuing. "Let me tell you about my last stand there. Because what happened to you? Just their latest campaign in a decades-long war against anyone who threatens their control."

He settled comfortably, rings catching light. "I'd been director almost three years. Built that ministry from twenty members who could barely carry a tune to over sixty voices getting regional recognition. Young people joining specifically for the music. Offerings increasing whenever we performed. Bishop Howard was thrilled."

Pride mixed with pain in his voice. "But Mother Bernice and Mother Jones hated everything I represented. Not just because I'm gay—though that was certainly a factor they hid behind biblical language. They hated that I was successful. Confident. Refused to perform the humility they expected from someone they viewed as fundamentally flawed."

"What did they do?"

"Everything they could while maintaining plausible deniability," Sage replied tightly. "Church doors would mysteriously lock before rehearsal, keys 'misplaced' for forty-five minutes. The sound system malfunctioning only during our practice time— perfect Sunday mornings, perfect Wednesday Bible study, mysterious technical difficulties every Thursday rehearsal. Music I'd ordered disappearing from the supply closet. Funds for new robes getting 'delayed' while every other ministry got budget approvals."

His hands gestured expressively. "Made my life absolute hell while smiling in my face Sunday mornings. Complimenting my suit while undermining my ministry. Psychological warfare disguised as Christian concern."

"What finally made you leave?"

"It came to a head during rehearsal one Wednesday," Sage replied, his eyes gleaming with a memory mixing trauma and triumph. "I'd arranged for praise dancers to join us—beautiful young ladies wanting to worship through movement. We were rehearsing a gorgeous contemporary piece set to 'Break Every Chain'—very tasteful, very anointed."

He paused dramatically, finishing his first sugar cube. "And here comes Mother Jones, storming into the sanctuary like an Old Testament prophet arriving to pronounce judgment. Bursts through those doors hard enough to rattle the hinges, face arranged in righteous fury that would have been impressive if it weren't so misplaced."

"What did she do?"

"Demanded we stop immediately," Sage replied, his voice rising slightly. "Declared that watching young women 'gyrate and shimmy' in God's house was ungodly. Said they looked like they were 'auditioning for some nightclub.' Announced that effective immediately, there would be no more dance rehearsals in the sanctuary."

His jaw clenched. "Lead dancer Crystal Martinez was a third-year divinity student at New Orleans Baptist Theological Seminary—more theological training than Mother Jones had received in fifty years of pew-sitting. Didn't matter. Mother Jones saw movement and assumed sin."

"What did you do?"

Sage's smile carried three years of satisfaction. "I snapped. Completely lost my religion right there. Told her if she wanted to worship like it was 1950, she could find herself a time machine, but the rest of us were living in the twenty-first century where dance had been part of worship since David danced before the ark."

Trange's eyes widened. "You did *not!*"

"Oh, I absolutely did," Sage confirmed proudly. "And when she tried quoting Scripture at me, I quoted right back—reminded her Miriam led women in dance after crossing the Red Sea, that Psalms repeatedly command praise with dancing, that even Jesus attended celebrations where people danced."

He stirred his drink. "But here's where I might have crossed the uncrossable line."

"What did you say?"

"I told her that her problem wasn't with praise dancing—it was with joy," Sage replied with conviction. "That she'd been bitter so long she'd forgotten what celebrating felt like. That her misery was trying to recruit company by shutting down everyone else's worship expression."

The bistro fell quieter, other patrons unconsciously tuning in. "Girl, the sanctuary went SILENT. You could have heard a communion wafer drop. Mother Jones's face turned seventeen shades of purple and red—I genuinely worried about a cardiac event right there."

"What happened?"

"She tried getting me fired, obviously. Emergency meeting with the deacon board, demanding my removal for 'insubordination' and 'disrespecting church mothers.' But Bishop Howard shut that down. Reminded everyone I was hired by pastoral leadership, not the Mother Board. That my ministry bore undeniable fruit—choir tripled, young people joining, offerings always increasing when we performed."

His voice softened with gratitude. "He protected me that day. But the harassment continued. Just more subtle, more careful to avoid direct confrontation Bishop Howard might address. Made it clear through a thousand small cruelties I would never truly belong. Eventually, I left. Not because they won, but because staying required surrendering pieces of my soul that weren't worth any fight."

He leaned forward intensely, his voice dropping to a conspiratorial whisper. "But here's what you need to understand about bullies—they only have power when targets are isolated and afraid. You, my darling, are neither."

"I'm not?" Doubt colored Trange's voice.

"Absolutely not," Sage declared with conviction. "You have resources they can't imagine. Connections they'll never access. Business acumen that could buy and sell their church politics ten times over. And most importantly—you have us."

He gestured broadly, rings sparkling. "Your sisters from the prayer circle. FaLessia fighting for you from inside leadership. And me—fabulous, fierce, occasionally inappropriate me who knows where the bodies are buried and has receipts to prove it."

His voice gained momentum like a sermon building to an altar call. "Plus, you're Trange' Moreau. You've survived things that would have broken weaker women. Foster care that would have destroyed most children. Built an empire from nothing. Conquered fashion weeks in three countries. Negotiated deals with people who make church mothers look like amateur hour."

He paused for effect, sipping his drink. "This is just another boardroom, honey—except this one has pews and a cross. Same politics, same power plays, same insecure people protecting territory. You've won bigger battles. These church mothers have no idea what real warfare looks like."

Trange' felt something shift—the wounded victim beginning to remember who she'd been, who she was becoming, who God was calling her to be.

"FaLessia told me about the women's group at church," she said, her voice gaining strength. "She thinks I should join."

"Are you INSANE?" Sage's voice exploded loud enough to make nearby diners jump. "You want to voluntarily walk back into that viper's nest? They tried blaming you for killing their pastor! What makes you think a women's group run by the same people would be anything except an elaborate ambush?"

Trange' caught herself mid-curse, the transformation new enough to require conscious correction. "I refuse to let them run me away from what God has for me. Don't they know who I am? I'm Madame Trange' Moreau, darling. I didn't build an international media empire by backing down from people who underestimated me."

"YAAASSS!" Sage's enthusiasm exploded, turning every head. "THERE'S my girl! I knew that spine was still there somewhere!"

His hands clapped with sharp precision. "You survived foster care—shuffled between seven different homes before twelve. Built a media empire from a receptionist job to a corner office. Conquered fashion weeks where models would literally stab each other with stilettos. These church mothers think they're something because they've sat in the same pew since Moses was in Pampers? PUH-LEASE. They have no idea what real warfare looks like!"

Trange' straightened in her chair, her hand moving to smooth the lapel of her blazer—a physical gesture signaling the mental shift occurring within. She took a breath, feeling the armor of her identity settling back into place.

"Nobody's keeping me from learning about God," she declared, her voice carrying the authority of a woman who'd conquered boardrooms across three continents. "These church people are about to accept me or move out of my way."

She paused, a smile playing on her lips. "Seriously, did you see what Mother Jones was wearing? That dress looked like it came from the Dress Barn clearance rack from 1987."

"I was trying to be charitable," Sage replied with mock seriousness. "But yes—that purple and green floral situation with the ruffled collar and bow that could double as a life raft? Fashion apocalypse. The kind of outfit that makes "Project Runway" judges weep."

They dissolved into healing laughter, releasing tension instead of holding it until it poisoned everything.

When they recovered, Sage turned serious. "And you know what? I'm coming back too. You're going to need backup, and those ladies have no idea what they're dealing with." He paused, his expression shifting to something knowing and strategic. "I've been sitting on information about certain church mothers for years now, waiting for the right moment when it might prove ... useful."

Trange's eyebrow arched—the same expression she'd used in boardrooms when sensing leverage. "What kind of information?"

"Let's just say," Sage's voice dropping to a whisper, "*that Mother Eartha Jones who preaches so loudly about biblical morality has some very interesting extracurricular activities that would scandalize the congregation if they became public. I clocked her tea years ago, filed it away for a rainy day. And watching her try destroying you while living her secret life? That's hypocrisy that makes the timing feel divinely appointed."*

Trange' wrestled with her ethics—old survival instincts versus new faith; learning grace, mercy, turning the other cheek.

"I want to do this right," she said carefully. "Handle them the way God would want. With integrity and wisdom."

"And God gave us brains for strategy," Sage countered, warming to the theological argument. "Nothing in the Bible says Christians must be doormats. Jesus flipped tables in the temple. Called Pharisees whitewashed tombs. Told them they strained gnats while swallowing camels. Sometimes righteous anger and strategic action are exactly what the situation requires."

He gestured expressively. "David didn't walk into battle with Goliath unarmed just because he had faith. He used intelligence, strategy, and weapons he knew how to wield. That's not lacking faith—that's being a good steward of the gifts God gave you."

Trange' couldn't entirely argue, even if the application made her spiritually uncomfortable. Maybe there was space between blind trust and calculated destruction—space for wisdom honoring both faith *and* reality.

"What exactly do you know about Mother Jones?"

Sage's smile carried the satisfaction of someone holding cards close until the right moment. "Oh darling, I know plenty. Receipts. Photographic evidence. Testimony from multiple witnesses. Documentation that would make investigative journalists weep with joy. But we'll save that conversation for when it's strategically necessary. The element of surprise is a powerful weapon."

He raised his glass, the lavender liquid catching afternoon light, creating prisms dancing across their table. "For now, let's toast to faith that doesn't require checking our brains at the sanctuary door. To fabulous fashion that honors both God and good taste. And to refusing to let religious hypocrites determine our destiny when God has already written a better story."

Trange' raised her own glass, feeling a smile break through the pain. The weight crushing her chest for three days lightened slightly, replaced by something like hope mixed with strategic determination.

"Darling," she said, her voice carrying old confidence and new conviction, "don't let this fabulousness fool you. They have no idea what I'm capable of."

But then she paused, catching herself, her conscience reminding her of the commitments made at the altar. Her hand moved instinctively to touch the small cross necklace Shaniece had given her—simple gold that cost nothing compared to her usual jewelry but carried value transcending any price.

"I mean ... " she corrected, her voice softening with genuine spiritual struggle, "I know God won't let this foolishness continue. I trust His timing and methods. But they better try God and not me. Because while I'm learning to turn the other cheek, I've got a really long neck, and eventually we run out of cheeks to turn."

Sage laughed—a genuine, joyful sound drawing smiles from other patrons. "THAT'S my girl! Spiritual, but strategic. Holy, but not helpless. Walking in faith while wearing Louboutins that could double as weapons if the situation requires—though we pray it doesn't because those shoes are too expensive to waste on church mother combat."

He stood dramatically, his linen suit billowing. "Now, I have a salon appointment with Jean-Claude I absolutely cannot miss. This platinum doesn't maintain itself. But call me the moment you need backup, support, or someone to read these church mothers using Scripture and shade in equal measure."

Trange' rose to embrace him, grateful for a friendship accepting her completely—both who she'd been and who she was becoming. The hug lasted longer than typical air-kisses, conveying a depth words couldn't capture.

"Thank you," she whispered. "I needed this more than I realized. Needed to remember who I am beyond what they tried making me believe."

"That's what best friends do," Sage replied, his voice softening. "We show up when it matters. Speak truth when lies are easier. Remind each other who we really are when the world tries making us forget our divine identity."

He pulled back, hands on her shoulders, looking into her eyes. "One more thing. When you walk into that women's group— and I know you will because you're too stubborn to let them win—remember their opinion is just that—an opinion. A limited perspective from limited people protecting a limited worldview."

His voice gained a prophetic quality. "God's truth about you is what matters. His truth says you're chosen, called, completely worthy of the transformation you're experiencing. Don't let their rejection make you doubt divine acceptance. They don't get to define your relationship with God—only He does."

Tears gathered—the good kind, the healing kind, the kind coming from being truly seen and valued by someone who knew her completely and loved her anyway. "How did I get lucky enough to have you as my friend?"

"Oh honey, luck had nothing to do with it," Sage replied with a wink. "God knew you'd need a fierce, fabulous, occasionally inappropriate prayer warrior who could quote Scripture and throw shade with equal effectiveness. I'm exactly the friend your journey requires at this precise moment."

With a final dramatic wave making his rings sparkle, Sage swept out, leaving traces of expensive cologne and a presence that made people wonder what exciting life he was living.

Trange' settled back, alone but no longer lonely. The isolation since Sunday had been replaced by something stronger—a community accepting her completely, a purpose transcending temporary opposition, a growing confidence that maybe God's plan included confronting religious hypocrisy rather than running from it.

She texted FaLessia with a decision made:

COUNT ME IN FOR THE WOMEN'S GROUP. WHEN DOES IT MEET? AND WHAT'S THE DRESS CODE? BECAUSE I'M DONE PRETENDING TO BE LESS THAN I AM TO MAKE INSECURE PEOPLE COMFORTABLE. THEY'RE ABOUT TO LEARN MADAME MOREAU COMES AS SHE IS—HAUTE COUTURE AND ALL. IF GOD CAN ACCEPT ME WEARING VALENTINO, THEY CAN LEARN TO DEAL WITH IT.

The response came almost immediately:

YAASSS! THAT'S THE TRANGE' I'VE BEEN PRAYING WOULD SHOW UP. WOMEN'S GROUP MEETS THURSDAY NIGHTS AT 7 PM IN FELLOWSHIP HALL. DRESS CODE IS TECHNICALLY "MODEST AND RESPECTFUL" BUT INTENTIONALLY VAGUE AND SUBJECTIVELY INTERPRETED.

SUGGEST SOMETHING HONORING BOTH YOUR PERSONAL STYLE AND THEIR SENSIBILITIES—FIND THE INTERSECTION WHERE YOU STAY TRUE WHILE SHOWING YOU UNDERSTAND THEIR VALUES EVEN IF YOU DON'T ACCEPT THEIR JUDGMENTS. WALK THE LINE BETWEEN PROPHETIC CHALLENGE AND PRACTICAL WISDOM.

FULL DISCLOSURE—MOTHER JONES AND MOTHER WILLIAMS RUN THE WOMEN'S MINISTRY WITH IRON FISTS IN LACE GLOVES. YOU'LL BE WALKING INTO THEIR TERRITORY, THEIR CAREFULLY CONTROLLED SPACE WHERE THEY'VE REIGNED UNCHALLENGED FOR OVER A DECADE. BUT I'LL BE THERE AS A TRUSTEE LIAISON. AND SEVERAL OTHER WOMEN ARE PRIVATELY FED UP EVEN IF TOO AFRAID TO SAY SO PUBLICLY. YOU WON'T BE ALONE.

BRING YOUR BIBLE. BRING YOUR CONFIDENCE. BRING YOUR ARMOR—BOTH SPIRITUAL AND FASHIONABLE. THIS IS GOING TO BE INTERESTING IN THE ANCIENT CHINESE CURSE SENSE. BUT I BELIEVE GOD IS POSITIONING YOU FOR PURPOSES BEYOND WHAT ANY OF US CAN SEE. TRUST THE PROCESS. TRUST HIM. TRUST THAT SOMETIMES DISRUPTION IS EXACTLY WHAT STAGNANT SYSTEMS NEED.

Trange' smiled, already mentally curating an outfit communicating exactly the message she wanted: she was here to stay, she refused to apologize for who God made her, and they had no idea what they'd started.

She paid her check—including a generous tip because service workers deserved better—and walked out into the French Quarter afternoon feeling more like herself than she had in days.

The battle for Greater Mount Calvary Cathedral had officially begun.

And Trange' Moreau was ready for war—spiritual warfare waged with prayer and strategy, faith and wisdom, grace and boundaries protecting divine purposes from religious gatekeepers.

She sent a group text to her prayer circle:

SISTERS, I NEED YOU. HEADING INTO THE WOMEN'S GROUP THURSDAY NIGHT. WALKING DIRECTLY INTO TERRITORY CONTROLLED BY CHURCH MOTHERS WHO BLAMED ME FOR BISHOP'S DEATH. NEED ALL THE PRAYER YOU CAN GIVE— SPIRITUAL COVERING, DIVINE PROTECTION, SUPERNATURAL WISDOM, PROBABLY ANGELIC REINFORCEMENT.

I'M SCARED. I'M ANGRY. I'M DETERMINED. I'M FAITHFUL. ALL OF IT SIMULTANEOUSLY. PRAY FOR ME. PRAY FOR THEM. PRAY GOD'S PURPOSES PREVAIL. AND PRAY I DON'T LOSE MY RELIGION AND SALVATION IN THE SAME EVENING BECAUSE MY FLESH IS WEAK AND MY MOUTH IS STRONG.

LOVE YOU ALL. SEE YOU ON THE OTHER SIDE OF WHATEVER THURSDAY BRINGS.

The responses came rapid-fire:

Samantha: *GIVE THEM HELL. RESPECTFULLY. IN JESUS'S NAME. WITH LOVE. BUT DEFINITELY GIVE THEM HELL. YOU'VE GOT THIS. WE'VE GOT YOU. GOD'S GOT ALL OF US.*

Renee: *REMEMBER—HURT PEOPLE HURT PEOPLE. MAYBE THEY'RE JUST TERRIFIED YOUR CONFIDENCE REMINDS*

THEM OF DREAMS THEY SURRENDERED. KILL THEM WITH
KINDNESS. OR JUST KILL THEM. DEALER'S CHOICE.

Moni: *PRAYING FOR YOU! REMEMBER WHAT BISHOP*
HOWARD SAID—JUDGE NOT. SHOW THEM THE GRACE THEY
DIDN'T SHOW YOU. THAT'S HOW TRANSFORMATION
HAPPENS.

Coko: *YOU'VE GOT THIS, BELOVED. WALK IN THERE LIKE*
YOU OWN THE PLACE—BECAUSE TECHNICALLY, YOU KIND
OF DO. EQUAL OWNERSHIP BEFORE GOD REGARDLESS OF
TENURE.

Shaniece: *BABY GIRL, YOU ARE CHOSEN, CALLED,*
COMPLETELY EQUIPPED FOR THIS EXACT MOMENT. GOD
DIDN'T BRING YOU THIS FAR TO LET CHURCH POLITICS
DESTROY YOUR JOURNEY. REMEMBER WHO YOU ARE—
WHOSE YOU ARE. YOUR VALUE COMES FROM HIM, NOT
THEIR APPROVAL.

AND IF YOU NEED ME TO SHOW UP AND REMIND THEM WHO
YOUR SISTER IS AND WHAT KIND OF BACKUP YOU HAVE, I
WILL GLADLY MAKE AN APPEARANCE WITH THE TWINS IN
TOW. NOTHING SAYS 'DON'T MESS WITH MY SISTER' QUITE
LIKE A SUCCESSFUL BUSINESSWOMAN WITH INFANT TWINS
WHO CAN AFFORD REALLY GOOD LAWYERS.

Trange' read through the responses with tears gathering—the
good kind again. Whatever happened Thursday, she wouldn't
face it alone.

She walked toward the parking garage, afternoon sun painting
the French Quarter in golden light. Street musicians played,
tourists photographed, locals navigated familiar paths.

This was New Orleans—a city that had always understood complexity, never demanded perfection as the price of belonging, made space for saints and sinners to coexist in uncomfortable but ultimately beautiful harmony.

Maybe Greater Mount Calvary needed the lessons this city had been teaching for centuries: grace accommodates diversity, love transcends judgment, and sometimes the people who look least like what religion expects are exactly who God chooses to reveal His character most powerfully.

Thursday was coming. And Trange' Moreau was going to teach some church mothers about grace—whether they wanted the lesson or not.

Chapter 4: Holy War and Divine Appointments

The Financial Weapon

FaLessia Shaw's heels struck marble with mounting fury. The letter in her trembling hand felt less like church correspondence and more like a declaration of war.

Patricia Jones sat behind her desk with studied nonchalance, fingers steepled, her smile suggesting she'd anticipated this confrontation.

"We need to discuss this." FaLessia dropped the letter hard enough to rattle Patricia's coffee cup.

Patricia's eyes—so much like her mother's—scanned the document. "The subcommittee's quarterly financial review? Standard procedure."

"*Standard?*" FaLessia leaned forward. "This letter—bearing *my* signature without authorization—suggests my tithing has 'declined significantly' and 'stresses the importance of continued faith and obedience.' You made me sound spiritually backsliding."

"The Tithing Subcommittee reviews giving patterns to ensure church solvency. You chair that committee, FaLessia."

"I chair a committee analyzing aggregate data, not one sending accusatory letters questioning spiritual commitment." FaLessia straightened. "My giving hasn't declined—I've redirected donations to my nonprofit rather than filtering everything through the church. Same stewardship, different distribution."

"Perhaps. But the bylaws are clear about tithing expectations for leadership. When commitment appears to waver, it raises legitimate questions."

63

Patricia was weaponizing church governance against FaLessia's credibility.

"How many letters went out?"

"Similar correspondence was sent to several members whose giving patterns raised concerns. Standard accountability measures."

"Bearing my signature stamp?"

"You're the committee chair. Your signature lends appropriate authority."

"This ends **now**. No more letters, no more unauthorized use of my signature, no more weaponizing financial data. **Understood**?"

Patricia's expression never changed. "Of course. Though I'm surprised you're so resistant to accountability practices. One might think you have something to hide."

Vivian Parker appeared with urgent sympathy. "FaLessia, six church members are waiting to speak with you. They're quite agitated about letters they received."

FaLessia's stomach dropped. "About their giving?"

"Yes ma'am. Mother Williams is demanding immediate audience."

Patricia's smile finally reached her eyes—satisfaction barely concealed. "Perhaps you should address these concerns. Member relations are so important."

As FaLessia exited, Vivian whispered: "The letters bear your personal stamp. Members believe they came directly from you."

Perfect. Patricia had created a situation where FaLessia would either defend unauthorized letters or publicly contradict a fellow trustee.

Lord, grant me wisdom, FaLessia prayed, *because my flesh wants to handle Patricia the way David handled Goliath—except I left my sling at home and church protocol frowns on physical violence. Your Word says that as much as lieth in me, I am to live peaceably with all men. I'm about to live VERY unpeaceably, Father.*

***

Divine Appointment at Ché Pierre

Trange' adjusted the emerald silk blouse, studying her reflection critically. The fabric caught light with subtle luxury—expensive enough to telegraph success, tasteful enough to avoid ostentation. Charcoal trousers provided structure while vintage Bulgari added sparkle reminding everyone that Madame Moreau didn't do dowdy.

This meeting carried weight. First Lady Clarice Howard had requested this conversation, and Trange' couldn't shake apprehension about its true purpose.

Renee had insisted on Ché Pierre—neutral territory where Trange' would have backup if needed.

The chauffeur opened her Bentley's door, cream and cookie-colored luxury that turned heads even in New Orleans' French Quarter, where extravagance was currency and understated wealth spoke louder than obvious displays.

"Thank you, Marcus."

Afternoon sun painted the Quarter golden as tourists and locals mixed while street musicians played. Ché Pierre's exterior impressed—wrought iron balconies with flowering vines, a vast fountain, gardens showcasing aggressive beauty. The maître d' recognized her immediately.

"Madame Moreau, what an honor. Your party is waiting."

She followed him past crystal chandeliers casting prismatic light. As she passed a gentleman studying his menu with focused intensity, their eyes met—brief contact stretching into significance.

Light caramel skin. Hazel eyes shifting between green and gold. Full lips curved into a smile revealing perfect teeth. Deep brown-slightly blonde hair into a trimmed low taper fade. African American with Creole accents. Not her usual type but, *My God,* she thought. Fitted shirt revealing gym-sculpted shoulders.

Something stirred in Trange's chest. When he licked his lips, she stumbled on flat flooring.

Thank You, God, for creating such beautiful specimens. And thank You I'll still have a view from my table.

First Lady Clarice Howard rose gracefully, offering an air kiss both formal and genuinely warm.

"Sister Trange' thank you for coming."

A waiter materialized with champagne. She reached instinctively, then paused. Should she drink in front of the First Lady?

Clarice's eyes tracked the hesitation with amusement.

Trange' decided authenticity trumped performance. She sipped—not defiant, not apologetic, simply honest.

Clarice raised an eyebrow. "So you're going to drink now?"

Before Trange' could respond defensively, Clarice called their waiter. "Well, she's not drinking alone. Bring a 1954 Château

Cantemerle and two glasses. Jesus's first miracle involved excellent wine."

Her smile was disarming, conspiratorial, completely unexpected.

"You drink?" Trange' asked.

"Occasionally. Do you know how many lunches I've had with stuffy church women who'd have heart failure if they saw me drink? Thank you for suggesting this restaurant where I can be myself."

They both laughed—genuine connection transcending formality.

The wine arrived with appropriate reverence. Across the room, Renee caught Trange's eye with expression mixing concern and curiosity. Trange' gave her a subtle look that communicated: *Everything's okay. Stand down. This might be enjoyable.*

After tasting, Clarice raised her glass slightly. "Would you invite your friend over? I'd love to meet the owner."

Trange' nearly choked. "How did you know?"

"Chile, I keep my ear to the ground. Very little gets past me—especially regarding women building empires while navigating expectations."

After brief introductions with Renee, Trange's eyes drifted back toward the gentleman.

"I like you," Clarice announced, drawing her attention back. "I wanted to tell you immediately. I like your spirit, your honesty, your refusal to perform humility you don't feel. The church needs women who challenge our comfortable categories."

Tears gathered—the healing kind.

"Call me Clarice. 'First Lady' makes me sound presidential."

"Clarice, I want to express how sorry I am about Bishop Howard—"

"Stop." Clarice's hand covered hers firmly. "You didn't contribute to anything except revealing hearts hiding behind religious performance. Marcus died from hypertension he'd ignored, stress he refused to manage. Not from your dress or altar call."

She paused. "But you need to understand—you represent progressivism the old guard hates. Nothing about you is objectively objectionable. Maybe cover the girls up slightly"— they both laughed— "but here's what those mothers can't handle: a full-figured woman with your confidence, turning heads like you did to that man over there."

Trange' felt heat rising—caught.

Clarice squeezed her hand. "Girl, I know all. They want you down not because you're ungodly, but because you mirror everything they've sacrificed to fit in."

She signaled the gentleman, who rose with smooth coordination. As he approached, Trange' felt apprehension rising.

"Trange', this is my son, Andre."

Oh Lord.

"Trange'," Clarice said with barely suppressed delight, "this is my son, Andre."

Oh Lord, Trange' thought, caught between appreciation and mortification. *Of course the finest man in this restaurant would be related to the woman I'm trying to impress.*

He extended his hand with old-world courtesy. "It is my absolute pleasure to meet you."

His voice—deep baritone dripping with sophistication—wrapped around words like velvet. Six-foot-two, 210 pounds of disciplined muscle. Everything about him communicated confidence tempered by genuine warmth: the way he held eye contact without staring, smiled without smirking, occupied space without demanding it.

When he lifted her hand to his lips in gesture that should have felt theatrical, but somehow landed as genuinely respectful, Trange' could have melted into her chair.

Clarice sat back with expression mixing maternal pride and strategic satisfaction, clearly enjoying every second of her son's effect on their guest.

"Mother, when you're ready.

Lady Trange', I will definitely be seeing you around." His hazel eyes met hers intensely. "Until we meet again."

After he returned to his table, Trange' reached for water with trembling fingers.

"Don't let these women run you off," Clarice said with authority. "God has purposes for you joining Greater Mount Calvary, and at least one person would love to see you there."

She glanced toward her son, who had returned to his reading but looked up as if sensing his mother's attention. He raised his glass in subtle salute that might have been directed at Clarice, Trange', or both.

"The women's meeting tonight—you should go. Walk in with head high, confidence intact, faith stronger than their judgment."

Trange' weighed risks against rewards. "I'll be there. And I won't be alone."

Clarice's smile suggested she'd anticipated exactly that. "Good. Because those mothers are about to learn that sometimes God sends prophets wearing Valentino."

The Fashionable Invasion

The stretch limousine pulled up to Greater Mount Calvary with the kind of arrival that made ushers straighten and deacons adjust ties. This wasn't transportation—this was a statement.

Trange' emerged first, entrance choreographed through decades of commanding attention. The flowing red Elie Saab moved like liquid fire—simultaneously modest and magnificent. But the hat—wide-brimmed crimson adorned with hand-sewn crystal crosses, ostrich feathers providing drama—that was her statement. Church lady millinery elevated to art form.

Samantha exited behind her like a chief petty officer—navy silk charmeuse, structured blazer, expensive jewelry. Hair catching breeze and dancing.

They weren't inappropriately dressed. They were two women who understood fashion and refused to apologize for presenting themselves with excellence.

Two female ushers materialized. "Excuse me, the women's meeting has reached capacity."

Trange's eyebrow arched. "*Capacity*? For a Wednesday evening women's group in a hall seating two hundred?"

"Fire code restrictions."

"I understand perfectly," Samantha interjected. "You've been told to keep us out."

First Lady Clarice materialized like divine intervention. "There must be some mistake," Clarice announced with voice carrying authority that brooked no argument. "We don't discriminate here at Greater Mount Calvary. If these women are good enough to be friends and guests of the First Lady, I know they would be welcomed to any church event."

The ushers exchanged panicked glances, their carefully constructed excuse crumbling under scrutiny that exposed it as the sham it was.

"First Lady, we were told—"

"I don't care what you were told," Clarice interrupted with gentle firmness that somehow felt more commanding than shouting. "Unless you're prepared to physically bar me from entering—which I assume you're not—these ladies are coming with me."

The ushers stepped aside with profuse apologies, their body language broadcasting relief that someone with greater authority had resolved their impossible situation.

"Well, well," Mother Jones began, her voice pitched to carry to anyone within earshot. "I see we have some very ... distinctive guests joining us this evening."

She moved closer, her eyes conducting inventory of their outfits with the precision of someone preparing a detailed critique. "That's quite an ensemble you're wearing, Sister Trange'. Very ... theatrical. Though I'm not sure a women's Bible study requires quite that level of drama."

"Good evening, Mother Jones," Trange' replied with tone matching her antagonist's artificial sweetness. "How kind of you to notice. I do believe in honoring God with excellence rather than approaching His house with careless disregard for presentation."

Samantha stepped forward slightly—protective positioning that communicated she was ready to intervene if this exchange escalated beyond verbal sparring. "The Bible says whatever we do, we should do as unto the Lord. That includes how we present ourselves when gathering in His name."

"Oh, I'm quite familiar with Scripture, dear," Mother Jones replied with condescension that could cut glass. "Including the passages about modest apparel and women not adorning themselves with costly array. Perhaps you'd benefit from reviewing 1 Timothy 2:9?"

"Perhaps *you'd* benefit from reading the rest of that passage," FaLessia interjected, appearing from the fellowship hall entrance like reinforcement arriving just in time. "The verse continues with 'good works, as is proper for women professing godliness.' Their works speak volumes—Trange's nonprofit donations, Samantha's mentorship of young businesswomen. When did expensive clothing become spiritual disqualification while expensive judgment got baptized as righteousness?"

Mother Jones's face flushed slightly, but her composure remained intact. "I'm simply trying to help our new sisters understand the culture here at Greater Mount Calvary. We maintain certain standards of dress and deportment that honor both God and our tradition."

"Standards that somehow only apply to certain women," Clarice Howard observed, positioning herself beside the guests she'd explicitly invited. "Interesting how Mother Williams's designer handbag doesn't warrant similar concern. Or how your daughter Patricia's salon-styled hair escapes critique about vanity. The selectivity of your 'standards' is rather telling, don't you think?"

The standoff might have continued indefinitely—a chess match of theological positioning and cultural criticism—but Minister Crystal Young appeared in the hallway with the bright desperation of someone trying to salvage an evening that was careening toward disaster before it officially began.

"Ladies! How wonderful to see everyone gathering for our W.O.R.D. meeting. That's Women Of Righteous Design," she added unnecessarily, as if the acronym's cleverness might diffuse the tension crackling through the air. "Please, come in, come in. We're about to begin."

As they moved toward Fellowship Hall, Mother Jones leaned close to Mother Bernice Williams, who had been observing from strategic distance. Their whispered exchange carried just far enough for those paying attention to catch fragments:

"... making a spectacle ..."

"... exactly what I warned about ..."

"... handle this appropriately ..."

First Lady Clarice heard them and made mental note. These church mothers were planning something beyond simple disapproval. The question was whether their conspiracy would be contained to social exclusion or escalate into active sabotage.

Lord, I'm going to need to pray before these ladies prey on this sister, Clarice thought, her protective instincts fully activated. Because if they think they're going to destroy another woman on my watch, they've forgotten who they're dealing with.

Women Of Righteous Design

Fellowship Hall filled with forty women in conservative fashion—crosses prominent, elaborate hats, colors projecting prosperity and propriety. Trange' and Samantha claimed middle seats—strategically positioned.

Minister Crystal Young summoned her practiced smile. "Welcome to Women Of Righteous Design. Tonight, we're discussing virtuous women in contemporary culture."

They read Proverbs 31 together. As Minister Young began unpacking verses, Mother Bernice Williams rose determinedly.

"If I may interrupt—we need to address the elephant in the room regarding virtuous womanhood."

She displaced Crystal at the podium. "Proverbs 31:30: 'Favor is deceitful, and beauty is vain.' External appearance—fancy clothing, elaborate hairstyles, expensive jewelry—these are meaningless compared to a gentle spirit."

Her eyes landed pointedly on Trange' and Samantha. "Some believe dressing to attract attention honors God. But Scripture tells us differently. Our adornment should be the hidden person of the heart."

The room grew silent.

"When we prioritize external appearance over internal character, we communicate wrong values. The virtuous woman isn't known for her wardrobe—she's known for works."

She returned to her seat with righteous satisfaction.

But Minister Crystal wasn't finished. She returned with something harder in her expression.

"When we read about the virtuous woman, verse 22 says: 'her clothing is silk and purple.' Purple was the most expensive dye—reserved for royalty. This woman wore the finest materials."

The observation landed like a stone in still water.

"Moreover, verse 25: 'Strength and honor are her clothing.' Her clothing communicated character. Why would we honor God by rejecting beauty when Scripture celebrates creation?"

She looked at Trange' and Samantha. "Jesus is coming for our souls, not our clothes. We need to embrace each other as fellow travelers, not projects to fix. Jesus reserved His harshest criticism for religious leaders who valued tradition over mercy."

Trange' felt something shift—tears gathering as truth penetrated her defenses. She didn't need to be extra. Before God, she was loved—not *despite* her fabulousness, but *including* it.

Across the room, Mother Jones leaned to Mother Williams: "Look at her fake crying. Jezebel performing repentance."

"I know that spirit. I'll take her down several pegs."

First Lady Clarice watched, her protective instincts activated. *Lord, I need to pray before these ladies prey on this sister.*

During small group discussion, Trange' spoke openly: "I've spent my life believing I was too much. Tonight, I realized God didn't make a mistake creating me with this personality. The issue isn't that I'm too much—spaces have been too small."

Her voice strengthened. "I'm learning authentic faith doesn't require performing someone else's acceptable. It requires becoming more fully who God created—not less fabulous, but more faithful."

FaLessia responded: "I'm grateful you're here. Your confidence and questions force us to examine whether traditions serve God's purposes or just preferences."

As the evening concluded, Mother Williams rose. "There's a spirit of rebellion tonight. I'm proposing standards for

W.O.R.D. participation—basic guidelines ensuring commitment to biblical modesty and traditional values."

First Lady Clarice rose with unmistakable authority. "Whose standards? Jesus welcomed women religious leaders rejected. His anger was reserved for religious leaders placing heavy burdens without helping carry them."

Her voice gained prophetic edge. "My husband built a church reflecting Heaven's actual diversity. And I'll be damned if I'll sit quietly while you transform his legacy into an exclusive club."

She placed a hand on Trange's shoulder. "This woman came seeking God. Instead of welcoming her, we blamed her for a death having nothing to do with her. That's un-Christian. I won't stand for it continuing."

"First Lady, with all due respect—" Mother Williams began.

"No." Clarice's voice cut through the attempted deflection like a blade. "I don't want respect—I want righteousness. *Real* righteousness. The kind that values mercy over sacrifice, includes the excluded, and remembers that we're all just broken people desperately needing grace we don't deserve."

She turned to address the entire room. "If we're going to implement standards for participation, let's make sure they're biblical rather than cultural. Let's measure hearts instead of hemlines. Let's examine whether we're serving the poor, loving our neighbors, and reflecting Christ's character—not whether our dresses come from the right stores or our hairstyles meet someone's subjective approval."

***

Minister Crystal Young seized the moment of stunned silence to offer closing prayer—words about unity, grace, humility, and divine guidance that everyone desperately needed.

After closing prayer, women divided—some approaching Trange' with encouragement, others clustering around Mother Williams.

Outside, Samantha linked arms with Trange'. "Well, that was eventful."

"Spiritually violent might be more accurate."

Trange's phone buzzed: *YOU WERE MAGNIFICENT TONIGHT. COURAGE LOOKS GOOD ON YOU. PERHAPS DINNER SOMETIME? - ANDRE*

She stared at the message, torn between delight and apprehension. The First Lady's son was interested—which was flattering, exciting, and potentially complicated given that she was still navigating her new faith and the church politics that came with it. *How did he get my number,* she wondered.

But as the limousine pulled away, something solidified: she was exactly where God wanted her.

The war for Greater Mount Calvary's soul had escalated.

And Trange' Moreau had just declared which side she was fighting for.

Chapter 5: Conspiracy and Compromise

Aftermath and Allies

Trange' Moreau's penthouse overlooked the French Quarter like a queen surveying her kingdom, but tonight the view felt less triumphant and more like strategic positioning. The city sparkled below—neon lighting and history mixing in that peculiar New Orleans alchemy where sacred and secular refused to stay separate.

Her phone sat on the marble counter, Andre's text message still glowing:

YOU WERE MAGNIFICENT TONIGHT. COURAGE LOOKS GOOD ON YOU. PERHAPS WE COULD CONTINUE OUR CONVERSATION OVER DINNER SOMETIME? - ANDRE

"Girl, you've been staring at that phone for twenty minutes," Samantha declared from the leather sofa where she'd planted herself with a glass of wine. "Either respond or don't, but this tortured contemplation is exhausting to witness."

"It's complicated." Trange' finally set the phone down, moving to join her friend.

"It's only complicated if you make it complicated. The First Lady's fine son is interested. You're interested. Both of you are single, saved, and clearly attracted to each other. What's the problem?"

"The problem is I just survived church mothers trying to run me out of God's House, and now I'm potentially dating into the family they're warring against. It's strategic suicide."

Samantha laughed mirthlessly. "Baby, you think staying away from Andre *protects* you? Those mothers already hate you. You could become a nun and they'd find something to criticize. At least this way, you get a gorgeous man and powerful allies simultaneously."

Before Trange' could respond, her phone rang. FaLessia's name appeared on the screen.

"Well, well," Trange' answered. "Calling to debrief the mission?"

"Something like that." FaLessia's voice carried exhaustion mixed with strategic urgency. "However, I also wanted you to know—tonight's board meeting got ugly. The church mothers are organizing something. I couldn't hear specifics, but Mother Williams, Mother Jones, and Patricia Jones stayed behind after everyone left. That's never good."

Trange' felt familiar tension returning to her shoulders. "Let me guess—they're planning to take me down?"

"You, the trustees, anyone threatening their control. But Trange', there's something else. I talked to Shaniece earlier about everything happening at Greater Mount Calvary."

"You called my *sister*?" Trange's voice warmed. The prayer circle that had formed around her included some formidable women, but Shaniece Mfume held special status—someone who'd survived her own church warfare and emerged victorious.

"I needed perspective from someone who's fought similar battles and won, and she had some wisdom I think you need to hear."

Trange' switched to speaker phone so Samantha could listen. "I'm all ears."

"Shaniece said the biggest mistake she made during her crisis was trying to fight every battle alone. She thought asking for help showed weakness, that true strength meant handling

79

everything herself. But she learned that sometimes God provides victory through community, not isolation."

FaLessia's voice gained intensity. "She also said something about church politics that hit me hard: 'They want you to fight on their terms, using their weapons, playing their game. But you win by changing the rules entirely—by being so authentically yourself, so genuinely faithful, that their attacks reveal their own spiritual poverty rather than your supposed inadequacy.'"

Samantha raised her wine glass, saluting the wisdom.

"Shaniece offered to come down to New Orleans if you need backup," FaLessia continued. "She said watching you walk into that W.O.R.D. meeting reminded her of her own journey, and she wants to support you however she can."

Tears gathered in Trange's eyes—the healing kind that came from unexpected solidarity. "Tell her I appreciate that more than she knows. And tell her I'm learning that being fabulous and faithful aren't mutually exclusive."

"She already knows. She said you're teaching church folks a lesson they desperately need but don't want to learn: that God's grace is big enough for women who wear Valentino to Bible study."

After they ended the call, Trange' sat in contemplative silence while Samantha refilled their wine glasses.

"Your sister is wise," Samantha finally said. "And she's right about community. You're not in this alone, Trange'. You've got me, FaLessia, the First Lady, and apparently the entire Mfume family ready to go to war for you."

"I know." Trange' picked up her phone, opening Andre's message again. "Which is why I need to stop overthinking and start living. Those church mothers want me diminished, apologetic, performing humility I don't feel. The best response is being exactly who God created me to be—fabulously, unapologetically, faithfully myself."

She typed quickly before courage could desert her:

DINNER SOUNDS PERFECT. WHEN AND WHERE? - TRANGE' '

The response came within seconds:

SATURDAY, 7 PM. I'LL PICK YOU UP. DRESS CODE: EXACTLY AS FABULOUS AS YOU ARE. - ANDRE

Samantha squealed with delight while Trange' allowed herself a smile mixing anticipation and strategic satisfaction. If the church mothers wanted war, she'd give them war—but on her terms, and by playing a game they'd never anticipated.

The War Council

The conference room erupted into chaos—voices colliding like storm fronts, accusations flying faster than anyone could track, decades of suppressed tensions finally detonating in the administrative heart of Greater Mount Calvary Cathedral.

"—absolutely unacceptable that trustees think they can—"

"—bylaws clearly state during pastoral transition—"

"—been running this church for thirty years before you—"

"—financial oversight requires board approval, not individual—"

"ENOUGH!" Trustee Marcus Webb's voice cut through the cacophony like a judge's gavel striking marble. At seventy-one, the retired judge still commanded courtrooms—or in this case, church boardrooms—with the kind of authority that made grown men remember their manners.

Silence crashed over the assembled leadership like a wave, leaving only the air conditioning's hum and someone's nervous pen-clicking.

Webb stood slowly, his six-foot frame still imposing despite age softening his edges. "We will conduct this meeting with decorum befitting God's house, or we will adjourn until everyone remembers how civilized people communicate. Your choice."

Mother Bernice Williams opened her mouth—probably to object that *she* had been perfectly civilized—but Webb's raised eyebrow suggested she reconsider.

"The trustee board has developed a ninety-day transitional plan," Webb continued, spreading documents across the conference table. "During this period, we'll maintain current ministries, address immediate financial concerns, and begin the pastoral search process through proper channels with representation from all three boards."

"*Maintain* current ministries?" Mother Eartha Jones's voice dripped skepticism. "Including the progressive agenda that's been dividing this congregation?"

"Including," Webb replied with judicial neutrality, "all ministries Bishop Howard established that serve our community and honor biblical principles. If you have specific concerns about any ministry's theological soundness, document them formally for board review rather than making vague accusations about 'progressive agendas.'"

Mother Jones's face flushed, but Deacon Harold Williams—Mother Bernice's younger brother—spoke before she could respond.

"Judge Webb, with respect, this plan concentrates significant power in trustee hands. The deacon and mother boards have always shared governance equally."

"With respect, Deacon Williams, that's historically inaccurate," April Richardson interjected, her attorney's precision slicing through revisionist history. "The bylaws—which I helped draft fifteen years ago—clearly give trustees expanded authority during pastoral vacancies specifically to prevent the kind of power struggles currently threatening this institution."

She pulled up the bylaws on her laptop, projecting them onto the screen. "Article VII, Section 3: '*DURING PASTORAL VACANCY OR INCAPACITY, THE BOARD OF TRUSTEES SHALL ASSUME PRIMARY ADMINISTRATIVE AUTHORITY INCLUDING BUT NOT LIMITED TO FINANCIAL OVERSIGHT, OPERATIONAL DECISIONS, AND INTERIM PASTORAL ARRANGEMENTS, SUBJECT TO ADVISORY INPUT FROM DEACON AND MOTHER BOARDS.*'"

"Advisory input?" Mother Williams stood abruptly. "We're being reduced to advisors in a church we've served for decades?"

"You're being asked to fulfill the role the bylaws always assigned," April replied without inflection. "If you find that diminishing, perhaps you should examine why you assumed authority the governance structure never actually granted."

The temperature in the room dropped ten degrees.

"This is exactly the kind of disrespect—" Mother Jones began.

"Sit down, Mother Jones." Deacon Marcus Spence's voice carried unexpected steel. At forty-eight, he was younger than most deacons but commanded respect through genuine spiritual depth rather than political maneuvering. "Judge Webb is offering a reasonable path forward. We can either work together during this transition, or we can destroy this church through infighting while pretending we're protecting it."

Mother Jones turned to stare Deacon Hearns, her expression unreadable but intense. Something passed between them—a look carrying layers of meaning that made several people shift uncomfortably, though no one could articulate exactly why.

FaLessia Shaw caught the exchange, her strategic mind filing away the observation. That wasn't the first time she'd noticed charged moments between Mother Jones and Deacon Hearns, and now Spence seemed to recognize something in their dynamic that made him uncomfortable. *Interesting.*

Before the standoff could escalate, the conference room doors opened.

First Lady Clarice Howard entered with the kind of presence that transformed spaces without announcement. Grief had carved new lines around her eyes, but her carriage remained regal—a woman who'd buried her husband three weeks ago and was now fighting to preserve his legacy.

"I apologize for the interruption," she began, though her tone suggested she wasn't actually sorry. "I know it's unconventional for the first lady to attend board meetings."

"It's more than unconventional," Deacon Thompson objected. "It's inappropriate. You're not an official board member."

"Neither was I officially invited to my husband's funeral, yet I managed to show up," Clarice replied with smile sharp enough to draw blood. "Funny how propriety becomes flexible when convenient."

Mother Delilah Chain raised her hand tentatively. "With all due respect, First Lady Howard, some might question whether you're still technically the first lady given we no longer have a pastor."

The silence that followed felt apocalyptic.

Trustee Richmond shot to his feet, face flushed with outrage. "How dare you question—"

"David, please." Clarice's raised hand stopped his defense mid-sentence. She turned to Mother Chain with an expression of pity mixed with steel. "You're absolutely right, Mother Chain. I'm not technically first lady anymore. I'm the widow of a man who gave thirty-seven years to this congregation. I'm the woman who watched him die serving this church. And I'm someone who knows his vision better than anyone in this room."

She moved to the head of the table, positioning herself beside Judge Webb. "I lined up guest speakers who could unite rather than divide, who could model the kind of leadership my dear bishop hoped you'd eventually accept."

"You've arranged guest speakers?" Mother Williams's voice carried accusation. "Without board approval?"

"I've secured someone for this Sunday who will demonstrate what Bishop Howard meant by progressive faith rooted in biblical truth. Someone who can bridge the generational and theological gaps currently tearing us apart."

FaLessia leaned forward, her expression mixing curiosity and strategic calculation. "First Lady, if this speaker can actually unite the congregation during this volatile period, I support bringing them in. The trustee board can vote right now to approve this interim arrangement."

"Agreed," Judge Webb declared. "All trustees in favor of authorizing First Lady Howard to arrange this Sunday's guest speaker, say aye."

Five trustees immediately responded: "Aye."

Patricia Jones remained conspicuously silent, her abstention noted by everyone present.

"The ayes have it," Webb announced. "First Lady Howard has authorization to proceed."

Clarice turned to the deacon board with expression suggesting this wasn't really a request. "I need the deacons' support as well. Not for my authority, but to show the congregation that leadership is united during this transition."

Deacon Spence stood immediately. "I move that the deacon board supports this arrangement. All in favor?"

Seven hands rose—not unanimous, but a clear majority.

"Thank you," Clarice said with genuine gratitude. "Your trust means more than you know."

As she prepared to leave, Deacon Hearns—who'd remained silent throughout—cleared his throat. "First Lady, you never mentioned who this speaker actually is."

Clarice paused in the doorway, her smile suggesting she'd been waiting for exactly this question. "A powerful vessel of God. Someone whose testimony will challenge comfortable assumptions while honoring biblical truth. You'll see Sunday."

Mother Jones shot Deacon Hearns a look that could freeze champagne—warning, possession, something that made FaLessia's earlier suspicions crystallize into near-certainty. Hearns's face flushed slightly, his gaze dropping to the table.

The First Lady noticed the exchange, her smile widening almost imperceptibly before she departed.

April Richardson stood, gathering her materials with efficient finality. "The bylaws clearly give trustees primary authority during this transition. Judge Webb's plan will be implemented as outlined. Any objections should be filed formally through proper governance channels—which means written documentation, not hallway conspiracies."

She looked pointedly at Mother Williams and Mother Jones. "Meeting adjourned."

The trustees—except Patricia Jones—rose and departed with coordinated efficiency.

Deacons and mothers filed out with grumbled disapproval, their body language broadcasting plans for continued resistance.

The Conspiracy Crystallizes

Three figures remained in the emptying conference room: Mother Bernice Williams, Mother Eartha Jones, and Trustee Patricia Jones. They sat in silence for several minutes, each processing the strategic defeat they'd just experienced.

Finally, Mother Bernice spoke, her voice carrying calculated strategy. "If we could get all the deacons and mothers together—really together, united behind our vision—we could unseat a few of these trustees. Then the balance of power shifts toward us."

She turned to Patricia. "Pat, I know you've got dirt. Between the three of us, we know everyone's business. We could use this as leverage—not maliciously, you understand, but strategically. To protect the church."

Mother Jones's face lit with something approaching glee. "I know where the bones are buried throughout this congregation." She slammed her palm against the conference table. "How about we shake the ground and see what comes up?"

But even as she spoke, anxiety flickered behind her eyes. If they started exposing secrets, would hers stay buried? Her relationship with Deacon Hearns had remained hidden for numerous years through careful discretion. But conspiracies had a way of becoming uncontrollable—bones shaken loose tended to scatter in unexpected directions.

Patricia leaned forward, oblivious to her mother's internal calculation. "We need a gathering that won't raise suspicion. Something traditional, expected." Her eyes brightened. "A bake sale. We'll organize a massive church bake sale. If all the old ladies come together, tea will *definitely* be spelled."

"Brilliant," Mother Williams declared. "We'll call it 'Supporting Church Ministries.' No one questions women organizing food events."

"And while we're decorating tables," Mother Jones added, forcing enthusiasm over anxiety, "we'll coordinate our campaign to remind these trustees who actually runs this church."

They gathered their belongings with renewed purpose. As they prepared to depart, Patricia suddenly stopped.

"I forgot my keys."

She rushed back while her mother and Mother Williams continued to their vehicles. But as Patricia approached the building's rear entrance, she noticed Deacon Marcus Spence's distinctive silver Lexus parked in shadows near the auxiliary offices.

Curiosity overwhelmed propriety. She moved closer, noticing an abandoned vacuum cleaner. The lights were off but sounds filtered through—unmistakable sounds of unrighteousness.

Patricia opened the door.

Deacon Marcus Spence was locked in passionate embrace with Libby Jean Hawthorne—Mother Hawthorne's supposedly virtuous daughter.

"Oh my God, Deacon!"

"Sweet Jesus, Usher Hawthorne!"

Patricia slammed the door shut. Within seconds, it flew open. Libby rushed past with mortified apology, clothing disheveled, sanctified composure shattered.

Patricia called sweetly: "Hope you have time to finish cleaning the church!"

She leaned against the wall, waiting. Deacon Spence emerged moments later, half-dressed, looking like a man whose world was ending.

"Well, well, well." Patricia's voice dripped theatrical delight. "That wasn't Deaconess Spence, was it?"

Spence jogged behind her, fumbling with clothes. "Please don't tell my wife. *Please.*"

"Your secret is safe with me," Patricia interrupted.

His relief was palpable.

"For now." She stopped, turning to face him. "As long as," Patricia continued, straightening his tie with maternal menace, "you help me out when the time comes."

"When?" His voice cracked.

"You'll know. I'll be in touch." She patted his chest. "And Deacon? Make sure your maid cleans that office thoroughly."

Inside her car, Patricia immediately dialed her mother.

"Girl, why you calling? I was in prayer," Mother Jones answered with irritation.

"Trust me, you don't want to miss this."

"Well, spill it then."

"I just caught Deacon Spence and Usher Libby having close fellowship on a desk in the auxiliary office. At church."

"That's just nasty." A pause. "Wait until I tell the girls."

"No, Mama." Patricia's voice sharpened. "We can use him. Since he supported Judge Webb so strongly, let's use him for information and to help turn the tides."

"Yes, Lord. We got that sucker." Mother Jones's voice carried vindictive satisfaction but underneath ran a current of fear. *If Patricia was this good at discovering secrets, how long before someone discovered hers?* "Mother Hawthorne acts like her daughter is so virtuous—all along she's Jezebel's understudy."

They revised their conspiracy to include blackmail. But Mother Jones's mind was already calculating contingencies. Maybe she needed to be more careful with Deacon Hearns. Maybe their stolen moments in his office after evening services carried more risk than she'd acknowledged. Maybe—

"Oh, and don't forget," Mother Jones forced her attention back to immediate targets, "that Triangle, STrange', Trange' — whatever her name is—needs to be taken down also. Can't have that woman prancing around here like she owns the place."

Patricia's smile could be heard through the phone. "Don't worry, Mama. We'll handle Miss Moreau. One way or another, she'll learn that Greater Mount Calvary belongs to us."

They ended the call with satisfaction that had nothing to do with serving God and everything to do with protecting territory.

Mother Jones sat in darkness, anxiety building. She'd encouraged her daughter to weaponize secrets while sitting on the biggest secret of all. And if this conspiracy spiraled out of control, if bones really did shake loose from unexpected places, her carefully constructed life could crumble faster than she could rebuild it.

Lord, what have I started? she prayed, though the prayer felt hollow. *Protect me from my own schemes.*

In the darkness of the church parking lot, Deacon Marcus Spence sat in his car, head against the steering wheel, wondering how his moment of weakness had transformed into leverage someone else now held over his entire future.

***

In her modest home, First Lady Clarice Howard knelt beside her bed, hands clasped but mind racing too much for coherent prayer. The house felt silent without Marcus—no sound of sermons being reviewed, no theological journals rustling, no soft snoring that had annoyed her for thirty-seven years.

She'd projected confidence during the board meeting, but now, alone with God and her doubts, the façade crumbled.

"No weapon formed against you shall prosper."

The verse from Isaiah had sustained her through countless crises. But lately, its actual words haunted her with uncomfortable precision. It didn't say weapons wouldn't be *formed*. Only that they wouldn't *prosper*.

Which meant weapons could be fashioned, sharpened, aimed directly at her heart. Could strike with devastating accuracy, drawing blood and creating permanent scars. The promise wasn't protection from pain—it was assurance that pain wouldn't achieve its ultimate purpose of destroying her. But the space between "formed" and "not prosper" felt vast enough to contain oceans of pain.

But Lord, how much destruction must happen before You intervene? How many weapons get formed and launched before the 'not prospering' part kicks in?

She thought about the conspiracy crystallizing—Mother Williams, Mother Jones, and Patricia coordinating attacks, gathering ammunition, preparing to weaponize decades of accumulated secrets. And she'd just made herself—and her son—primary targets.

Am I strong enough for this?

She moved to the window where moonlight painted the garden Marcus had planted. He'd designed it to bloom year-round so she'd always have beauty during difficult seasons.

Her reflection showed a woman grief and stress had aged beyond seventy-three. Fear—honest, bone-deep fear—shadowed her eyes despite her public confidence.

What if my faith wavers when the weapons strike? What if I watch my son get destroyed by church politics and break under the weight of knowing I put him there?

The doubts felt blasphemous—the kind a First Lady wasn't supposed to entertain. She was supposed to model unwavering faith, demonstrate unshakeable confidence in God's protection.

But tonight, she was just Clarice—a scared widow facing enemies who knew every vulnerability, every place where armor didn't quite cover exposed flesh.

Lord, I know Sunday's showdown is coming. I know those mothers are planning something devastating. And I'm terrified—not just of what they'll do to me, but of what it might do to my faith.

She stood there wrestling with questions that had no easy answers, doubts that felt too honest to be holy.

Finally, she whispered the only prayer her broken faith could manage: *"I don't know if I'm strong enough. But You do. So I'm trusting not in my strength, but in Yours. Because mine feels inadequate right now."*

It wasn't the confident prayer of a First Lady. It was just honest—raw, vulnerable, terrifyingly honest.

And somehow, in that honesty, something shifted. Not peace. Not confidence everything would work painlessly. But something quieter: acceptance that weapons would be formed, battles fought, wounds inflicted—and that God's promise wasn't immunity from pain but redemption through it.

She returned to her bedside where Marcus's Bible lay open to Philippians 1:6: ***"BEING CONFIDENT OF THIS VERY THING, THAT HE WHICH HATH BEGUN A GOOD WORK IN YOU WILL PERFORM IT UNTIL THE DAY OF JESUS CHRIST."***

God had started something at Greater Mount Calvary—through Marcus's ministry, through progressive inclusion, through women like Trange' who challenged comfortable categories. And what God started, He would finish.

Even if the finishing involved walking through weapons and fire.

Okay, Lord. I'm still scared. Still not sure I'm strong enough. But I'm showing up anyway. For Marcus. For this church. For that fabulous sister in Valentino. And maybe because You're asking me to.

She climbed into bed, exhaustion finally overwhelming anxiety. Tomorrow would bring new battles, new conspiracies, new weapons being formed.

But tonight, she'd rest in the uncomfortable truth that faith wasn't immunity from warfare—it was courage to fight anyway, trusting that weapons might wound but wouldn't ultimately win.

The conspiracy had crystallized.

The weapons had been gathered.

And First Lady Clarice Howard had just decided that her fear wouldn't determine her faithfulness.

Sunday was coming.

And with it, a reckoning none of them could fully anticipate.

Chapter 6: A Church That Preys

Sweet Deception

The church's fellowship kitchen hummed with domestic harmony—the kind of scene that belonged on Southern Living covers. Flour dusted countertops like fresh snow, mixers whirred their mechanical hymns, and the air carried intoxicating scents: vanilla extract, brown sugar caramelizing, butter melting into perfection.

Mother Delilah Chain rolled pie dough with practiced precision, her movements synchronized with decades of muscle memory. Beside her, Sister Patricia Chen measured ingredients with accountant's exactness while Mother Hawthorne—blissfully ignorant of her daughter's recent auxiliary office indiscretions—piped decorative frosting onto cupcakes with artistic flair.

"I do love our baking days," Mother Chain sighed contentedly. "Reminds me why I joined this ministry thirty years ago. Simple fellowship, serving together, no drama or politics."

"Amen to that," Sister Chen agreed, though her tone suggested she knew better than to expect drama-free existence at Greater Mount Calvary.

The fellowship hall's double doors swung open with theatrical timing. Mother Eartha Jones and Mother Bernice Williams entered like generals surveying battlefields, their smiles fixed with deliberate sweetness that immediately transformed the atmosphere from harmonious to hazardous.

Something shifted in the air—subtle but unmistakable, like barometric pressure dropping before storms.

Mother Heady Mitchell sensed it immediately.

At six-foot-one and built like the semi-professional basketball player she'd been fifty years ago—one of Louisiana's first African American women to break that barrier—Mother Heady commanded respect through presence alone. Her height made her formidable. Her prayer life made her dangerous. Her willingness to deliver tongue-lashings that would make demons cower made Jones and Williams typically avoid direct confrontation.

She stood at the front of the room, hand on hip, watching the facade as Jones and Williams greeted everyone with artificial warmth. This behavior fell so far outside their typical patterns that alarm bells rang in her spirit.

Lord, reveal what these two are plotting, she prayed silently, her eyes tracking their movements with predator's precision.

Jones and Williams began circulating, pausing at various stations with compliments that dripped honey-coated poison.

"Sister Causey, those cupcakes look absolutely divine," Jones cooed. "You have such talent."

"Mother Hawthorne, that frosting technique is magazine-worthy," Williams added with smile that never reached her eyes.

But their attention kept drifting back to Mother Heady, calculating glances that suggested they were measuring threats and planning approaches.

Mother Heady had heard about their recent scheming—FaLessia had quietly warned her that something was brewing, that the church mothers were organizing beyond normal political maneuvering. And now here they were, performing sweetness with Oscar-worthy commitment.

She charged across the room with strides that scattered lesser women. "This is church ground," she announced without preamble, positioning herself between them and the other mothers. "And I won't stand for foolishness. I've heard about your antics."

Jones's expression cycled through surprise before settling on wounded innocence. "Mother Heady, we're simply fellowshipping and admiring your confectionary contributions. Nothing nefarious, I assure you."

"Absolutely," Williams chimed in, gesturing toward the display table where Mother Heady's legendary desserts commanded attention. "Your German chocolate cake is the talk of New Orleans. And those triple chocolate creations—what do you call them?"

"Death and Salvation by Chocolate," Mother Heady replied automatically, her guard lowering slightly at genuine appreciation. The cake would kill you with richness and resurrect you with flavor—a reputation earned through decades of perfecting the recipe.

"And these pecan bars," Jones continued, leaning in to examine the buttery confections. "Glorious doesn't begin to describe them."

Mother Heady felt herself blushing despite strategic instincts screaming warnings. She glanced over her three-tiered presentation of treats that represented forty hours of baking— and couldn't suppress pride at her culinary accomplishments.

Jones caught Williams's eye. A look passed between them— silent coordination that Mother Heady missed while admiring her own handiwork.

"You know," Jones announced to the assembled women, "while we're all gathered here, and with our great prayer warrior Mother Heady present, this seems the perfect time for corporate prayer. We need divine guidance for our church during this transition."

"I'm always down to talk to my God," Mother Heady declared, her spiritual authority reasserting itself. She called the women to gather, forming a circle that felt both holy and strategic.

They joined hands while Mother Heady launched into prayer that would have impressed revival tent preachers. Her words rose with power, calling down Heaven's intervention, binding spirits of division, loosing peace and unity across Greater Mount Calvary.

But Jones and Williams kept their eyes open.

Another "eye-sation" passed between them—silent countdown to coordinated chaos.

Midway through Mother Heady's most passionate supplication, Williams suddenly screamed in pain, grabbing her hip. "My trick hip! It's giving out!"

Everything happened in slow motion yet too fast to prevent. Williams's falling trajectory aimed directly at Mother Heady's display table. Her flailing arms struck the edge with devastating accuracy. The table tipped. Cakes airborne briefly before gravity claimed them. German chocolate glory splattering across tile. Death and Salvation by Chocolate living up to its name as it died spectacularly across the floor. Buttery pecan bars scattering like shrapnel.

Williams crashed to the ground in theatrical collapse, moaning with Oscar-worthy commitment despite remaining completely unscathed.

Mothers rushed to help. Deacons poured through doors, drawn by commotion.

But Mother Heady stood frozen, tears filling her eyes, fists slowly clenching as she surveyed the destruction of forty hours' work.

"LOOK AT WHAT YOU DID!" The scream erupted from depths that transcended anger into righteous fury. She locked eyes on Williams sprawled dramatically across tile. "We about to have some close fellowship! I am about to lay hands on this—"

"Heady, no!" Deacon Samuel Fry appeared from nowhere, wrapping strong arms around her before maternal violence could manifest. At seventy-three, he still possessed the strength that had made him semi-professional boxer forty years ago.

He'd been her companion for five years—eating dinner together five times weekly since his wife died the same year as her husband. Everyone knew he loved her. She liked him back, enjoyed his company, appreciated his steady presence. But she'd committed herself to God after her husband's death, refusing to date or remarry despite Deacon Fry's patient hope.

He'd accepted this arrangement if he could spend time with her and eat her delicious food. This made watching her culinary masterpieces destroyed particularly painful for both of them.

"Baby girl, you're a great cook," he whispered urgently, restraining her while she struggled toward Williams. "You can whip up replacements in no time. I'll stop over tonight to help. We'll bake together, and it'll be even better."

His voice—gentle, loving, completely sincere—penetrated her rage. Mother Heady took shuddering breath, then another. Finally nodded.

She snatched her apron off with enough force to rip fabric, threw it at Williams's prone form, and stormed out with dignity that somehow transcended fury.

Miraculously, Mother Williams's hip felt better immediately. She rose with assistance from Jones, brushing off her dress while deacons cleaned the spectacular mess.

Tea Time

The mothers gathered outside for respite, clustering beneath ancient live oaks that had witnessed seventy-five years of church politics. Humid air carried jasmine scent mixed with something heavier—anticipation of secrets about to surface.

Mother Jones waited until Mother Heady's car disappeared from the parking lot before beginning her performance. "You know," she announced with calculated casualness, "I've been troubled by changes at our church lately."

Several mothers leaned in—gossip's siren call irresistible.

"Women preachers," Jones continued, voice dripping disapproval. "That gay choir director who thinks his agenda belongs in God's house. And loose women parading around in inappropriate clothing."

The group erupted with whispered affirmations, each mother adding observations they'd stored like ammunition for exactly this moment.

Mother Chain: "I heard Minister Young is dating someone outside the church—"

Sister Chen: "And did you see what Sister Renee wore last Sunday—"

Mother Hawthorne: "My Libby said the youth ministry is teaching things that don't align with scripture—"

Jones and Williams exchanged satisfied glances. Mission accomplished. The tea they'd been waiting for was spilling with perfect timing.

"And that Trange' girl," Williams added with theatrical disgust, her voice pitched to command attention.

"I think she's pretty," one younger mother ventured timidly. "I like her style. Makes church feel less stuffy."

Mother Jones shot her a look that could freeze baptismal water. "Women should be modest as the Lord commanded." The pronouncement landed with enough authority to silence further dissent.

Mother Rose Washington leaned forward, her seventy-eight-year-old frame bent but formidable around the African walking stick she gripped with both hands. Her dark skin had weathered decades of Louisiana sun, her eyes sharp as the day she'd first arrived at Greater Mount Calvary fifty years ago.

"I knew I'd seen that girl from somewhere," she announced with voice carrying swamp wisdom and generational memory. "She's not from around these parts originally."

This caught Jones and Williams's immediate attention. "Go on," they said almost in unison, predators sensing wounded prey.

"I know her people. Her *real* people." Mother Rose's voice dropped to conspiratorial whisper that somehow carried perfectly. "Sad people. Ungodly people. Down there in the muck—them Caldwell Parish folks. Not a dime or penny to their names. Don't know how she became so fancy. Nothing but harlots and tramps down in those parts."

She paused for effect, enjoying the rapt attention. "But I know some people down there. Let me place a call. I'll have the whole story by evening."

Mother Jones's face gleamed with vindictive satisfaction barely concealed beneath spiritual concern. This was better than she'd hoped—actual dirt from Trange's past, verifiable through

101

sources, ammunition that could be weaponized with plausible deniability about protecting the church from deception.

Across the courtyard, through glass windows, they spotted movement. A cookie-and-cream colored Bentley pulled into the circular drive with the kind of arrival that announced wealth beyond typical church member means.

Trange' emerged wearing an oversized black and white hat that would have looked ridiculous on anyone else but somehow worked perfectly on her. The form-fitting black dress featured a white lightning bolt through it—dramatic, slightly dangerous, absolutely Trange'.

Three men in professional attire emerged behind her, each carrying ornate boxes.

Mother Jones felt disgust warring with excitement. The woman was insufferable, yes, but about to walk directly into a trap so perfectly constructed she'd never see it coming.

"Come with me, Bernice," Jones commanded, rising with predatory grace.

They approached while other mothers watched from the courtyard, anticipating confrontation that would provide entertainment for weeks.

Trange' saw them coming and braced for battle—shoulders straightening, chin lifting, armor activating beneath her fashionable exterior.

But instead of attacks, she received warm welcomes that shocked her into temporary speechlessness.

"Sister Trange'!" Mother Jones's voice carried genuine-sounding delight. "What a wonderful surprise!"

Williams watched in admiration. Her friend was Oscar-worthy in this performance.

"What do we have here?" Jones asked with what seemed like sincere curiosity.

"These are my assistants," Trange' replied cautiously, testing dangerous waters. "We're donating desserts to the bake sale. I trust that's acceptable?"

The first assistant stepped forward, presenting a box with theatrical flourish. "Artisan French macarons in lavender, rose, and champagne flavors. Imported ingredients, hand-crafted by New Orleans' premier patisserie."

The second assistant revealed his offering. "Deconstructed tiramisu—espresso-soaked ladyfingers layered with mascarpone cream infused with Italian liqueur, topped with dark chocolate shavings and edible gold leaf."

The third completed the presentation. "And finally, individual crème brûlée tarts with vanilla bean custard and caramelized sugar, garnished with fresh berries."

Each dessert probably cost more than the entire bake sale's projected revenue. The offerings screamed wealth, sophistication, and subtle message: *I belong here, and I have resources you can't match.*

Mother Jones examined the confections with expression mixing appreciation and calculation. "How lovely! We thank you so much. I know we got off to a rough start, but this gesture is wonderful. Please, place these over here with the other contributions."

Trange' felt tears gathering—the healing kind that came from unexpected acceptance after weeks of rejection. The tension that had lived in her shoulders since Sunday's traumatic altar call began dissolving. *Could they be welcoming me?*

"You know," Jones continued, her hand finding Trange's shoulder with what felt like maternal warmth, "there's a special service this Sunday. New speaker, testimony time—something you definitely shouldn't miss. We'd love to see you there."

The invitation landed like benediction. Trange' felt walls crumbling, hope rising, the possibility that maybe—finally— she'd found genuine acceptance. Her eyes misted as she nodded enthusiastically.

"I wouldn't miss it for the world," she managed, voice thick with emotion.

Jones moved in for a hug, and Trange' returned it gratefully— two women who'd been at odds now embracing like sisters reconciled. "Thank you so much, sweety. However will we pay you back for this charitable gift?"

"I'll hear nothing of it," Trange' replied, blinking back tears. "I'm a member now. I want to serve. This is what sisters do for each other."

Williams caught Jones's eye over Trange's shoulder—a look Trange' couldn't see, filled with satisfaction at how perfectly their prey was swallowing the bait.

"We need to finish preparations," Jones said warmly, pulling back from the embrace. "But Sister Trange' , we're so glad you're becoming part of our family. Everyone will be getting their just desserts very soon—all this delicious food you've brought will be such a blessing."

Trange' laughed at what seemed like a playful comment about the bake sale offerings. "I'm just happy to contribute."

Williams stepped forward, taking both of Trange's hands in hers with what appeared to be genuine affection. "We'll see you Sunday then? Bright and early?"

"Absolutely. I'll be there." Trange' squeezed back, her guard completely down, her heart open to what felt like the acceptance she'd been desperately seeking.

"Wonderful," Williams said with smile that looked warm to Trange' but carried edges visible only to those watching carefully. "It's going to be a service no one will ever forget."

As Trange' turned to leave with her assistants, she glanced back one more time. Mother Jones waved with what looked like genuine fondness. Mother Williams smiled broadly, mouthing "See you Sunday" with enthusiasm that seemed completely sincere.

Trange' waved back, practically floating on air as she walked toward her Bentley. Her assistants exchanged glances but said nothing, unsure how to process the dramatic shift from expected confrontation to what appeared to be genuine reconciliation.

"Ma'am, that went surprisingly well," the first assistant ventured as Marcus opened her door.

"It did, didn't it?" Trange' settled into leather luxury, her smile genuine and unguarded. "Maybe I was wrong about them. Maybe they just needed time to see past the exterior to recognize genuine faith."

She pulled out her phone, texting her prayer circle with joy instead of distress:

SISTERS, YOU WON'T BELIEVE WHAT JUST HAPPENED. THE CHURCH MOTHERS WELCOMED ME! THEY INVITED ME TO

Rev. Dr. Mario DeSean Booker

TESTIMONY SERVICE SUNDAY AND ACTUALLY SEEMED GENUINE. MAYBE THINGS ARE FINALLY TURNING AROUND. GOD IS SO GOOD! - TRANGE'

The responses came quickly:

Samantha: *REALLY? THAT SEEMS ... SUDDEN. ARE YOU SURE?*

FaLessia: *TRANGE', BE CAREFUL. THOSE TWO DON'T CHANGE THAT FAST. THIS MIGHT BE—*

But Trange' was too happy to process warnings. She typed back:

I KNOW IT SEEMS SUDDEN, BUT YOU SHOULD HAVE SEEN THEM. REAL HUGS, GENUINE SMILES. SOMETIMES PEOPLE JUST NEED TO SEE YOU'RE SERIOUS ABOUT FAITH. I'M CHOOSING TO BELIEVE THE BEST. SEE YOU ALL SUNDAY! ❤️

She set her phone down, watching the French Quarter slide past her window as Marcus navigated familiar streets. For the first time since that traumatic Sunday when Bishop Howard collapsed, she felt genuine peace about her place at Greater Mount Calvary.

Thank You, Lord, she prayed silently, *for softening their hearts. For opening doors I thought were permanently closed. For showing me that persistence and authenticity eventually win people over.*

As the Bentley disappeared around the corner, Mother Jones and Mother Williams stood at the fellowship hall window, watching her departure.

"She actually believed us," Williams marveled, shaking her head. "Hook, line, and sinker."

"Of course she did," Jones replied with satisfaction that bordered on glee. "Desperate people believe what they want to believe. She's been so hungry for acceptance that she couldn't see the trap even when we laid it right in front of her."

"And Sunday?"

"Sunday, Mother Rose's information will be ready. Sunday, we'll have testimony service where Sister Trange's real background gets exposed in front of the entire congregation. Sunday, she'll learn that some doors close for good reasons."

They turned away from the window, their laughter carrying through the fellowship hall like crows celebrating a successful hunt.

Behind them, scattered mothers began cleaning up, most oblivious to the conspiracy that had just tightened its noose. Only a few—like Mother Chain—had caught the subtle wrongness in Jones and Williams's behavior, the calculated quality of their warmth that felt more like strategy than genuine reconciliation.

Lord, protect that girl, Mother Chain prayed silently as she boxed up her pies. *Because something wicked this way comes, and she has no idea what's waiting for her.*

Sunday was coming.

Testimony service awaited.

And Trange' Moreau walked toward it with joy in her heart and complete blindness to the public execution being prepared specifically for her destruction.

The conspiracy had moved from planning to execution.

The trap had been set and baited.

Rev. Dr. Mario DeSean Booker

And the prey had swallowed the bait whole, mistaking poison for nourishment, destruction for acceptance, calculated cruelty for answered prayer.

Chapter 7: Sunday Morning Warfare

Mother Rose's voice crackled through the phone line with barely contained excitement, each word dripping with the kind of satisfaction that comes from holding explosive information. "Girl, you won't believe what I found out about Miss-High-and-Mighty Trange' Moreau."

On the other end, Mother Jones reclined in her favorite armchair, her weathered fingers wrapped around a delicate China cup filled with Meyer lemon tea—the kind she imported specially because regular lemons simply wouldn't do for a woman of her refined sensibilities. Her eyes sparkled with anticipation as she took a deliberate sip, savoring both the citrus notes and the promise of scandal.

"Go ahead, Rose. I'm listening."

The words that followed painted such a vivid picture of Trange's past that even Mother Jones—who prided herself on maintaining composure in all circumstances—nearly choked on her tea. Names, dates, business dealings that skirted the edges of propriety, relationships that would make the sanctified sisters clutch their pearls until their knuckles turned white.

"Hold on, Rose." Mother Jones set her cup down with a sharp clink against the saucer. "We need Bernice on three-way. This is too good for just the two of us."

She conference-called Mother Williams, her thick fingers navigating the phone buttons with surprising dexterity for someone who claimed technology was the devil's playground.

"Bernice? Girl, hear this mess. Rose, tell her everything. Don't leave out a single detail."

Rose launched into her recitation again, this time with even more theatrical flair, knowing she had a larger audience. Mother Williams listened in stunned silence, her shock genuine even though she'd suspected Trange's past contained skeletons. But this? This exceeded even her most creative assumptions about what worldly women got into before finding the Lord.

"Sweet Jesus," Mother Williams breathed when Rose finally paused for air. "That woman walked into Greater Mount Calvary like she was visiting royalty, and all this time ... "

"Oh, it gets better," Rose interrupted, her voice dropping to a conspiratorial whisper that somehow carried more weight than her earlier volume. "I got her people to agree to come up here. Told them we're honoring their family members—some nonsense about community appreciation and wanting them to introduce themselves and her at Sunday service."

The silence that followed lasted exactly three heartbeats before all three women burst into laughter—the kind that comes from somewhere dark and satisfied, the sound of crows celebrating a successful hunt.

"Rose, you are absolutely diabolical," Mother Jones managed between gasps. "Getting them to publicly present her background to the whole congregation? Under the guise of family honor?"

"Sunday morning," Mother Williams added, her voice hardening with resolve. "Testimony service. When the sanctuary is packed and every ear is listening. The whole church will finally see what kind of woman has been prancing around here acting like she belongs."

They spent the next twenty minutes finalizing details with the precision of generals planning a military campaign. Who would sit where. When the "family introductions" would happen. How to ensure maximum attendance and impact. By the time they ended the call, the conspiracy had crystallized from malicious impulse into coordinated execution.

Mother Williams hung up and immediately texted Patricia Jones: ***SUNDAY MORNING. BE READY. EVERYTHING CHANGES.***

Patricia read the message and smiled. Finally, that worldly woman would be exposed for who she really was. No more strutting around the church like she owned the place. No more catching the attention of men who should know better. After Sunday, Trange' Moreau would be finished at Greater Mount Calvary.

The conspiracy was set. The trap was baited. And the prey had no idea Sunday morning would become her public execution.

The First Date Debrief

Trange' kicked off her Louboutins the moment she walked through her penthouse door, phone already pressed to her ear before the shoes hit the marble floor.

"Shaniece? Girl, I need to tell you about this date before I explode."

On the other end, Shaniece Mfume settled deeper into her sofa, recognizing the breathless quality in her friend's voice. This wasn't Trange' the business mogul or Trange' the strategic socialite. This was Trange' the woman—vulnerable, excited, slightly terrified.

"I'm all ears. Start from the beginning and don't skip any details."

Trange' poured herself a glass of wine—her last glass before officially giving up alcohol, she'd promised herself—and began narrating the evening with Andre with the kind of detail usually reserved for merger negotiations.

He'd taken her to Commander's Palace, which should have been predictable but somehow felt perfect. Not trying too hard, not slumming it, just confident enough to choose a classic. They'd talked for three hours—actual conversation, not the performance art that usually passed for dates in her social circle. He'd asked about her business with genuine curiosity rather than the calculating assessment most men brought to discussions of her success. She'd asked about his calling to ministry, and his answer had been refreshingly free of religious performance.

"He listens, Shaniece. Like, really listens. Not just waiting for his turn to talk or looking for openings to impress me. He asked follow-up questions. He remembered details from things I mentioned in passing."

"Okay, but what about the chemistry?" Shaniece asked, knowing her friend well enough to cut through the romantic preamble to the question that mattered.

Trange's laugh held notes of embarrassment and delight. "Oh, the chemistry is ridiculous. We're talking combustible. He walked me to my door, and I invited him in."

"Trange'!"

"I know, I know. But Shaniece, I was thinking like the old me for a second. Just one nightcap, what's the harm? But he declined. Said as a minister, it wouldn't be appropriate. Which should have been the end of it, except ... "

She paused, remembering the moment with perfect clarity. "He kissed my hand. So old-fashioned and sweet. Then my cheek. And I don't know what possessed me, but I guided his mouth to mine. Just grabbed this fine man and kissed him like we were in some romance novel."

Shaniece gasped. "You didn't."

"I absolutely did. And Shaniece? He kissed me back. *Really* kissed me. His lips—I mean, this man has the most perfectly full, juicy lips—and through that cinnamon-brown complexion, I watched him blush. Actually blush! He thanked me, which was adorable and confusing, and then he walked away."

"Wait, he just left?"

"He texted me before I even got my shoes off." Trange' pulled up the message, reading it aloud with girlish excitement that would have shocked her business rivals. *YOU'RE DANGEROUS AND A CHALLENGE. I LIKE BOTH. LOOKING FORWARD TO OUR NEXT DATE.*

"Oh, you in trouble now," Shaniece teased, but her voice carried genuine happiness. "I haven't heard you sound like this about a man in ... ever, actually."

"That's because I've never felt like this about a man," Trange' admitted, her voice dropping to something more vulnerable. "It's new. It's terrifying. It's wonderful. I don't know how to do this—the whole faith-based relationship thing where you actually court instead of just sleeping together and sorting out feelings later."

"You'll figure it out," Shaniece assured her. "And I'll be there Sunday to see this man who's got my girl acting like a teenager. What time does service start?"

"Eleven. But come early—I want you to meet some people. And I might need moral support. Those church mothers are still giving me trouble."

"They're always going to give you trouble, sis. That's what church mothers do when they feel threatened. But you've got friends in that building. You've got First Lady Clarice on your side. And apparently, you've got her son very interested. Focus on that."

They talked for another twenty minutes—dissecting every moment of the date, analyzing every word of Andre's text, planning Trange's outfit for Sunday. By the time they hung up, Trange' felt grounded again, ready to face whatever Greater Mount Calvary threw at her next.

She had no idea what Sunday morning actually had in store.

Strategic Lunch

The bistro—Café Amelie, tucked away in a French Quarter courtyard where brick walls and hanging plants created intimate atmosphere—provided the perfect setting for strategic conversation. Mother Heady had chosen it deliberately, knowing they needed privacy for discussions that couldn't happen at the church.

FaLessia arrived first, claiming their usual corner table beneath a spreading oak tree that filtered afternoon sunlight into lace patterns across the tablecloth. She ordered sweet tea and checked her phone, reviewing notes from the previous night's women's meeting that had devolved into thinly veiled warfare.

"Sorry I'm late," Mother Heady announced, settling into her chair with the careful movement of someone whose joints occasionally reminded her of her eighty-three years. "Traffic on Rampart was ridiculous."

"You're not late—I'm early. Nervous energy."

Mother Heady studied FaLessia over her reading glasses, those sharp eyes that could read spirits, missing nothing. "The church mothers."

"The church mothers," FaLessia confirmed. "Heady, they're planning something. I can feel it. The way Mother Williams and Mother Jones stayed behind after the board meeting, whispering. The looks they were giving Trange' during women's meeting. Patricia Jones practically vibrating with satisfaction about something."

"That girl never got over Andre breaking up with her in high school," Heady observed, signaling the waiter for coffee. "Now she sees him paying attention to Sister Moreau, and all those old feelings are coming back twisted up with jealousy and entitlement."

"It's more than jealousy though. This feels coordinated. Calculated."

Before Heady could respond, Samantha Williams burst through the courtyard entrance, her energy preceding her like a force field. She spotted FaLessia and headed straight for their table, her smile warm and unfiltered.

FaLessia stood to embrace her, genuine affection evident in the hug. "Samantha! I didn't know you'd be here."

"I was in the neighborhood doing some errands and thought I'd grab lunch. Is it okay if I join you?"

"Of course." FaLessia gestured to the empty chair, then turned to make introductions. "Samantha, this is Mother Heady—"

The moment she heard the last name, Heady's entire demeanor shifted. Her body tensed, her eyes narrowed, and her hand paused halfway to her coffee cup. "Williams?"

Samantha noticed the change immediately, confusion flickering across her face even as she maintained respectful posture toward her elder. "Yes, ma'am."

The temperature at the table dropped perceptibly. Samantha looked between FaLessia and Heady, trying to understand what she'd done wrong.

FaLessia jumped in quickly. "Oh, she's not related to Mother Bernice Williams."

The relief that washed over Heady's face was almost comical. She exhaled dramatically, her shoulders dropping. "Good. I just can't."

Samantha's confusion transformed into understanding, then amusement. She laughed, settling into the chair with newfound confidence. "Oh, that old biddy who was giving Trange' attitude at church? Trust me, I wanted to let her have it. Only reason I didn't is because she's my elder and we were in God's house. Otherwise?" She made a gesture that suggested Mother Williams would have gotten more than respectful silence.

Heady's expression remained neutral for several long seconds, giving Samantha the kind of thorough visual examination usually reserved for suspicious spirits or questionable testimonies. She looked over her glasses, into Samantha's eyes, assessing something beyond surface presentation.

Samantha sat perfectly still, instinctively understanding she was being evaluated according to criteria she couldn't quite identify. The silence stretched.

Finally, Heady picked up her coffee, took a long sip, and pronounced, "She's good."

"Well, okay then. Thanks?" Samantha joked, relief evident in her laugh.

FaLessia joined her, shaking her head. "Oh, Heady."

"What?" Heady's tone suggested she saw nothing unusual about her behavior. "I had to look into the spirit of this young lady. Discern what kind of energy she carries. I saw nothing wrong." She bit into her danish with satisfaction.

"You just passed the Heady test," FaLessia explained to Samantha. "That's actually a compliment."

"I'm honored," Samantha replied, and she meant it. Something about the old woman's presence commanded respect despite— or perhaps because of—her unfiltered approach.

Samantha ordered lunch, and conversation shifted to the reason they'd all been thinking about this gathering: Trange' .

"I'm worried about Sunday," FaLessia admitted once the waiter departed. "The way those mothers have been moving, I feel like they're setting something up."

"They definitely are," Samantha confirmed. "I overheard Mother Jones on the phone yesterday. She was talking about 'Sunday morning revelations' and 'family introductions.' Whatever that means."

Heady's eyes sharpened. "Family introductions?"

"That's what she said. And she was laughing about it—that mean kind of laugh that gives you chills."

The three women exchanged looks that communicated shared concern without needing elaboration. They all knew church warfare when they sensed it approaching. And they all cared about Trange' enough to want to protect her from whatever ambush was being prepared.

"We need to warn her," FaLessia said.

"And we need to be there," Samantha added. "Whatever they're planning, she shouldn't face it alone."

Heady nodded slowly, her mind already working through spiritual strategies and prayer coverage. "Sunday morning is about to get interesting. We better make sure we're armed and ready."

They spent the rest of lunch discussing logistics—who would sit where, how to provide support without being obvious about it, ways to counter whatever the church mothers might attempt. By the time they finished, they'd formed their own conspiracy— one built on protection rather than destruction.

The battle lines were drawn. Sunday morning would determine which side had planned better.

Sunday Morning: The Calm Before

Greater Mount Calvary Cathedral swelled with bodies long before the morning service officially began. The organ's prelude music filled the sanctuary—traditional hymns that invited worship while the congregation gathered, the Hammond B-3 producing those rich, churchy tones that made even skeptics feel something spiritual stirring.

People came for different reasons. Some arrived seeking genuine encounter with God, their hearts hungry for the kind of word that might shift their week or their life trajectory. Others came specifically to hear the guest speaker—someone special who'd been announced in last week's bulletin but whose identity had been kept surprisingly quiet. But a significant number came for entertainment, drawn by whispers and promises of drama that had circulated through church circles all week like viruses jumping from host to host.

"I heard she used to be an escort," one sister whispered to her neighbor while pretending to read her bulletin.

"That's not what I heard. I heard she ran some kind of pyramid scheme," another voice countered.

"Whatever it is, we're finally going to know the truth," a third added with satisfaction.

Outside, a black Cadillac Escalade glided into the church parking lot with the kind of smooth elegance that made people turn their heads. The vehicle's presence alone communicated importance, money, status—things that Greater Mount Calvary's members both appreciated and resented in equal measure.

The driver's door opened, and Andre Howard stepped out wearing a charcoal gray suit that had definitely been tailored specifically for his frame. He moved with unhurried confidence around the vehicle, opening the rear passenger door with old-world courtesy that was becoming rare even in the South.

First Lady Clarice emerged first, her elegance understated but undeniable. She wore a lavender suit that honored her mourning without drowning in it, her bearing regal despite grief still visible in her eyes.

But it was the second woman who captured everyone's attention.

Trange' Moreau stepped out of the Escalade like she was arriving at a premiere. Her outfit represented a masterful negotiation between modesty and magnificence—a cream-colored dress with three-quarter sleeves that covered everything that needed covering while still making it clear that the body beneath the fabric was spectacular. The hemline hit just below the knee, appropriate by any church standard. But the fit—the way the fabric draped and sculpted—that was pure Trange'.

And then there was the hat.

The cream and gold fascinator perched at a carefully calculated angle could only be described as architectural. Not the oversized, view-blocking monstrosities that some church mothers favored, but a precisely designed statement piece that complemented without overwhelming. It proclaimed simultaneously: *I respect your traditions* and *I'm not apologizing for my style.*

Parishioners gathered outside the sanctuary doors stopped their conversations mid-sentence. Some stared with open admiration. Others with barely concealed disdain. But everyone noticed. That was unavoidable.

Andre offered his arm to his mother first, escorting her up the cathedral steps with visible pride. Trange' followed a step behind, close enough to be clearly part of their party but respectful of First Lady Clarice's position. The positioning was deliberate—studied without appearing calculated.

"Is that Bishop Howard's son walking in with that woman?" someone stage-whispered loud enough for half the parking lot to hear.

"I heard they're dating," another voice supplied, tinged with scandal.

"Good morning, Minister Howard!" various members called out as Andre passed, their greetings carrying the enthusiasm usually reserved for celebrities or politicians. He smiled and nodded, shaking hands and greeting people by name with the kind of pastoral attention that endeared him to congregations.

One sister—Sister Marcus, who'd served as church secretary for twenty years—greeted them warmly but pointedly ignored Trange's presence. Her eyes skipped over Trange' like she was invisible, her smile fixed on Andre alone.

Andre stopped mid-stride. "Sister Marcus, I don't believe you've officially met Trange' Moreau. Sister Moreau, this is Sister Marcus—she essentially runs this church from the administrative office."

The rebuke was gentle but unmistakable. Sister Marcus had no choice but to acknowledge Trange', extending her hand with reluctance that bordered on rudeness. "Welcome to Greater Mount Calvary."

"Thank you," Trange' replied, her smile warm despite recognizing the coldness beneath Sister Marcus's greeting. "I've heard wonderful things about how you keep everything organized."

They continued into the sanctuary, Andre greeting members while ensuring Trange' felt included in each interaction. The usher at the door—Deacon Thompson, whose wife was firmly in Mother Williams's camp—directed First Lady Clarice toward the front pew reserved for her, then made to direct Trange' toward seating further back.

"Sister Moreau will be sitting with me," Clarice interrupted smoothly, her tone brooking no argument. "She's my friend and a special guest of today's speaker."

Several nearby deacons gasped audibly. The sound rippled through the sanctuary as word spread: *Trange' Moreau would be sitting on the front row.* With the First Lady. While the Bishop's son preached.

Mother Williams and Mother Jones, positioned strategically in the third pew where they could observe everything, exchanged looks loaded with malicious satisfaction. Their whispers carried just far enough:

"So bold."

"No shame."

"We'll see how long that lasts."

First Lady Clarice walked over to the trustees' pew, leaning down to whisper something to the Master of Ceremonies. Whatever she said made his eyes widen, but he nodded respectfully. She then approached Andre, who'd been waiting near the pulpit entrance, and spoke quietly to him as well.

Then Andre climbed the three steps into the sacred desk, settling into his father's chair—the high-backed throne where Bishop Marcus Howard had sat for twenty-three years. The symbolism wasn't lost on anyone present. This wasn't just guest preaching. This was a son claiming his father's legacy.

He looked out over the congregation, his eyes scanning faces until they found Trange'. Their gazes locked. He smiled—warm, intimate, promising—and winked.

Trange' felt heat rise from her chest to her face, a blush that probably showed through her makeup. She couldn't suppress her smile, that giddy feeling that made her feel like a teenager despite being a successful businesswoman approaching forty.

First Lady Clarice caught the exchange and smiled with maternal satisfaction. Her son had excellent taste, she thought. If only these narrow-minded church folk could see past their prejudices long enough to recognize a quality woman when God placed one in their midst.

But across the aisle, Patricia Jones witnessed the same interaction with entirely different emotions. Rage. Jealousy. Determination. She'd loved Andre since they were sixteen—a persistent, patient love that had survived his rejection, her marriage to someone else, her eventual divorce. His father's death had reopened possibilities she'd thought permanently foreclosed. She'd been planning her strategy, rebuilding their connection, positioning herself as the kind of traditional, church-appropriate woman who could help him carry forward his father's ministry.

And then Trange' Moreau walked in with her designer wardrobe and worldly confidence and stolen Andre's attention like he was some prize she could just claim.

Mother Rose leaned over from her seat next to Patricia, whispering urgently. "Don't worry, baby. We got something for Miss Moreau. Everything's set."

"For sure?" Patricia's whisper carried desperate hope.

"For sure. Trust me—after this morning, Andre won't be looking at her the same way ever again."

Mother Williams joined their huddle, her satisfaction visible. "Everything's in place?"

"Everything," Rose confirmed with vindictive glee. "Her people are in the building. They think they're here for family honor recognition. They have no idea what we've got planned."

The three women shared knowing looks before settling back into their pews with expressions of mock piety. To casual observers, they appeared to be faithful church mothers settling in for worship. But anyone looking closely would have recognized predators waiting for their prey to wander into the killing zone.

Meanwhile, Trange' felt a touch on her shoulder. She turned to find Shaniece sliding into the pew behind her, the twins— Israel and Imani—trailing behind their mother with the reluctant energy of teenagers dragged to church.

"You made it!" Trange's joy was genuine, immediate.

"Of course I made it. Told you I'd be here." Shaniece hugged her friend, then nodded respectfully to First Lady Clarice. "First Lady."

"Shaniece Mfume," Clarice responded with warmth. "I've heard wonderful things about you from my son. And these must be your children."

Before Shaniece could respond, FaLessia appeared from the side aisle, making her way over to greet her friend. "Shaniece! And my favorite niece and nephew!" She hugged Israel and Imani.

The scene should have been perfect—almost was perfect. Trange's almost-man about to preach from his father's pulpit. One of her best friends there with her godchildren. First Lady Clarice showing public support. FaLessia's friendship visible for the whole congregation to see. She was being welcomed at her new church in the front row, surrounded by people who actually cared about her.

Life was good.

Then Trange's peripheral vision caught movement. She glanced over her shoulder toward the back entrance.

Her heart stopped.

The old man stood near the rear doors, leaning on a cane. He wore a dusty but familiar top hat that belonged to another era, another lifetime. Dark sunglasses masked most of his face, but they couldn't hide the scar running underneath his left eye—a scar Trange' had witnessed being carved, had heard the man scream as the knife opened his flesh.

That scar was as familiar as her own reflection. That man was supposed to be dead. She'd been told he was dead. She'd *seen* the news reports of his death five years ago in a prison hospital in Angola.

But there he stood, solid as sin and twice as terrifying.

Sweat broke across Trange's forehead and upper lip. Her breath caught in her throat. The temperature in the sanctuary seemed to spike despite the aggressive air conditioning.

First Lady Clarice noticed immediately. "Sister Moreau? Are you alright?"

Shaniece leaned forward, her hand on Trange's shoulder. "Trange'? What's wrong?"

Trange' stood abruptly, twisting around to get a better look, to confirm what her eyes were telling her couldn't possibly be true.

Nothing. No one. The spot where the old man had been standing was empty—just a group of teenagers chatting animatedly, completely unaware they were standing where a ghost had appeared moments before.

"Trange'?" Shaniece's concern deepened.

"I ... I think I saw a ghost." Trange's voice shook despite her attempts to control it.

First Lady Clarice turned in her seat, scanning the back of the sanctuary with the calm assessment of someone who'd dealt with spiritual warfare before. "Better be the Holy Ghost, Sister Moreau."

The women laughed—First Lady Clarice, Shaniece, FaLessia who'd leaned in to check on the commotion. But Trange's laugh was hollow, unconvincing even to her own ears. Because she knew what she'd seen. And she knew ghosts didn't wear top hats and carry canes.

Which meant either she was losing her mind, or something from her past had crawled out of its grave and followed her to church.

She looked over toward where Mother Williams, Mother Jones, and Patricia sat. All three women were staring at her with expressions that could only be described as amused. Satisfied. They waved—fingers waggling in that condescending way that church mothers perfected, smiles that didn't reach their eyes.

Something was wrong. Trange's instincts—honed through years of navigating dangerous business deals and predatory social circles—screamed warnings her conscious mind couldn't quite articulate. These women were too satisfied. Too confident. Too much like cats who'd successfully cornered prey.

She forced herself to turn around, to focus on Andre who sat in the pulpit watching her with concern that softened into relief when he saw she was okay. Their eyes met again, and his smile disarmed her defenses, made her feel safe despite every warning bell ringing in her subconscious.

Just then, Sage slid into the pew behind Trange' with the dramatic flair he brought to everything. "Had to show up today. I heard some grumbles about a few sisters and brothers, so I came to clock the tea."

He hugged Shaniece with genuine affection. "Hey, queen."

"No tea but communion today, Sage. This is church," Shaniece replied with mock severity.

"Girl, this is Mount Calvary. All the hellions go here," Sage shot back, his voice just loud enough to make several people turn around with various expressions of offense and amusement.

Trange' turned in her seat, trying to match Sage's playful energy despite the anxiety still churning in her gut. "Excuse me, my man is talking."

"Oh, it's your man now?" Sage's eyebrow arched with theatrical interest.

"That's what I heard," Shaniece confirmed, joining the teasing.

Samantha Williams slid into the pew at that moment, slightly breathless from rushing. "Hope I'm not late."

"No, her man is still doing the introductions," Shaniece supplied, emphasizing "her man" with comedic timing.

"Yeah, Miss 'My Man, My Man, My Man,'" Sage added, making everyone laugh.

First Lady Clarice listened to the playful exchange behind her and smiled. Hearing Trange' call Andre "her man" with such genuine affection warmed something in her grieving heart. After watching her husband pour his life into building a church that valued grace over legalism, watching her son find a woman who embodied that same bold faith felt like divine confirmation.

But Mother Heady, seated a few rows back, caught the entire scene with different eyes. She watched Sage's theatrical energy and shot him a look—the kind of look that held decades of spiritual authority and exactly zero tolerance for nonsense.

Sage, recognizing that look, immediately shot Mother Heady a look back. She cocked her head in warning. He cocked his head in response, countering her unspoken challenge. She made a movement like she was about to get up and handle him physically.

Sage mouthed silently, "Sorry, Mother Heady, girl."

She smiled a particular smile that said, *"I see you, I love you, but don't try me."*

Sage was her spiritual son. She'd mentored him through his coming out, through the church's attempts to exorcise his "demons," through his own journey toward accepting that God could love gay people without requiring them to stop being gay. She loved him fiercely. But she also didn't play games in God's house.

Trange' felt good despite the lingering unease. Her friends surrounded her. First Lady Clarice provided visible endorsement. Andre beamed at her from the pulpit with undisguised affection. This was what she'd been praying for—acceptance, community, belonging.

But she couldn't shake the feeling that something was wrong. That presence in the air—heavy, expectant, malicious. She glanced back over her shoulder again. No top hat. No old man. Nothing but regular church folk finding their seats.

"It must have been a ghost," she thought, trying to convince herself. Stress manifesting as hallucinations. Nothing more.

Andre stood, moving to the podium as the MC prepared to introduce him. The congregation settled, anticipation building. Trange' locked her eyes on Andre, letting his presence ground her, push away the anxiety threatening to ruin this moment.

"Let's bow our heads and usher in the Spirit," Andre instructed, his voice carrying pastoral authority tempered with warmth.

The congregation complied. Heads bowed. Hands clasped. Hearts—at least some of them—opened to receive whatever word God had prepared for this morning.

But in the third row, three women sat with their heads bowed and smiles playing at the corners of their mouths. They weren't praying. They were savoring. Anticipating. Waiting.

Because what was coming wasn't heavenly. What was about to unfold wasn't divine. And the woman in the front row, surrounded by friends who loved her and hopeful about a man who clearly wanted her, had walked straight into an ambush.

The trap had been set with precision. The executioners sat ready. And testimony service awaited—where truth and lies would tangle into whatever narrative served the church mothers' purposes.

Sunday morning worship was about to become Sunday morning warfare.

And Trange' Moreau had no idea she was the primary target.

Chapter 8: Hell in the Sanctuary

Andre Howard commanded the pulpit like he was born to it—which, in many ways, he was. His voice rose and fell with the kind of rhythm that only came from growing up in the Black church, from watching his father weave scripture and soul into sermons that changed lives.

"Romans chapter eight!" His voice carried to the cathedral's rafters. "Paul tells us something revolutionary, church. Something that should make every believer jump out of their seat with joy."

He paused, letting anticipation build.

"Therefore, there is now no condemnation for those who are in Christ Jesus, because through Christ Jesus the law of the Spirit who gives life has set you free from the law of sin and death!"

The organ punctuated his declaration. In the front pew, Sister Matthews shouted, "Hallelujah!" Several members rose to their feet.

"Free!" Andre repeated, his voice gaining power. "Not partially free. Not conditionally free. Not free-with-an-asterisk. FREE! Set free by the Spirit of God from sin and death!"

The congregation erupted. Tambourines shook. Hands clapped. Bodies swayed. Even Mother Jones—who'd been sitting with pursed lips and folded arms—couldn't resist the anointing. She rose to her feet, hands lifted, tears streaming down her face. Mother Williams beside her wept openly, caught up in something bigger than her conspiracy, swept away by the same Spirit her scheming had tried to resist.

First Lady Clarice sat beside Trange' in the front pew, slowly waving her ornate church fan—the one with Bishop Howard's face printed on it, a memorial gift from the church after his homegoing. She watched her only son command that pulpit, and the resemblance nearly broke her. The same gestures. The same cadence. The same way of pausing to let a point settle before delivering the knockout punch of Scripture.

Tears streamed down her face, though her smile never wavered. Her bishop would be so proud. Their son had inherited not only his father's pulpit but his anointing, his passion, his heart for God's people.

Beside her, Trange' sat mesmerized. She'd attended church a few times since her conversion, but this was different. This wasn't just good preaching—this was Andre, the man who'd kissed her goodnight and texted her sweet messages, now transformed into a vessel of divine fire. Every few minutes, their eyes would meet. He'd smile—just a slight upturn of his lips— before returning to his message. And every time, Trange' felt heat rise in her cheeks.

Shaniece leaned forward from the pew behind them, unable to resist. "Girl, he sure can't keep his eyes off you."

Trange' tried to suppress her smile but failed miserably.

Andre's sermon built toward its crescendo. His voice grew hoarse from shouting. Sweat beaded on his forehead despite the sanctuary's aggressive air conditioning. He paced the pulpit like a caged lion, unable to contain the message burning in his spirit.

"The Spirit of God!" He shouted, his voice cracking. "The same Spirit that raised Jesus from the dead dwells in you! That means every addiction, every shame, every sin—IT'S UNDER YOUR FEET!"

Then it happened.

Andre's knees buckled. His eyes rolled back. He staggered, reaching for the podium but missing. His body went limp,

131

collapsing backward into the high-backed chair that had been his father's throne for over two decades.

Church nurses and ushers rushed forward—a coordinated response practiced through years of catching people slain in the Spirit. They surrounded him with fans, pressed bottles of water into his slack hands, covered him with white cloths that signified the presence of God.

Trange' bolted upright, alarm flooding her system. "What's happening? Is he okay?"

She tried to stand, but First Lady Clarice's hand caught hers, firm and reassuring. "It's okay, honey. God is working with him."

"But he—he collapsed—"

"He's slain in the Spirit," Clarice explained, her voice calm despite the chaos. "His sermon was so powerful, so anointed, that the Holy Ghost took over. He's not hurt. He just needs to come down from the glory."

Trange' slowly lowered herself back into the pew, but her eyes never left Andre's slumped form. The nurses fanned him. Deacons prayed over him. The congregation praised God with renewed fervor, recognizing they'd witnessed something holy.

But Trange' had never seen anything like this. The spiritual warfare she'd been learning about in Bible study suddenly felt terrifyingly real.

The Announcement

Trustee Marcus Webb and church attorney April Richardson approached the podium while Andre remained slumped in the pastor's chair, two nurses still attending him with fans and whispered prayers.

Webb—always one for humor even in serious moments—gestured toward Andre with a wry smile. "We want to announce this while he was conscious."

The church erupted in laughter. Andre, barely conscious himself, managed a weak wave that brought another round of chuckles.

"The brother brought the house down, didn't he, church?" Webb's voice carried pride and satisfaction.

"Amen!" Multiple voices responded. Applause swelled.

April stepped to the microphone, her professional demeanor firmly in place despite the emotional service. "I am so glad. Now, at the request of our current First Lady and in line with our dearly departed Bishop's wishes, the Greater Mount Calvary Trustee Board—as authorized by the church bylaws—has formally decided to extend Reverend Andre Howard an offer and appointment as interim pastor."

She paused, letting the information sink in.

"This is a ninety-day appointment, after which time a formal offer will be extended pending a church vote. Church, let's give a hand of praise to our new pastor, Reverend Andre Howard!"

The sanctuary exploded.

Shouts of "Hallelujah!" and "Glory to God!" competed with applause that shook the walls. The organist launched into a triumphant hymn. People leaped to their feet. Hugs and tears flowed freely as members celebrated what felt like divine confirmation—the son stepping into his father's mantle, continuity of leadership, hope for the future.

Mother Heady shouted from her seat, hands raised. "God is faithful!"

FaLessia stood with tears streaming down her face, clapping until her hands hurt. This was the move she and the trustees had strategized for weeks, prayed over, protected from interference. And now it was done. Public. Official.

But not everyone celebrated.

Patricia Jones stood at the podium as MC, her face suddenly ashen. She hadn't known. The board had moved without telling her—without consulting the Deacon and Mother Boards who should have had input on pastoral selection. FaLessia caught her eye from across the sanctuary, saw the confusion and hurt there morph into something harder. First Lady Clarice met Patricia's gaze, offering a subtle nod that communicated both acknowledgment and resolve.

Patricia swallowed her wounded pride and fury, her hands gripping the podium edges. "I know we have so much left to do, so I will pass it over to Trustee Jones for the remainder of the program."

She stepped back from the microphone, her mind already racing. They'd kept this from her deliberately. Moved in secret. Made her look like a fool standing up here while decisions were made behind her back.

Mother Jones, Mother Williams, and Mother Rose huddled together in their pew, the euphoria of worship evaporating like morning mist under harsh sunlight. This wasn't what they wanted. They'd envisioned selecting a pastor themselves— someone from the old-time faith, someone they could control, someone who would restore the "traditional values" Bishop Howard had supposedly compromised.

Not this young, progressive, good-looking man who'd walked into the church with a worldly woman on his arm like it was the most natural thing in the world.

Mother Williams felt a flicker of regret. What they were about to do would explode in multiple directions, potentially causing collateral damage she hadn't fully considered. But this news—this unilateral decision by the trustees to install Andre without consulting the other boards—warranted a counterstrike.

She caught Mother Jones's eye. Jones nodded. The plan would proceed.

Patricia took back the microphone, her voice carrying an edge that made several people shift uncomfortably. "It is time for testimony. I know we have a couple who want to get up and tell the church how good God has been to them. Come tell the good news. As the good Bishop used to say—" her voice caught slightly "—come on up here to testify. Don't 'testi-lie.'"

The church chuckled at the familiar phrase, one of Bishop Howard's trademark sayings.

"Who wants to start?" Patricia scanned the congregation.

Sister Mary Thomas stood first, a retired schoolteacher whose gentle spirit made her beloved throughout Greater Mount Calvary. "I want to thank God for healing," she began, her voice wavering with emotion. "Y'all know I was diagnosed with Stage Three breast cancer last year. Doctors said I'd need aggressive chemotherapy, radiation, the whole nine yards. But I'm standing here today to tell you—" she paused, tears flowing freely "—my last scan came back completely clear. No cancer. *None.* My oncologist called it a miracle, and church, that's exactly what it was. God spared my life!"

The sanctuary erupted in praise.

"Hallelujah!"

"Thank you, Jesus!"

Members shouted while Sister Thomas wept openly, overwhelmed by gratitude and the memory of her battle.

Next came Brother Jerome Washington, a construction worker in his mid-thirties who'd joined Greater Mount Calvary six months earlier. He approached the microphone with the shy energy of someone unused to public speaking.

"I, uh, I just want to say God is good," he began, his deep voice barely above a whisper. Then, gaining confidence: "A lot of y'all don't know my story. I was released from Angola State Penitentiary fourteen months ago after serving eight years for armed robbery. Eight years, church. I came home to nothing— no job, no place to stay, family wanted nothing to do with me. But Bishop Howard—" his voice broke "—rest his soul, that man saw me sleeping outside the church one morning and didn't call the police. He bought me breakfast, helped me find a job, connected me with a halfway house. This church took me in when nobody else would."

He wiped his eyes with the back of his hand. "I got promoted to foreman last week. I'm saving money for my own place. And I'm three hundred and seventy-two days clean and sober. God gave me my life back through this church, and I'll never forget it."

The applause was thunderous. Several deacons stood to shake his hand. Mother Heady waved her handkerchief, shouting "Glory!"

Finally, Sister Chen Rodriguez stood—a young Latina woman in her early twenties whose family had immigrated from Honduras. She approached the microphone nervously, her accent thick but her testimony clear.

"I want to thank God for provision," she said simply. "My family, we come to America four years ago with nothing. No

English, no money, just hope for better life. Bishop Howard, he let my father clean the church to make money. My mother, she help in the kitchen. They pay us when they don't have to. They teach us English in the community center. Last month—" her voice swelled with pride "—I graduate from community college. First person in my family with college degree. And I start nursing school in the fall, all because this church invest in my family when we was nobody."

She clutched the microphone, tears streaming. "This church change our life. Gracias a Dios. Thank you, God. And thank you, Greater Mount Calvary, for showing us Jesus with your actions."

By the time she finished, half the congregation was crying. These testimonies—raw, authentic, powerful—reminded everyone why they'd come to Greater Mount Calvary in the first place. This was what church was supposed to be: a community of broken people made whole by God's grace, supporting each other through hell and celebrating together in breakthrough.

But the moment was about to shatter.

The Ambush

The adjacent sanctuary doors—the ones that led from the fellowship hall—opened slowly.

Two ushers entered first, their faces uncertain, almost apologetic. Behind them came three figures who caused immediate disruption simply by their appearance.

The first was an older Black woman, probably in her late fifties but looking sixty-five, her body ravaged by years of hard living. She wore a faded floral dress that had been nice once, maybe a decade ago, now hanging loose on her thin frame. Her movements were jerky, agitated, fingers constantly scratching at

137

her neck and arms—telltale signs of drug use that several recovering addicts in the congregation recognized immediately.

Behind her came a middle-aged man in a dingy black suit that might have been pulled from a donation bin. His cinnamon-brown skin was weathered, scarred. And perched on his head—incongruous and somehow menacing—sat a beat-up top hat that had seen better decades. He walked with a cane, and as he entered the sanctuary, he smiled, revealing gold teeth and chewing tobacco that he periodically spit into a plastic bottle he carried.

The third figure was a young woman in her mid-twenties wearing a hot-pink crop top and a skirt so short that several church mothers gasped audibly. She never looked up from her phone, her fingers flying across the screen, completely oblivious to or unconcerned with where she was.

"Oh Lord," Mother Williams muttered, loud enough to be heard. "There's more of them."

Sage leaned toward Shaniece. "Well, this should be interesting. They came to church like this?"

Shaniece nudged him sharply. "This is church. People are supposed to come as they are."

Sage shrugged, but his eyes tracked the trio with fascination as they made their way down the center aisle.

The older woman waved her hands as if she were on a red carpet, occasionally calling out "Hey, baby!" to random congregation members who stared back in confused horror. The man—Henry Earl, based on what happened next—kept smacking his lips wetly around his chewing tobacco. And the young woman maintained her phone fixation, nearly tripping over a pew but catching herself without ever looking up.

Patricia stood at the podium, her expression carefully neutral despite the satisfaction gleaming in her eyes. "I heard that you all have a few words you want to say."

The older woman approached the microphone, scratching around her neck with visible agitation. Her pupils were dilated, her movements twitchy. "We sho' do, don't we, Henry Earl?"

She elbowed him sharply.

"Cora Jean!" His voice carried irritation mixed with something darker. "You know better than be hitting me. Gon' up and tell people what you got to tell. Let's go."

Their little performance was almost comical—like characters from a sitcom stumbled into the wrong set. Nervous laughter rippled through parts of the congregation. Others sat frozen, sensing something terrible approaching but unable to look away.

Patricia stepped away from the podium, making eye contact with her mother in the third pew. Mother Jones nodded slightly. Everything was proceeding according to plan.

"Hello, everybody." The woman's voice crackled through the microphone, too loud, distorted. "My name is Cora Jean Burns. And I was asked to come here and give a few words about my baby girl, Octavia Shanika Burns."

The congregation exchanged confused looks.

"Who is Octavia?" someone whispered.

"And why is this lady with no teeth taking over the microphone?" another voice added.

Cora Jean squinted at the assembled faces, searching. "I don't see her here, but we were asked to come and talk about our baby girl. Ain't that right, Henry Earl?"

She elbowed him again, harder this time.

"Cora Jean, I done told you about elbowing me!" His voice rose with genuine anger now.

"Okay, so Octavia was born in the parish with us." Cora Jean continued as if nothing had happened. "This is her sister, Leanne Marie. But we call her Lee Lee for short."

She gestured to the young woman, who finally looked up from her phone long enough to give a lackluster wave before returning to her screen.

Sage couldn't help himself. "Girl, not Lee Lee," he whispered to Shaniece, who shook her head in warning but couldn't suppress her own horrified fascination.

"Now, we ain't some people who like to put on a front," Cora Jean continued, warming to her subject. "I used to be a dancer and a prostitute. Baby, I used to have them lined up back in my days. I remember this one time—"

Patricia stepped in quickly. "Well, thank you. You can skip over those details."

"Naw…I want to hear!" One of the sisters in the back shouted, bringing scattered laughter from the less spiritually mature members.

"We could talk after church," Cora Jean shot back with surprising quickness, pointing toward the fellowship hall. Her comeback brought more chuckles from the congregation, though the laughter had an edge of discomfort now.

"Now, my Octavia was a special girl." Cora Jean's voice dropped into something that might have been maternal pride but sounded more like satisfaction at possessing valuable property. "Now I hear she's all sanctified in the church now, and I'm happy for her because I remember back in the day, even as a little teenager, she would always be running around with all the boys."

First Lady Clarice's fan stopped moving. Beside her, Trange's body went rigid.

"I remember one time I caught her in the back shed with a little pile of boys on top of her." Cora Jean laughed as if sharing a fond memory. "Just couldn't keep that girl's skirt down. I wasn't the best mother, but I did what was best for me and my family. And you see, Henry Earl took in me and my two girls. He used to be my pimp, so we all had to chip in."

Gasps echoed through the sanctuary.

"But he loved him some Octavia. I couldn't keep them two away from each other. Ain't that right, Lee Lee?"

Without looking up from her phone, Lee Lee nodded agreement with her mother.

"Octavia always looked older for her age, so the men loved her too." Cora Jean continued, oblivious to--or energized by--the horror spreading through the congregation. "She would help her dear Mama out on some of these nights, helping me—let's just say—handle the men. Do you know what I mean?"

She started chuckling. Henry Earl joined her, his laugh wet and obscene.

"I needed her to help out, you know? This girl started running the brothel. Yeah, this little fifteen-year-old girl out here booking appointments and running me and my girls. She then dropped out of school. It became a full-time thing—madam. Got to be one of the first down here in Louisiana, I tell you."

The church sat in stunned silence now. No more nervous laughter. Just horror building with each word.

"Yeah," Henry Earl interjected, his voice dripping with something vile. "She ended up being one of the sweetest girls in the house, I'll tell you." He licked his lips, and several people in the front row visibly recoiled.

"She was always so ambitious—couldn't stop her for nothing," Cora Jean continued. "She started dancing at the club with me. Always a businesswoman. She even started turning tricks off the strip club. I didn't even think of that. I miss her."

Trange's tears started flowing silently, mascara tracking down her cheeks.

"We had a falling out because her and Henry Earl started messing around, and she ended up getting herself pregnant." Cora Jean's voice carried no emotion—just stating facts. "You can't be a pregnant trick."

"Sho can't," Henry Earl agreed with a nod.

"What am I witnessing?" FaLessia whispered to herself, looking over at First Lady Clarice and Trange'. Both women were pale, frozen, barely breathing.

"Now, after I took her to take care of the business with the baby—" the casual reference to abortion hung in the air like poison "—she wanted to try and talk about retiring. But she was one of Henry Earl's best girls. He couldn't let that go. So then she helped us have a business where her and a couple other girls would do private dancing for parties and then take care of the men afterward."

Cora Jean paused for effect.

"This was all before she was eighteen years old. That girl had a business mind on her if I ain't seen no one else. I can keep going on and on about how Octavia was such a wild child. But

I'm so happy that she found the Lord now, and she's up in here with all you good fancy people."

Patricia took the microphone, her voice dripping with false sweetness. "Well, thank you, Mrs. Burns."

"Girl, call me Coco!" Cora Jean did a little shimmy that would have been funny in any other context.

"Well, okay, Coco. Thank you for talking about your daughter, Octavia Shanika Burns. But you did forget one thing." Patricia paused, savoring the moment. "She is here! I know you said it's been—what is it—fifteen years since you've seen her?"

Cora Jean, Henry Earl, and Lee Lee all nodded.

"Well, she's right here in the first row." Patricia pointed like a prosecutor presenting evidence. "Miss Burns, your daughter is called Trange' Moreau. Well, that's what she told us her name was. That's her sitting there next to the First Lady."

The sanctuary erupted.

"WHAT?!"

"Lord have mercy!"

"That can't be true!"

"Octavia girl!" Cora Jean's voice carried across the chaos. "Come on up here and say hi to your Mama!"

Trange' sat frozen. Completely immobile. Every muscle locked. Her mind screamed at her body to move, to run, to do something—anything—but she couldn't. She was fifteen again, trapped in that shed. She was seventeen again, being dragged to the clinic. She was every age she'd ever been when she'd had no power, no choice, no voice.

Seeing her stepfather. Her mother. Her sister. Remembering the hell she'd survived—not lived, survived. And now it was on display for the whole world, told as a modified version that somehow made it sound like she'd been a willing participant in her own destruction rather than a child being trafficked by the people who should have protected her.

"Baby girl, is that you?" Cora Jean squinted toward the front row. "You look all fancy. Don't she, Henry Earl?"

"Mmm, yeah, looking really good there, 'Tavia." Henry Earl's voice carried implications that made several men in the congregation shift uncomfortably, recognition dawning that they'd just heard a man sexualize his stepdaughter.

Trange' started hyperventilating. Her chest heaved. Tears poured down her face, taking her carefully applied makeup with them.

"Why aren't you going to come up and give your Mama and Paw a hug?" Patricia added, her voice sickeningly sweet.

The church erupted in whispers, comments flying faster than anyone could track:

"I knew she was too worldly!"

"That dress made sense now!"

"Poor First Lady, sitting next to that!"

"Bishop Howard must have been deceived!"

"Demon in designer clothes!"

"Should have known better!"

Shaniece, Sage, Samantha, and FaLessia sat in shocked silence behind them, trying to process what they'd just witnessed.

Shaniece leaned forward and shook Trange's shoulder. "Trange'? Trange', say something!"

But no words came. Trange's mouth opened and closed like a fish gasping for air.

Mother Jones rose from her pew and walked to the front, taking the microphone with the satisfied air of someone who'd orchestrated everything perfectly. "I think we all have some questions. And I think we all deserve some answers. Right, church?"

Several people responded with "Amen!"—though whether they were agreeing out of genuine concern or mob mentality was unclear.

Samantha stood up, her voice cutting through the chaos. "She doesn't owe anybody any explanation!"

"You sit and be quiet in the House of the Lord!" Mother Williams shot back. "You ain't no better than her anyway!"

Samantha's hands went to her earrings. She started removing them with deliberate slowness. "Oh, I'll hit an old woman. Try me."

Sage immediately took her earrings, holding out his hand for her purse. "I got you, Sis."

"Sage, you are not helping!" Shaniece hissed. "Samantha, sit down!"

Mother Jones continued as if there'd been no interruption. "We got to be careful who or *what* we bring into the church." She turned toward Trange', speaking slowly, deliberately, each word a knife thrust. "Is this true? Octavia. Shanika. Burns." She paused between each name. "You are a loose, drug-addicted trick from the parishes down south who got pregnant by her

145

stepdad—who was her mother's pimp—and then had an abortion. Is that correct?"

Before Trange' could respond—not that she could have spoken—Cora Jean approached Mother Jones with surprising speed.

"Now you're going to be talking about my baby?" She looked over at Trange', her expression shifting as memories infiltrated her drug-addled mind. "Well, oh my Lord. Cookie, is that you?"

"Cookie?" Multiple voices echoed the word.

"Who is Cookie?" Mother Jones asked, confusion breaking through her satisfaction.

"Well, I'll be!" Cora Jean's eyes widened. "If it ain't Miss Cookie Lookie, looking all fancy over there next to my baby girl!"

Mother Jones's face flushed red. "Who are you calling Cookie? The woman next to your daughter is our First Lady!"

"First Lady?" Cora Jean laughed. "I don't know what she go by now, but that's my girl Cookie! I knew her when she was 'Cookies and Cream.' We used to dance together. That was my road dog. I was Coco, and she was Cookie, and when we danced together, they would call us Chocolate Chip Cookie!"

She slapped her hands together, laughing at the memory.

Mother Jones almost passed out. The goal had been to expose Trange'. But *this*? This was an unexpected bonus. The First Lady herself!

The congregation's shock multiplied exponentially. Heads swiveled between Cora Jean and First Lady Clarice like spectators at the world's most horrific tennis match.

First Lady Clarice sat composed. Stunned, certainly—but composed. She'd known this day might come eventually, though she'd hoped it would be on her terms, in her time, with her framing.

Andre, who'd regained consciousness several minutes earlier and had been watching the unfolding disaster with growing horror, made eye contact with his mother. His face showed sympathy, confusion, and—underneath it all—hints of anger.

But Clarice remained rigid, her posture perfect, her expression neutral.

Patricia took the microphone, barely suppressing her glee. "First Lady, do you have anything to say?"

Trange' looked at Clarice, confusion across her tear-stained face. The weight of this service broke something in Trange'.

She stood abruptly, her movement so sudden that people in nearby pews flinched. Then she ran.

Not walked. Not hurried. Ran—full sprint down the center aisle in heels that weren't made for running, her hat flying off, her carefully chosen modest-yet-stunning outfit catching on pews as she fled.

"Trange'!" Samantha bolted after her.

Sage followed immediately, his longer legs helping him catch up.

The scene played out like a movie—Trange' fleeing down the aisle in obvious distress, her three friends chasing her, the congregation erupting in a cacophony of judgment and speculation:

"You can't outrun Jesus!"

"Or your past!"

"Don't run now!"

"Look at them demons just running out of church!"

Sage turned, ready to snap back with something cutting, but Samantha grabbed his arm. "We need to get to Trange'. That's what matters."

They burst through the sanctuary doors into the bright Sunday sunshine, leaving chaos in their wake.

With them gone, all eyes turned to First Lady Clarice.

The sanctuary went silent—that particular silence that comes when a mob is waiting to see if their prey will fight or flee.

Andre stood at the podium, his hands gripping the wooden edges so hard his knuckles turned white. He made eye contact with his mother. Sympathy warred with confusion, confusion with hints of anger. But underneath it all—love. Whatever she'd done, whatever her past held, she was still his mother.

Clarice felt that love like a lifeline. She folded up her church fan with deliberate slowness, tucked it gently into her purse, and cleared her throat. Then she rose—slowly, gracefully, like royalty addressing peasants.

Mother Heady immediately stood as well, positioning herself at Clarice's side without being summoned. The two women had been friends for over thirty years. Heady had known about Clarice's past—had helped her walk away from it, had discipled her through transformation, had stood as godmother at Andre's baptism. She would stand with her now.

The silence stretched. Finally, Clarice spoke.

"Yes, Coco. It's me."

The church erupted in gasps and exclamations.

Clarice raised one hand, and somehow, the gesture commanded silence. "I did not know this was your daughter. But it's nice seeing you." She paused, her voice taking on steel. "But please, call me First Lady Clarice."

She walked toward them—not away, but toward—with the confidence of someone who'd faced her demons and won. She pulled a small card from her purse and handed it to Cora Jean.

"While you're in town, give me a call. Let's catch up."

Then she turned to face the congregation. Every eye was on her. Every ear waited. The moment hung suspended—would she crumble? Apologize? Flee like Trange' had?

"Everyone has a past," Clarice said clearly, her voice carrying to the rafters. "And I will not allow mine to be weaponized against me."

She turned, looking directly at Mother Jones. "What you have done here, in the name of 'unveiling demons,' merely shows who the true devil is in this church."

Mother Jones's face went purple with rage and embarrassment.

"May God have mercy on your soul," Clarice continued, her voice dropping but somehow becoming more powerful. "But I will say this, and I say this in front of the whole church—I am saved, sanctified, and filled with the Holy Ghost."

She took a step closer to Mother Jones, who actually backed up.

"But if you ever pull a stunt like this again, it's going to take Heaven, several angels, and all the disciples to pull me off your behind."

Gasps and a few barely suppressed chuckles rippled through the congregation.

Clarice looked up to the pulpit where Andre stood. "Go ahead and give the benediction, son. I'll be in the car."

She picked up her purse and walked down the aisle with her head held high, that pleasant First Lady smile on her face—but with an edge that clearly communicated: *Don't try anything.*

As she exited through the doors, every head turned back to the podium where Andre stood, befuddled and confused.

For a moment, silence held. Then, like a dam breaking, everyone started talking at once.

"The First Lady was a dancer?"

"She was a stripper!"

"That explains why she defended that Trange' woman!"

"Birds of a feather!"

But others rose to Clarice's defense:

"She's been nothing but gracious to this church!"

"Bishop Howard loved her! That's all that matters!"

"We all have a past!"

"Judge not lest ye be judged!"

The arguments escalated rapidly. What began as raised voices became shouting. Shouting became accusations. Accusations became confrontations.

Sister Harris and Sister Mitchell—who'd been feuding for months over a church kitchen dispute—used this chaos as cover to finally settle their differences. Sister Harris shoved. Sister Mitchell shoved back. Within seconds, they were grabbing each other's wigs while their respective supporters jumped in.

In the back, Brother Thomas—who'd been harboring resentment over a perceived slight from Deacon Williams—used the mayhem to settle that score. A punch was thrown.

Then another. Soon, three or four men were tangled together while their wives screamed.

Brother Jenkins, usually mild-mannered, grabbed Deacon Morris by his collar. "You been talking about my wife for weeks! Say it to my face now!"

"Your wife IS a gossip!" Morris shot back, and suddenly they were wrestling in the aisle.

Sister Rodriguez tried to separate two women fighting near the choir stand and got shoved backward into a pew. Her husband jumped in, and the altercation spread like wildfire.

The ushers and deacons who tried to restore order found themselves pulled into the chaos. Church nurses abandoned Andre to attend to bloody noses, torn clothes, and scratched faces. One of the stained-glass windows rattled as bodies slammed against the wall beneath it.

Mother Williams stood on her pew, shouting, "Order! We need order!" But her voice was drowned out by the pandemonium.

The organ player, in a moment of either inspired brilliance or complete panic, began playing—loudly—as if music could somehow restore sanctity to the space. But the hymn "Amazing Grace" competed with shouting, crying, and the sounds of physical violence.

Andre stood at the podium, ready to give his benediction on his first official day as pastor of Greater Mount Calvary Cathedral. He looked out at the pandemonium—fistfights in the sanctuary, people screaming at each other, the unity his father had spent twenty-three years building crumbling in real-time.

He hung his head. A single tear tracked down his face.

He wondered if he'd made a grave mistake accepting this appointment. Did he have the fortitude? The grace? The power from God to heal this church and cleanse it of the unrighteousness that plagued it?

The legacy his father had built so carefully was burning down and Andre Howard wasn't sure he had what it took to save it.

Outside in the parking lot, Trange' ran blindly through rows of cars, her breath coming in ragged gasps that sounded like drowning. Her shoes—beautiful Louboutins, red-soled proof of her success, now instruments of torture—twisted on the asphalt. One heel caught in a crack, and she stumbled, catching herself against a silver Lexus.

She leaned there, trying desperately to catch her breath, but the air wouldn't come. Hyperventilation. Panic attack. Complete system failure.

Her makeup was destroyed, tracking down her face in rivulets of black and bronze. Her carefully chosen outfit—the one that had balanced modesty with magnificence—was torn at the shoulder where it had caught on a pew during her flight. The fascinator that had proclaimed both respect and style lay somewhere back in that sanctuary, abandoned like everything else she'd tried to build.

But worse than the physical destruction was the humiliation. The hurt. The exposure of wounds she'd spent fifteen years covering with designer labels, business success, and the carefully constructed identity of Trange' Moreau.

She'd built an entire persona—mogul, sophisticate, woman who'd pulled herself up from nothing through sheer determination and business acumen. And in fifteen minutes, three people from her past had reduced her back to Octavia

Shanika Burns: trafficked child, sex worker survivor, a victim with no voice and no power.

Everything she'd run from. Everything she'd buried. Everything she'd tried to kill through reinvention and relocation and ruthless compartmentalization—it had all just been dragged into the light and displayed for public consumption.

Her body slid down the side of the Lexus until she was sitting on the hot asphalt, knees pulled to her chest, rocking slightly. The sounds coming from her throat weren't quite sobs and weren't quite screams—something more primitive, the noise of a wounded animal.

A royal blue Yukon Denali pulled up beside her, tires screeching slightly.

The passenger window rolled down. "Get in. Let's get out of here." Samantha's voice was firm, commanding, leaving no room for argument.

Trange' looked up but couldn't process the words. Couldn't move. Couldn't function.

Sage jumped out of the back seat and crouched beside her, his voice gentle despite the urgency. "Come on, queen. We got you. But we need to get you out of here."

He helped her up, his hands careful with her torn dress, mindful of her dignity even when she couldn't protect it herself. He guided her into the vehicle where she immediately collapsed into the seat, curling into the fetal position, body wracked with sobs that came from somewhere primal.

Shaniece sat in the driver's seat, her hands gripping the steering wheel so tightly her knuckles had gone white. She looked in the rearview mirror, first checking on her babies—who sat in the far back, their faces shocked and confused but mercifully silent.

153

They'd witnessed something they shouldn't have; heard things no child should hear.

Then she looked at Trange' through the mirror.

For a moment—a brief, terrible moment—Shaniece wondered if she truly knew who her friend was. The woman sobbing in her back seat was Octavia Shanika Burns, a name she'd never heard. A past she'd never suspected. A history of trauma so profound that Shaniece couldn't fully process it.

The details Cora Jean had shared—said so casually, like recounting a family vacation instead of child trafficking—they reframed everything. Every time Trange' had shied away from touch. Every time she'd overshared about her business success but revealed nothing about her childhood. Every time she'd thrown money at problems instead of building genuine intimacy.

It all made horrible sense now.

But as quickly as that moment of disconnection came, it fled.

She had known Trange' for seven years. Seven years of friendship, of late-night conversations, of watching this woman build an empire while battling demons Shaniece had never seen but had always sensed lurking beneath the surface. The woman she knew—the one she loved like a sister—was the one in pain right now.

The past didn't erase the present. Octavia didn't negate Trange'. And childhood trauma—no matter how horrific—didn't define the woman who'd survived it and built something beautiful from the ashes.

This wasn't the time to dissect what had happened. This wasn't the moment for questions or judgment or trying to reconcile two names that belonged to the same person at different points in her journey.

This was the time for healing. For protection. For being the kind of friend who stays when everything falls apart.

"Where are we going?" Sage asked quietly from the middle seat, one hand resting gently on Trange's shoulder.

"My place," Shaniece replied, putting the Denali in drive. "She needs somewhere safe. Somewhere those vultures can't get to her."

Samantha reached back and took Trange's hand, squeezing gently. "We got you. You hear me? *We got you.* Whatever you need, however long it takes—we got you."

But Trange' couldn't respond. Couldn't speak. Could barely breathe through the pain of having her past weaponized against her in the one place she'd hoped to find sanctuary.

The God she'd been learning to trust had led her into a church that destroyed her. The faith she'd been building had delivered her into the hands of people who'd rather expose than embrace. The grace she'd been promised had been withheld by gatekeepers who measured worthiness by pedigrees they'd never had to overcome.

As the Denali merged into Sunday afternoon traffic, Trange' continued to weep—deep, body-shaking sobs that sounded like grief, like rage, like fifteen years of carefully constructed walls finally crumbling under the weight they were never meant to carry.

Shaniece drove carefully, one eye on the road and one on the rearview mirror where she could see her broken friend. She prayed silently—not the eloquent prayers she'd learned in Church, but raw, desperate pleas: *God, hold her together. God, don't let her give up. God, show her You're not like Your people.*

The truck carried them away from Greater Mount Calvary Cathedral, away from the sanctuary that had burned, away from the man in the pulpit who'd watched the woman he was falling for run screaming from his church.

Behind them, a building full of people wrestled with what they'd done. Ahead of them, an uncertain future where Trange' would have to decide if faith could survive this kind of betrayal.

But at this moment—in this car, with these friends—she was safe. Broken, but safe. Exposed, but protected. Destroyed, but not alone.

Sometimes that has to be enough.

Chapter 9: The Truth Beneath the Lies

The guest bedroom in Shaniece's home had become a tomb. Trange' Moreau—or Octavia Shanika Burns, or whoever she was supposed to be now—lay curled beneath Egyptian cotton sheets that cost more than most people's monthly rent, staring at nothing.

Three days since the sanctuary burned.

Three days since her past was weaponized and displayed like evidence at a trial where she'd already been convicted.

Three days of barely eating. Barely moving. Barely existing.

The elegant diamond-encrusted circular mirror on the opposite wall had witnessed her decline. That mirror—a $15,000 piece she'd commissioned from a Belgian artist, one of the few possessions she'd had Samantha retrieve from her penthouse—reflected someone she didn't recognize. Not Trange' the mogul. Not Octavia the victim. Just a shell, hollowed out and discarded.

Shaniece had brought food on delicate china plates: gumbo, jambalaya, beignets from Café Du Monde—all of Trange's favorites. The plates sat untouched on the nightstand, food congealing into unappetizing masses that had to be thrown away and replaced with fresh attempts that met the same fate.

The phone—that lifeline to her empire, her business, her carefully constructed world—sat powered off on the dresser. No emails. No calls. No notifications demanding her attention or confirming her importance. Just silence.

She'd turned down every visitor. Business associates who wanted to discuss the "unfortunate incident" at church. Clients who'd heard rumors and wanted to "check in" while really just hunting for gossip. Even well-meaning acquaintances whose sympathy felt more like morbid curiosity.

Only her inner circle had been granted access: Shaniece, Samantha, Sage. FaLessia had stopped by twice, sitting quietly outside the bedroom door when Trange' refused to let her in, praying aloud until her voice cracked.

But today felt different. Today, the weight pressing on her chest felt slightly less suffocating. Today, she could breathe without feeling like broken glass was lodged in her lungs.

Trange' pushed back the covers—heavy, expensive, useless— and swung her legs over the side of the bed. Her bare feet touched the cool hardwood floor, grounding her in something physical when everything emotional felt untethered.

She stood, her silk nightgown hanging loose on a frame that had lost weight over three days of refusing food. She walked to the mirror, each step requiring conscious effort, and finally looked at herself.

Really looked.

The woman staring back was a stranger. Hair uncombed, natural curls matted and tangled. Face bare of the armor she usually applied with precision—foundation, contour, highlight, the war paint of a woman who'd learned to hide behind beauty. Eyes red-rimmed and swollen from crying. Lips chapped from dehydration.

But underneath the physical destruction, something else flickered. Something angry. Something refusing to stay buried.

"I am Madam Trange' Moreau," she whispered to her reflection, her voice rusty from disuse. "Couture designer. Socialite. Fashion icon."

She leaned closer to the mirror, watching her own lips form the words.

"Queen of the French Quarter."

The titles felt hollow. Costumes she'd worn so long she'd forgotten they weren't her skin. But they were still hers. She'd earned them. Built them. Claimed them from nothing.

"How did I let them win?" The question came out stronger, anger bleeding through the grief.

A soft knock interrupted her communion with her reflection. She turned, instinctively wrapping her arms around herself, protective.

The door opened slowly. Shaniece entered first, her eyes assessing, taking inventory of Trange's physical and emotional state. Behind her came the others: Samantha, whose protective energy filled the room before she'd fully crossed the threshold. Renee, whose return after their near-falling-out felt like divine timing. Moni, steady and solid. Coko, carrying her Bible and that brand of spiritual authority that came from surviving her own hell.

Her sisters. Not by blood—blood had failed her repeatedly— but by choice. By showing up. By refusing to let her disappear.

For a moment, Trange' considered retreat. The bed was right there, offering escape back into unconsciousness. But something in their faces stopped her. Not pity—she would have fled from pity. Something harder. Something that demanded she meet them as an equal rather than a victim.

Still, old habits die hard. She turned away and climbed back into the bed, pulling the covers up to her chin like a child hiding from monsters.

Samantha grabbed the covers and yanked them back with zero ceremony. "You're not hiding from us today. It's time to get out of this room, out of this bed, and back into the land of the living."

Moni sat on the edge of the bed and took Trange's hand, her grip firm and warm. "We've heard the rumors. We've been giving you space, but I think it's time we hear your side of the story."

She paused, her eyes locking onto Trange's with an intensity that made looking away impossible.

"But before we do, I want you to know—we love you regardless. Whatever you're about to tell us, whatever happened, whoever you were, doesn't change who you are to us. You're our sister. Nothing changes that."

Trange' felt tears gathering but refused to let them fall. She'd cried enough over the last three days to flood the Mississippi.

"Can we pray first?" Coko's voice carried that blend of gentleness and authority that made people bow their heads without thinking. "My sister, the floor will be yours. But let's invite God into this space before we start."

They formed a circle around the bed—some sitting, some standing, all connected. Coko began to pray, her words washing over the room like cleansing water:

"Father God, we come before You broken but not destroyed. Wounded but not dead. We ask that You would fill this space with Your presence. That You would give our sister the courage to speak her truth and us the grace to receive it. That You would heal what's been broken and restore what's been stolen. We bind up every spirit of shame, every demon of condemnation, every lie that says her past defines her future. In Jesus' Name, amen."

"Amen," the others echoed.

The room fell silent, waiting.

The Story Beneath the Story

Trange' hesitated, her throat tight. Where did she even start? How did you explain a childhood that shouldn't exist? A past that most people couldn't fathom? A survival story that got told as a cautionary tale?

She closed her eyes, and suddenly she was back there. Not in the sanitized version Cora Jean had performed for the congregation's entertainment, but in the real place. The muck. The parish. The hell she'd clawed her way out of.

When she finally spoke, her voice was small—the voice of Octavia, the child who'd been silenced for so long.

"The story they told in church—Cora Jean's version—it's not completely wrong. But it's not right either. It's like describing a hurricane by talking about how the rain felt refreshing."

She opened her eyes and looked at her friends. "I was born into foster care. My mother—Cora Jean—was already too deep into drugs and prostitution to keep me. The system bounced me around for seven years. Different houses. Different families. Some okay. Some ... " She trailed off, shaking her head. "Some not okay at all."

Renee squeezed her hand, encouraging her to continue.

"Then, when I was seven, my grandmother—my father's mother, Hattie Burns—she got custody. She was the first person who ever loved me. Really, truly loved me, not because she had to or because the state paid her, but because she wanted to."

A genuine smile flickered across Trange's face—the first smile in three days. "Miss Hattie was something else. Old-school religious woman. Took me to church three times a week—

Sunday morning, Wednesday night, and Saturday youth service. She cooked these huge meals even though it was the two of us. She taught me to read using her Bible and recipe cards. She called me her 'unexpected blessing.'"

The smile faded. "Those five years with her were the only time in my childhood I felt safe. Protected. Like maybe God actually saw me and cared that I existed."

She paused, steeling herself for what came next.

"I was twelve when I found her. I'd heard her moving around the night before—she had trouble sleeping sometimes—but when I woke up, the house was too quiet. You know that kind of quiet? Where the silence feels wrong?"

Her friends nodded, understanding the kind of dread that precedes discovering something terrible.

"I knocked on her bedroom door. No answer. Called out to her. Nothing. So I went in."

Trange's voice dropped to barely above a whisper. "She was in bed, lying on her side like she was sleeping. But something was off. The way her skin looked. The smell in the room. I tried to wake her up—shook her shoulder, yelled in her ear, even slapped her face like I'd seen people do in movies."

Tears were falling freely now, but she barely noticed. "She wouldn't wake up. So I ... I just stayed there. I climbed into bed with her and laid there, praying to the God she'd taught me about. Begging Him to wake her up. Promising I'd be better, read my Bible more, stop talking back."

"Oh, baby," Moni whispered, her own tears starting.

"I stayed in that bed for four days," Trange' continued, her voice hollow. "Four days with my grandmother's body, waiting for the miracle Miss Hattie had always told me God could do. I only left once, when I got so hungry I couldn't stand it. Went to the neighbor, Miss Margaret, and asked for some bread so I could make sandwiches for me and my grandmother."

She laughed—a bitter, broken sound. "Miss Margaret asked why Miss Hattie didn't come ask herself. I told her Grandma had been sick for four days and wouldn't wake up, but maybe a sandwich would help. That's when Miss Margaret figured out what happened."

The room was silent except for quiet sniffles. Coko had her hand over her mouth, tears streaming down her face. Shaniece's eyes were closed, her lips moving in silent prayer.

"They came and took Miss Hattie away. The police, the ambulance—everybody. And then they started asking questions: Where was my mother? Who would take care of me? Miss Margaret—sweet lady, but practical—she told them she couldn't take me in. She gave them the address to where my mother was staying."

Trange's jaw clenched, anger replacing grief. "A place they called the muck. Down in the worst part of the parish. Where people went to disappear into drugs and crime and whatever else you did when you'd given up on everything else."

"I remember sitting in the back of that police car as we drove away from Miss Hattie's house. Watching Miss Margaret standing in the doorway. And thinking—for the first time ever—that God had abandoned me. Left me just like everyone else."

Into the Muck

Samantha shifted closer, her presence a silent anchor as Trange' continued.

"My mother was less than pleased to see me." The understatement was almost funny if it wasn't so horrific. "She seemed less concerned that her own mother had died and more concerned with getting the death certificate so she could collect the insurance money. She actually asked the police officers how long that would take while I was standing right there."

Trange's eyes went distant, seeing something the others couldn't. "The house—if you could call it that—was this dingy shotgun shack that smelled like mold, cigarettes, and something chemical I later learned was crack being cooked. Furniture that looked like it had been salvaged from the dump. Mattresses on the floor. No doors on the bathroom. Holes in the walls."

"There were always people there. Coming and going at all hours. Men who looked at me in ways that made my skin crawl. Women who were too high to remember their own names. And presiding over it all was Henry Earl—Pops—who ran the whole operation like some twisted businessman."

Her voice hardened. "Over the next few weeks, I learned my place. I was the maid. It was my job to clean up after everyone. Especially after Cora Jean and Pops were coming down off a high, which meant I was cleaning up vomit, drug paraphernalia, and things a twelve-year-old shouldn't even know existed."

Renee made a sound of distress, but Trange' continued, needing to get it all out before she lost her nerve.

"Pops was a pimp. A well-known one in the parish. Cora Jean was his top girl—the one who brought in the most money. He only married her to keep her, because she tried to run away once and he tracked her down and beat her so bad she couldn't work for a month. After that, she was his wife, and nobody touched her without paying him first."

The clinical way Trange' described it made it somehow worse—like she'd had to detach from the horror to survive it.

"When I turned thirteen, Pops started looking at me differently. Not like a stepdaughter. Like property he was evaluating for profitability. Cora Jean noticed and instead of protecting me, she encouraged it. I was eating their food, using their electricity, taking up space. It was time I started earning my keep."

"No," Shaniece breathed, her hands covering her face. "Please, God, no."

"That's when the business arrangement started," Trange' said, her voice flat, emotionless—the only way she could tell this part. "I was told it was temporary. Just until I could save up enough to leave. They'd help me get out if I'd just help them for a little while."

She laughed again—that same bitter, broken sound. "I was thirteen years old and still believed people kept their promises. Still thought there was some bottom line that even the worst people wouldn't cross. I was wrong."

Coko's Bible had fallen to the floor, forgotten. She was openly weeping now, her body shaking with sobs. Moni held her, tears streaming down her own face, while keeping her other hand locked with Trange's.

"That story Cora Jean told in church—about me in the shed with boys—that wasn't me being promiscuous. That was me being gang raped." The words came out sharp, cutting. "A group of local boys heard that I was working. They figured if I was giving it away for money, they would get it for free. Five of them in broad daylight in a shed behind our house while Cora Jean and Pops were inside getting high."

Samantha stood abruptly and walked to the window, her shoulders shaking. Trange' could hear her cursing under her breath—all the words she wanted to say but was trying to restrain herself for the sake of the moment.

"When I finally got back inside, covered in dirt and blood and shame, you know what happened? Cora Jean beat me. Said I was stupid for giving it away for free. That I'd just cost them money because now those boys would tell everyone and nobody would pay for what they could get for nothing."

The room was heavy with grief and rage—grief for what had been done to a child, rage at the adults who'd failed to protect her.

"For the next five years, that was my life. Prostitution. Stripping at parties. Whatever Pops said I needed to do to pull my weight. I tried to be smart about it—came up with business ideas, ways to streamline the operation, strategies for making more money. I thought if I proved I was valuable in other ways, maybe they'd let me just manage things instead of ... " She trailed off, unable to finish.

"But they took my ideas and turned them into a house of ill repute. Made it bigger, more organized, more profitable. And kept me working because I was one of their best earners."

Trange' looked up at her friends, her eyes dry now, cried out. "The abortion Cora Jean mentioned? That was real. I got pregnant by Pops when I was fifteen. Cora Jean dragged me to some back-alley clinic where they didn't ask questions or require parental consent. I hemorrhaged afterward. Nearly died. Spent three days in that same bed where I'd found Miss Hattie, delirious with fever, while Cora Jean got high and Pops complained about lost revenue."

"I'm going to be sick," Renee whispered, pressing her hand to her mouth.

"After that, Pops got tired of Cora Jean. She was aging out, using too much product, bringing in less money. So he set his sights on me as his new 'wife.' Not legally—he was already married to Cora Jean. But in all the ways that mattered in that house."

The words hung in the air like smoke from a fire, choking everyone in the room.

"When I was seventeen, they left town for a funeral. Took Lee Lee—she was just a baby then—but left me behind to 'watch the house.' Which really meant keep the business running while they were gone. The moment that car was out of sight, I packed a bag with everything I could carry and ran."

Becoming Trange'

For the first time since she'd started talking, something like strength entered Trange's voice.

"I made it to New Orleans with forty-three dollars, a fake ID, and clothes that screamed exactly what I'd been doing. I slept in a park the first night. Got mugged the second night and lost half my money. By the third day, I was ready to give up and go back because at least there I had food and a roof."

She shook her head at the memory. "But then I met Delacroix. He ran a drag house in the Quarter—one of those places where queens performed and the boundaries of gender got beautifully blurred. He found me digging through the dumpster behind his club, looking for something to eat."

A real smile, soft and grateful, crossed her face. "Most people would have chased me off. Delacroix took one look at me and said, 'Child, you look like you've been through hell and back. Come inside and let me feed you properly.'"

"He took me in. Gave me a job cleaning the club. Let me sleep in the storage room. And slowly, over weeks and months, he and the other queens taught me that I could be whoever I wanted to be. That my past didn't have to determine my future. That I could literally reinvent myself."

Trange's eyes were bright now, animated by the memory of that transformation. "They taught me about fashion, about presentation, about carrying yourself like you belong anywhere you go. They showed me how makeup could be armor. How the right walk could communicate power. How a well-chosen name could become a whole new identity."

"'Trange'," Shaniece said softly, understanding dawning. "It sounds fierce."

"Exactly!" Trange's voice gained energy. "I didn't want to be Octavia anymore—poor, pitied, victimized Octavia. I wanted to be someone fierce. Someone ostentatious. Someone revered, not someone people felt sorry for. Trange' sounded like strength. Like money. Like power."

She sat up straighter, her posture shifting from broken to defiant. "I added Moreau because it sounded French and sophisticated. Like I came from old money and good breeding instead of the muck and drug houses. I created her from nothing—every gesture, every mannerism, every carefully curated detail."

"The queens helped me put together fashion shows. Small ones at first—just in the club for the regular clientele. But I had an eye for design, for knowing what would make people look twice. Those shows got bigger. Started attracting attention from

outside the drag community. And then one day, a modeling
agent showed up."

Trange's smile was almost wicked now. "She thought I was one
of the models. Asked if I'd ever considered professional work. I
lied and said yes, that I'd modeled before but was new to New
Orleans. She believed me because Trange' Moreau was designed
to be believed. Gave me her card. Within six months, I'd
booked my first real campaign."

"The rest—the business, the success, the empire—I built that
brick by brick. Every meeting where someone tried to
underestimate me, I proved them wrong. Every door that tried
to close, I kicked open. Every person who tried to remind me
where I came from, I showed them where I was going."

She looked at each of her friends in turn. "So yes, everything
Cora Jean said in church was technically true. But it wasn't the
truth. The truth is that I survived something most people can't
even imagine. The truth is that I took nothing and built
something extraordinary. The truth is that I'm not the victim
they tried to make me on Sunday—I'm the victor who refused
to stay dead."

The Weight of the Past

The women sat in stunned silence, processing what they'd just
heard. Finally, Coko spoke, her voice thick with emotion.

"You know what I hear in your story? I hear Job. I hear Joseph.
I hear every person in the Bible who went through hell but
came out refined like gold." She picked up her Bible from where
it had fallen. "The enemy meant it for evil, but God meant it for
good."

"Did He though?" Trange's voice carried years of doubt.
"Because from where I'm sitting, it feels like God left me in that

house. Left me with those people. Let them do whatever they wanted to a child who prayed to Him every night for rescue that never came."

"I understand that feeling," Renee said quietly. All eyes turned to her—Renee, who'd been through her own hell with her ex-husband's abuse. "I felt abandoned by God too. Wondered why He let my husband beat me. Why He didn't intervene when I was lying on the floor bleeding, praying for death or deliverance, whichever came first."

She moved closer to Trange'. "But here's what I learned: God didn't cause what happened to you. Evil people made evil choices, and you bore the consequences of their sin. But God— He's the reason you survived. He's the reason you found Delacroix. He's the reason you had the strength to reinvent yourself when most people would have stayed broken."

"She's right," Shaniece added. "Your story isn't about God abandoning you. It's about God sustaining you through the unsurvivable. Every time you should have died—the abortion complications, the violence, the streets—you lived. That's not luck. That's God's hand of protection."

Moni nodded emphatically. "And the skills you developed, the business acumen, the eye for fashion—those are gifts. Gifts that got twisted and exploited by evil people, but gifts nonetheless. God gave you what you needed to not just survive but thrive."

Trange' wanted to believe them. Part of her—the part that had walked down that aisle to altar—did believe them. But another part, the part that had learned to trust no one and expect nothing good, resisted.

"This is why you have such a hard time trusting people," Samantha observed, her voice gentle. "Why you keep everyone at arm's length. Why you'd rather throw money at a problem than let someone get close enough to help you emotionally."

"Can you blame me?" Trange' shot back. "Everyone who was supposed to protect me either abandoned me or exploited me. The system. My family. Even the church—Miss Hattie's church knew something was wrong when I stopped coming, but nobody came looking for me. Nobody checked."

"And now the church has done it again," Coko said sadly. "Instead of being a place of healing, it became a place of exposure and shame. Instead of covering you, they stripped you bare for entertainment."

The women sat with that truth, the weight of Sunday's violence hanging heavy in the room.

"But not all churches," Shaniece reminded her. "Not all church people. FaLessia was horrified. First Lady Clarice—she defended you and herself with grace and strength. Mother Heady tried to stop it. There are good people in that building who are just as devastated as you are about what happened."

"And there's Andre," Moni added carefully.

Trange's entire body tensed. "Don't."

"We have to talk about him eventually," Samantha pressed. "He's been texting you nonstop."

"How would you know? My phone's been off."

Renee picked up the device from the dresser and held it out. "Then I think it's time you rejoined the world."

Trange' stared at the phone like it was a venomous snake. "I'm sure he wants nothing to do with me now. He knows who I really am. What I really am."

"What you really are," Coko corrected firmly, "is a survivor. A warrior. A woman of God who's been through the fire and came out purified. If he can't see that, then he's not the man we thought he was."

"And if he can't handle your past," Samantha added with characteristic bluntness, "then he doesn't deserve your future."

"We all have a past," Shaniece reminded her. "Every single person in that church has done something they're ashamed of. The only difference is yours got put on display while theirs stayed hidden. That doesn't make their sins smaller or your redemption less real."

Trange' reached for the phone with a trembling hand. "What if he's different? What if seeing the real me changed everything?"

"Then you'll know," Moni said simply. "But you won't know if you keep hiding in this room with the phone off."

Trange' powered on the device. It took a moment to boot up, connecting to Shaniece's WiFi, syncing with the cloud. Then the notifications started.

The sound was overwhelming—ding after ding after ding, a barrage of texts, voicemails, emails, all flooding in simultaneously. Dozens of them. Maybe hundreds. Three days of messages compressed into thirty seconds of constant alerts.

Her friends watched as Trange' scrolled through the chaos, her face unreadable.

Business associates checking in. Clients expressing concern. Acquaintances fishing for gossip. Social media notifications from people she'd never met commenting on her life. News outlets requesting interviews about "the incident at Greater Mount Calvary Cathedral."

But one name appeared more than any other. One sender whose messages dominated her screen.

Andre Howard.

Her heart hammered as she opened the thread, reading from the earliest to the most recent:

CALL ME.

TRANGE', PLEASE. LET'S TALK ABOUT THIS.

I CAN'T BELIEVE THEY DID THIS TO YOU.

I'M SO SORRY. THIS SHOULD NEVER HAVE HAPPENED.

PLEASE CALL ME.

I NEED TO HEAR YOUR VOICE. NEED TO KNOW YOU'RE OKAY.

After several more messages: I WANT TO MEET WITH YOU TO TALK THIS OVER. I NEED TO UNDERSTAND.

AND I NEED TO SEE YOU.

The final message had been sent two hours ago: *I KNOW YOU PROBABLY DON'T WANT TO HEAR FROM ME. I KNOW SUNDAY WAS TRAUMATIC AND MY CHURCH CAUSED THAT TRAUMA. BUT PLEASE, IF YOU CAN, JUST LET ME KNOW YOU'RE ALIVE AND SAFE. THAT'S ALL I NEED. JUST ONE WORD SO I KNOW YOU'RE OKAY.*

Trange' stared at the screen, emotions warring across her face. Hope. Fear. Anger. Longing. Doubt.

"What do I do?" She looked up at her friends, these women who'd just heard her darkest secrets and hadn't run. "What if he's just being polite? What if he feels obligated because his church hurt me?"

"There's only one way to find out," Shaniece said gently. "You have to talk to him."

"But what if—" Trange's voice broke. "What if I let myself believe he still wants me, and then I see his face and realize the truth? I don't think I can survive that kind of rejection right now."

Samantha sat on the bed beside her. "You survived things that would have killed most people. You survived rape, abuse, trafficking, poverty, abandonment, and three days ago, you survived public humiliation in God's house. You can survive one conversation with a man."

"Besides," Coko added with a knowing smile, "something tells me that man isn't trying to let you go."

Trange' looked down at the phone in her hand, at Andre's messages filling the screen, at the evidence that maybe—just maybe—not everyone would abandon her when they saw who she really was.

Her thumb hovered over the keyboard. Three days of silence about to be broken. Three days of hiding about to end. Three days of assuming the worst about to be tested against reality.

She typed one word: *ALIVE.*

Then, before courage could desert her, she added: *CAN WE TALK?*

The response came within seconds: *WHEN AND WHERE? I'LL BE THERE.*

Trange' looked up at her friends, fear and hope warring in her eyes. "He wants to meet."

"Then meet him," Shaniece urged. "Hear what he has to say. Give him a chance to prove he's different."

"And if he's not?" Trange's voice was small, vulnerable, the voice of Octavia rather than Trange'.

"Then we'll be right here," Moni promised. "Ready to pick up the pieces and remind you that one man's inability to see your worth doesn't diminish it."

"But something tells me," Renee said with a smile, "that conversation is going to surprise you."

Trange' looked in the mirror across the room—that expensive, diamond-encrusted monument to everything she'd built. For three days, it had reflected her brokenness. But now, surrounded by women who knew her truth and loved her anyway, it reflected something else.

Possibility.

Maybe faith could survive betrayal. Maybe grace was bigger than shame. Maybe redemption wasn't just a church word but a lived reality.

Maybe God hadn't abandoned her after all—He'd just been positioning her for a testimony that would set other captives free.

She typed: *TOMORROW. 2PM. CAFÉ AMELIE.*

Andre's response was immediate: *I'LL BE THERE. THANK YOU FOR GIVING ME A CHANCE.*

Trange' set the phone down and looked at her friends—her sisters, her chosen family, her evidence that love existed even in a world that had tried to teach her otherwise.

"Okay," she said, strength returning to her voice. "Let's get me ready to rejoin the world."

They surrounded her—Shaniece, Samantha, Renee, Moni, Coko—their hands on her shoulders, their prayers rising like incense, their love a fortress against every lie that said she was unworthy of good things.

Tomorrow she would face Andre and whatever truth that conversation revealed.

But today, she had survived telling her story. And in the telling, she'd discovered something crucial: her past was powerful, but it wasn't determinative. It was testimony, not identity. Evidence of survival, not proof of unworthiness.

Octavia Shanika Burns had died in that muck.

Trange' Moreau had risen from the ashes.

And whoever she was becoming through faith—that woman was still being formed, still being refined, still being loved into existence by a God who specialized in resurrections.

The sanctuary had burned three days ago.

But from the ashes, something new was beginning to grow.

Chapter 10: When God Calls You Home

Mother Heady's Visit

Mother Heady Mitchell gripped the iron railing, her knuckles whitening with each labored step up the sloping driveway toward the Howard estate. Seventy-three years old, and they had her climbing what felt like Jacob's ladder just to check on somebody.

"These people ought to be ashamed," she muttered, adjusting the heavy casserole dish balanced in her free arm. "Got a seventy-three-year-old woman hiking up Mount Sinai just to bring some food."

But she kept climbing because that's what church mothers did—they showed up, invitation neither desired nor required.

In her other hand swung a canvas tote bag stuffed with Tupperware containers: thin-cut fried pork chops (Marcus's favorite, seasoned with her secret blend of paprika and garlic salt), collard greens cooked low and slow with smoked turkey necks until they sang, sweet potatoes candied with real butter and brown sugar, deviled eggs with just enough mustard to make your tongue happy, and—wrapped carefully in foil—six of her legendary pecan bars that had won the church bake-off three years running.

"Clarice and Marcus better appreciate this meal," she huffed, finally reaching the landing. "All this work I put in—"

She stopped mid-complaint as reality crashed over her like a rogue wave.

Marcus.

Bishop Howard. The man she'd mentored when he first took the pulpit at Greater Mount Calvary twenty-three years ago, all raw potential and nervous energy. The godson she'd claimed when his own family couldn't see his calling. The man who'd made Clarice so happy, who'd built that church from three hundred members to three thousand, who'd preached funerals and officiated weddings and prayed over hospital beds until his own body gave out.

Marcus was dead.

Her eyes welled up, tears threatening to spill over and ruin the mascara she'd carefully applied that morning more out of habit than vanity. She shook her head hard, a physical rejection of the grief trying to take root.

"No ma'am," she said aloud to no one. "Not now. Clarice needs me strong, not blubbering like a baby."

Before she could ring the bell, the door swung open. Andre stood there, startled, his hand still on the doorknob.

"Mother Heady? I didn't know—we weren't expecting—" He stammered like a teenager caught sneaking in past curfew. "Mother really isn't up to seeing anybody. She's been—"

"I ain't got time for a dissertation on what your mama is or isn't up for." Heady shoved the casserole dish into his chest with enough force to make him step backward. "I'm here, and she *will* see me. Now take this food to the kitchen. Where she at?"

She breezed past him into the foyer before he could mount a defense, her sensible orthopedic shoes clicking against the travertine tile that probably cost more than her car.

The Howard residence was a study in contemporary elegance—all clean lines and floor-to-ceiling windows that flooded the space with natural light. The open-concept design flowed seamlessly from the two-story entryway into a living area furnished with mid-century modern pieces: a low-slung gray sectional, a marble coffee table with gold accents, abstract art that probably had names she couldn't pronounce mounted on pristine white walls. Everything spoke of money spent with intention rather than ostentation, of taste refined by travel and exposure to beauty.

But Heady had been coming here long enough that she didn't pause to admire the aesthetics. She knew exactly where Clarice would be.

"She in that parlor right now, ain't she?" Heady called over her shoulder, not waiting for confirmation.

Andre chuckled despite himself, following her with the food. "Yes ma'am. But Mother Heady—"

"But nothing. This is just how I am—a warrior wrapped up in an Afghan."

She found the parlor exactly as she'd expected: Clarice's sanctuary within the modern house, the one room Marcus had let her design according to her own sensibilities. Here, contemporary gave way to tradition. Crown molding hugged walls painted a warm cream. A Persian rug in rich burgundy and gold covered the hardwood floor. The furniture leaned Victorian—a velvet settee in hunter green, two wingback chairs upholstered in damask, an antique secretary desk that had belonged to Clarice's grandmother. Fresh flowers—Marcus's tradition, continued now by Andre—sat in a crystal vase on the side table: white lilies and yellow roses, their scent mixing with the bergamot notes of the tea Clarice was sipping.

The First Lady sat in her usual chair by the French doors that opened to the garden, still in her nightgown and robe at two in the afternoon. Her usually immaculate silver-streaked hair was pulled back in a simple ponytail. No makeup. No jewelry except her wedding ring, which she kept twisting around her finger like a worry stone.

She looked up as Heady entered, surprise flickering across features otherwise dulled by grief.

"Heady? How did you—"

"Imma sit down." Heady commanded, plopping herself into the opposite chair with a grunt that spoke to both her age and her exhaustion. "Lord have mercy, got an old woman doing all this work."

She leaned back, pulled off her crocheted shawl—her signature Afghan that had seen her through forty Louisiana winters—and set down her oversized purse that could double as an overnight bag.

"Is that tea fresh?" Without waiting for an answer, she reached for the elegant teapot on the table and poured herself a generous serving in one of Clarice's bone china cups. "I do love me some good tea."

Her eyes scanned the room with the practiced surveillance of someone who'd been conducting home visits for fifty years. Instinctively—as if pulled by muscle memory—she reached into that cavernous purse and extracted a silver flask. With the smooth efficiency of a bartender working happy hour, she unscrewed the cap and poured a healthy shot of bourbon into her tea.

Clarice couldn't help it—she laughed. The sound surprised them both, rusty from disuse but genuine.

"You know," Clarice said, a hint of her old self creeping back into her voice, "no one's here but me. You don't have to be sneaky."

Heady took a deliberate sip, closing her eyes as the bourbon-laced tea warmed her chest. "Mmm-hmm. But I don't need nobody talking. You know how they would judge if they saw me having a little nip. These church folk got the discernment of a prophet when it comes to everybody else's business but can't see their own mess if it hit them in the face."

She set the cup down with a soft clink. "Besides, I brought you some food. Andre got it in the kitchen—pork chops, greens, the works. Your favorites. And Marcus's favorites too." Her voice caught slightly on his name but she powered through. "Made sure to fix it just how y'all like it."

"Thank you, Heady." Clarice's voice was soft, genuinely grateful.

"Don't 'thank you Heady' me." The older woman's finger shot out, pointed like a weapon straight at Clarice's chest. "I've been calling you for days. *Days*, Clarice. I don't care what's going on in this house, what grief you're drowning in, what shame you're feeling from Sunday's foolishness—you take my phone calls."

Her voice had shifted from playful to drill sergeant in seconds flat.

"Yes ma'am." Clarice responded automatically, the way you do when someone who earned your respect a long time ago calls you out.

Heady was only twelve years her senior—hardly a generation's gap. But those twelve years carried weight. Heady had been there when Clarice first arrived at Greater Mount Calvary as the new First Lady, young and overwhelmed and trying to figure out how to be herself in a role that felt like it came with a manual she'd never received. Heady had been there through Clarice's struggles to conceive, through the joy of Andre's birth, through every church split and power struggle and political maneuvering that came with leading a growing congregation. She'd earned her

181

place as spiritual mother through consistency and fierce love and the kind of honesty that hurt but healed.

As if the wind had been knocked out of her, Heady sat back in her chair. She took a few more sips of her fortified tea, letting the silence settle around them like dust after a storm.

They sat like that for several minutes—two women who'd walked through enough of life together that they didn't always need words.

Finally, Heady broke the silence. "That sure was a hellish service Sunday."

"Yes." Clarice's voice was barely above a whisper. "I can't believe they did that. In Marcus's church. At his memorial."

"What I can't believe," Heady interrupted, her voice rising with the righteous anger she'd been tamping down for days, "is that they think they're gonna get away with it. We ain't gonna just let this slide, even if we can't do anything immediate about it. God sits high and looks low! For them old dingy women to come up in the Lord's House and cause all that confusion, bring that girl's family up in there like some kind of Jerry Springer ambush—" She shook her head, disgust written across every line of her face. "May God have mercy on their souls, because I sure wouldn't!"

Clarice set down her cup, her hands trembling slightly. "I've never been so embarrassed in my life. The whole church. Watching. Judging. And that poor girl—Trange'—she just sat there frozen. I wanted to do something, say something, but I was so shocked I couldn't even move."

"That child ain't the one who should be embarrassed." Heady's voice softened. "She's the victim in all this. You're the victim. The church is the victim of their mess. But those women who orchestrated that? They're the ones who should be hanging their heads in shame."

"I probably should have told the church sooner about my past," Clarice said, her voice small. "Maybe if I'd been honest from the beginning—"

"Stop it." Heady's command cut through Clarice's spiraling. "Stop that right now. Your past is your testimony, not their entertainment. You don't owe them nothing. The people who needed to know about your journey knew about it. Marcus knew. Andre knows. The people who love you and support you—we knew. The rest of them? They don't get access to your story just because they sit in the same building on Sunday mornings."

She reached over and grabbed Clarice's hand, gripping it with surprising strength.

"Besides, half them folk got skeletons in their closets that would make your past look like a Sunday school lesson. The difference is, you got free. You found Jesus, you found Marcus, you built a good life. They're still locked up in their mess, which is why they're so eager to dig up everybody else's."

Clarice squeezed back, tears finally spilling over. "I miss him, Heady. I miss him so much it physically hurts. I wake up and forget for a second that he's gone, and then I remember and it's like losing him all over again."

"I know, baby. I know." Heady's own eyes glistened. "Frederick been gone eleven years and I still reach for him some mornings. But you got to keep living. Marcus wouldn't want you locked up in this house, drowning in grief and shame. That man loved you fierce, and he'd be furious if he knew you were letting them church vultures make you feel less than the queen he crowned you."

They sat in companionable silence again, both thinking about the men they'd loved and lost.

"So what you know about Trange'?" Heady finally asked, her tone shifting to the practical. "I know Andre sweet on her. Anybody with eyes can see that boy is smitten."

"He is." A small smile played at Clarice's lips. "And honestly? I like her. I know that probably shocks you—"

"Ain't nothing about you shocks me, Clarice Howard. I know you better than you know yourself sometimes."

"She's got fire. Spirit. She doesn't let people push her around. And she's genuine—I can spot a fake from a mile away, and that girl is the real deal. Rough edges and all." Clarice paused. "She reminds me of myself at that age. Before I learned to soften myself to fit into church folk's expectations."

"Where she at now?" Heady asked. "Andre been trying to reach her?"

"He finally got through to her this morning. That's where he's headed now—to meet her." Clarice's smile widened slightly. "Knowing my son, he's probably already planning how to make this right."

"Good." Heady nodded with satisfaction, refilling her mug with tea and an equal measure of bourbon. Clarice's eyebrows shot up, a look that clearly communicated, *that's too much*.

Heady caught the expression and laughed. "Girl, I'm just sitting up here talking to you. You trying to turn me into a full wino?" They both laughed—deep, cleansing laughter that felt like medicine.

Clarice needed this. Needed the awakening from her cocoon of grief. Needed the gentle kick in the rear that only someone who loved you could deliver.

"Speaking of young love," Clarice ventured, her eyes twinkling with mischief for the first time in weeks, "how are things with you and Deacon Fry? He's a younger man compared to you, isn't he?"

Heady almost choked on her bourbon-enhanced tea. "Now you stay out of old folks' business! Samuel is my *friend*. And I'd appreciate you keeping it right there." The finality in her voice would have shut down most people.

But Clarice wasn't most people. "I'm just saying, if Andre and Trange' are finding love, I can't see why the Reverend Mother Heady and the good Deacon Fry can't find love together."

"Child, I'm not going to cheat on the Lord. I'm married to God." Heady's voice had gone quiet, reflective. "Been there, done that with earthly marriage."

Her mind drifted to Frederick—her Fred. They'd grown up together in the early forties in rural Louisiana, two Black kids who found each other despite (or maybe because of) the world trying to crush them both. She'd known him since they were children running barefoot through creek beds, stealing kisses behind the schoolhouse, promising forever when they didn't even understand what forever meant.

She'd never dated another man. Never kissed another man. Frederick had been her first date, her first kiss, her first everything. Their families had been close, so at sixteen—with her mama's blessing and her daddy's stern lecture about respect—she'd married him.

They hadn't had children of their own—the Lord had other plans in that department. But Heady had never felt the lack because she'd adopted every child who needed her. Her nieces and nephews. The neighborhood kids who showed up hungry.

The teenagers from church who needed guidance. Anyone who needed help found it at Heady and Frederick's door.

For sixty years, they'd been a dynamic duo. He'd been her person, her partner, her peace. When he died nine years ago, it left a void in her heart and soul that no amount of prayer could completely fill. That space was his, would always be his, could never be occupied by another man.

Not now. Not ever.

But—and she hated to admit this even to herself—she did enjoy spending time with Sammy. Samuel Fry. Deacon Fry, as she insisted on calling him in public to maintain propriety.

"Well now that you mention it," Heady said abruptly, standing and gathering her things with the hurried efficiency of someone fleeing an uncomfortable conversation, "I gotta get on back to the house. Sammy's coming over tonight. Our shows are coming on, and I've got fish to fry and peach cobbler to finish off."

"*Sammy*?" Clarice seized on the nickname like a prosecuting attorney spotting a confession. She'd never heard Heady refer to him so casually. It had always been "Deacon Fry" or "Mr. Fry" with rigid formality. "Sounds like you've got yourself a really nice *date* tonight."

She swayed slightly in her chair, sipping her tea with exaggerated innocence.

Heady whipped around, eyes flashing. "Now I told you to stay out of my business! And I also told you—he's just a friend. Now you get yourself out of this parlor and go eat some of that food I brought. Lord knows it's cold by now. And don't you dare just throw my pork chops in the microwave and get them all steamed and soggy. Put them in that fancy air fryer you got to crisp them up a little bit. And save some of those pecan bars for Andre."

She gathered her shawl and purse with the speed of someone making a tactical retreat. As quickly as she'd entered—like a ravaging tornado touching down with purpose—she exited with equal force.

Clarice sat alone in the parlor, thinking about Marcus. About the church. About the mess that Sunday had become. She said a quiet prayer—asking God to continue watching over her and the congregation, praying that Marcus was looking down from Heaven and still proud of the woman he'd married.

Her phone rang. She glanced at the caller ID and smiled despite herself.

"I don't even know why I looked. I know who it is."

"Child, get your butt up and go eat that food like I told you to!" Heady's voice came through the speaker before Clarice could even say hello. "And don't you sit there wallowing. Marcus wouldn't want that and you know it. Now bye."

The line went dead before Clarice could respond.

Laughing softly—another small miracle—Clarice stood and headed toward the kitchen to follow orders.

The Church Mothers' Strategy

The parlor at Mother Eartha Jones's house was a shrine to Black church lady culture circa 1985—doilies on every surface, Bible verses in ornate cursive, plastic slipcovers that squeaked with each shift. A European-looking Jesus with blue eyes surveyed the room from above the mantle, his expression caught somewhere between blessing and judgment.

Mother Bernice Williams settled into her usual spot on the sofa. Mother Rose Washington followed, her African walking stick clicking against hardwood as she claimed the wingback chair.

Three old women. An unholy trinity of church politics.

Jones poured sweet tea from a crystal pitcher, ice cubes tinkling into glasses from her fifty-year-old wedding china.

"Well," she said, satisfaction dripping from her voice, "I'd say Sunday went exactly as planned, wouldn't you ladies?"

Williams leaned back, cat-like. "Better than planned. Did you see that girl's face? Frozen like a deer. And First Lady Clarice not knowing whether to run or stay—" She cackled. "Priceless."

"The look on Andre's face though," Rose added, her voice raspy from age and menthol cigarettes. "Like somebody slapped his mama. Which, in a way, we did."

Their laughter held no joy. Only malicious satisfaction.

"I still can't believe Cora Jean showed up," Williams said. "When you tracked her down in Caldwell Parish, I thought she'd be too strung out."

"Five hundred dollars and a promise of five hundred more." Jones dismissed it with a wave. "Money talks to addicts. And that Henry Earl was ready to come just for the drama."

"The whole family's a mess," Rose interjected. "Can you imagine *them* at church functions? Pastor appreciation dinners? Front row at Easter service?"

They shuddered dramatically.

"We saved Greater Mount Calvary from embarrassment," Jones declared. "From having its good name dragged through mud by associating with such low-class people."

Rose sipped her tea. "And that Clarice. Butter wouldn't melt in her mouth and come to find out she's got her own sordid past. Marcus Howard was too good for her."

"If Marcus had listened to us from the beginning," Williams agreed, "he would have married someone from a good church family. Someone with proper breeding."

"Someone like Patricia Jones," Rose said with a knowing look.

Jones bristled. "My daughter understands ministry. She knows the church. She's been preparing to be a First Lady her whole life. But instead, Andre's making googly eyes at some jezebel who probably slept her way to success. You saw those clothes. Those labels. She's worldly to her core."

"But we can't let up now," Rose cautioned, her voice strategic. "We struck a blow Sunday, but we can't let this story die. Every time someone sees her or hears her name, they need to remember what we revealed."

Williams nodded. "And we need to expand our target. It's not just Trange'. We need to address this whole progressive movement. All these women who think they can preach, lead, teach men."

"Like that Crystal Young," Jones said, lip curling. "Writing books, speaking at conferences. A woman teaching men—it's biblical disorder."

"Now that Bishop Howard's gone," Williams added, "we have the opportunity to restore proper biblical hierarchy. No more women preachers. No more women on the trustee board."

Rose leaned forward, gripping her walking stick. "We need a comprehensive strategy. Drive out everyone who doesn't align with our vision."

Jones stood, pacing. "We start with Trange'—keep that story circulating. Subtle reminders. Questions about her family. Comments about her clothes. References to 'troubled backgrounds'."

"Target her relationship with Andre directly," Williams suggested. "Make him understand that pursuing her means damaging his ministry before it begins."

"We also pressure First Lady Clarice," Rose added. "Make her understand that defending that girl means dredging up her own past. We've been polite about what we know, but we don't have to stay polite."

The threat hung in the air like smoke.

Jones smiled slowly, viciously. "And Crystal Young. We need to have a serious conversation with the ministers' council about whether women should hold ministerial licenses at all. Frame it as returning to biblical values. Make her choose between her calling and her comfort."

"Some people need to know when they're not wanted," Williams said with finality.

"Exactly," Jones agreed. "We're not being mean. We're protecting the church. Maintaining standards."

Rose raised her glass in mock toast. "To tradition. To biblical order. To protecting our church from the world's influence."

They clinked glasses, three old women who'd convinced themselves that cruelty was righteousness, that exclusion was protection, that judgment was discernment.

"We have to keep this going," Jones declared, setting down her glass with a decisive clink. "Can't let the story die. We have to drive out Trange'—or Triangle, or Octavia, or whatever name that girl's using—" She paused for maximum effect. "And Crystal too."

She laughed—a sound devoid of warmth or grace, empty of anything remotely resembling the love of Christ they claimed to serve.

The other two joined in, their laughter echoing through the plastic-covered parlor, bouncing off walls adorned with Bible verses about love and forgiveness that they'd long ago twisted to serve their own purposes.

Outside, the sun set on Baton Rouge, painting the sky in shades of orange and purple. But inside Mother Jones's house, there was only darkness.

Café Amelia

Café Amelia occupied a converted Creole cottage in the Garden District, its soft yellow exterior catching the afternoon light. Inside, exposed brick walls held local art, vintage fixtures cast warm glows, and the scent of coffee and fresh-baked bread made the space feel like a hug.

Andre had arrived twenty minutes early, which gave him too much time to second-guess himself. After three outfit changes, he'd settled on dark jeans and a crisp white button-down, sleeves rolled to his elbows. He ordered coffee he didn't drink, checked his phone every thirty seconds, rehearsed words until they lost all meaning.

Lord, give me the right words. Help me fix this. Help her see—

The door opened. Trange' entered.

She was beautiful—but today her beauty felt different. Guarded. Her designer handbag hung like armor. Her posture perfect, almost rigid. Cream silk blouse and tailored black pants—

professional, expensive, carefully chosen to project success and self-sufficiency.

But her eyes betrayed her. They carried hurt, wariness, and underneath it all, a flicker of hope she probably wished she could extinguish.

She spotted him, squared her shoulders, and walked over with measured steps.

"Andre." She sat across from him, setting her bag on the empty chair—a barrier, an escape route.

"Thank you for coming." His voice came out rough. "I wasn't sure you would."

"I almost didn't." Her honesty landed between them like a stone. "I've been preparing a speech all morning. Practicing how to tell you that I understand if you need to walk away. That I know what Sunday revealed changes things—"

"Stop." He held up his hand. "Please, let me talk first. I need to say this before I lose my nerve."

She fell silent, her perfectly manicured hands folded on the table.

Andre took a deep breath. "I need to apologize. Not for what those women did—I can't control that. But I'm sorry I didn't stand in the gap for you. I didn't interrupt it, didn't protect you, didn't do *something*. I sat there frozen, and you deserved better."

Trange' blinked rapidly, clearly not expecting this.

"I've been praying," he continued, his voice gaining strength. "Asking God what He wanted me to do, how to move forward. And the answer I kept hearing was that you're for me. That's what God said. 'She's for you.'"

Tears welled in Trange's eyes, spilling over before she could stop them. She swiped at them angrily.

"How can you say that?" Her voice cracked. "Now that you know—now that the whole church knows—"

"The story they told isn't the whole story, is it?" Andre asked gently.

She looked at him sharply, defensive walls snapping into place. "What do you mean?"

"I mean it didn't sit right in my spirit. The way they presented it—like you were some willing participant in your own destruction. Like a child could be blamed for the sins committed against her." His hazel eyes held hers steadily. "That wasn't the truth, was it?"

Something in her broke. The careful façade crumbled. Words flooded out like water from a broken dam.

"I didn't choose that life. I didn't want any of it. I was twelve when my stepfather—" Her voice caught. She forced herself to continue. "I was twelve when he first came into my room. My mother knew. She knew and she didn't stop it because he brought money into the house."

She stopped, struggling for composure. "Yes, I did things. Despicable things. Things I'm ashamed of. But there was a reason behind it. Survival. Escape. Trying to claw my way out of a hell I didn't ask to be thrown into."

Her words came faster now. "I left that life. I rebranded myself. Changed my name, changed my look, changed everything because I couldn't stand to see Octavia Shanika Burns—that scared little girl who couldn't save herself. I became Trange' Moreau because she was strong. Successful. Everything that broken child could never be."

193

She looked up, suddenly realizing she'd been staring at the table. "I forgot you were even here. I'm sorry—"

But Andre's eyes were glistening with unshed tears. He'd been clinging to every word, his face a mixture of grief and rage—not at her, but for her.

He reached across the table and took her hand. His touch was gentle but firm.

"I'm glad you told me," he said quietly. "And I want you to know—after you left Sunday, my mother had a conversation with yours. I overheard it. She tried to get through to them, tried to persuade them to see your pain, to recognize what you'd overcome. But they're so caught up in their addiction they couldn't see past their own needs."

He squeezed her hand. "And what I heard about my mother's past—that wasn't shocking to me. Not the facts. It was shocking they would weaponize it like that. But I've known most of my mother's story for years. Mother Heady told me when I was a teenager, angry and frustrated. She explained that my mother came from a rough past, that she didn't want her son to experience what she'd experienced."

He paused, his gaze intense. "You and my mother have similar backgrounds. You should call her. Tonight, if you're comfortable. I think you'd find more understanding there than you expect."

They sat back, the immediate crisis passed. But a question still lingered.

Trange' asked softly, "So what does this make us? Where do we go from here?"

Andre looked at her directly. "God said you're my woman. So you're my woman." He stated it matter-of-factly, as if it were the most obvious thing in the world.

A smile tugged at her mouth despite everything. "So like your girlfriend?"

His face remained serious. "I don't see a girl in front of me. I see a whole woman." He grabbed her hand again, his thumb tracing circles on her palm. "I'm a man of God. I'm led by the Spirit. And the human man in me finds you incredibly desirable. The physical attraction is real and strong."

Heat flooded Trange's face.

"But more importantly," he continued, "the spirit man in me has been given a green light from the Father. The woman in front of me is for me. I don't believe in long dating just for the sake of it. I don't believe in fornication or shacking up. I'm a minister and now a pastor, so I must do things decently and in order. If you can respect that, I see a bright future for us."

Tears streamed down her face again—but these were different tears. Healing tears.

She'd had beautiful men before. Rich men. Powerful men. Men who wanted her body, her connections, her money, her status. But she'd never had a man who chose *her*. Who saw her completely—past and present, broken pieces and all.

Not love yet, maybe. Too soon for that word. But desire. Fire. Intention. Commitment. Coupled with God's approval, this courtship was transforming into a relationship right before her eyes.

"I've been loved before," she said quietly. "But I've never been loved in plain sight. Out loud. You're willing to claim me. To elevate me. Despite my past. Despite how they tried to

195

weaponize my pain. You're telling me that God turned their mess into a message."

"That's exactly what He did," Andre confirmed. "If I call you, I clean you and qualify you. That's what the Lord does. What God has cleansed, let no man call common."

That verse struck a chord so deep inside her that she felt it vibrate in her bones. *If God has cleaned me, then I'm clean. If the Father says I'm acceptable, then I'm acceptable.* No amount of judgment from church mothers could change what God had declared.

Andre leaned across the small table. His eyes held a question, a permission sought.

She nodded, almost imperceptibly.

He kissed her. Deeply. Passionately. Not the chaste peck of a first date, but the kiss of a man staking a claim. When he finally pulled back, she was melting into her chair.

She looked around nervously. "People will see. People will talk."

"Let them talk." His voice carried authority that sent shivers down her spine. "Let them see. I kissed a woman that God told me was my woman."

My woman. Those words resonated deep within her. Typically, she'd bristle at anyone claiming possession. But coming from his lips—in that voice that carried both tenderness and certainty—she'd accept it.

A thought crossed her mind. *Can he truly handle a woman like me? Someone who pairs Chanel with church praise, who claims victory in Vuitton, who praises God in Gucci? Who'll also read someone for filth if necessary?*

Andre's phone rang, interrupting her thoughts. He glanced at the screen, his expression shifting to concern. "I need to take this. I'm sorry—"

"It's fine." She waved him on, turning to look out the window.

She glanced back at Andre and froze.

His caramel skin had gone pale. The phone fell from his hand to the table with a clatter that made nearby patrons look over.

"Andre? What's going on? What's wrong?"

He looked at her, devastated. "My grandmother. My father's mother. The lady I was staying with in Michigan." His voice cracked. "She just passed away."

"Oh my God." Trange' moved instinctively, sliding into the chair beside him. "I'm so sorry. I'm so, so sorry."

"She was like a second mother to me. She raised my dad. She—" He couldn't finish. His face crumpled. Tears streamed down his face as grief hit him in waves.

Trange' pulled him to her chest, not caring about propriety or appearances. She held him as he broke down, sobbing into her expensive silk blouse, his body shaking.

"She was my last connection to my father on that side," he managed between gasps. "The last person who knew him as a boy. And now she's gone. They're both gone."

"I know. I know." She held him tighter, one hand stroking his back, the other cradling his head. "I'm here. I've got you. You're not alone."

While she comforted him with one arm, her other hand reached for her phone. Quickly, efficiently, she texted her assistant: **NEED THE JET FUELED AND READY TO GO IMMEDIATELY.**

Rev. Dr. Mario DeSean Booker

FLIGHT PLAN TO MICHIGAN—WILL SEND DETAILS IN 30 MINUTES. NO QUESTIONS.

She set the phone down and lifted Andre's tear-stained face to look at her. "Whatever you need, I'm here for you. And I'm going to Michigan with you. I'm going to help you through this entire process. I'll have my assistant coordinate everything—flights, hotel, whatever logistics need handling. You don't have to do this alone."

He nodded, unable to speak, tears still flowing.

"I'm going to take care of you," she continued, her voice strong and sure. "The way you just took care of me. That's what partners do, right? They show up. They stay. They fight for each other."

They sat like that for several more minutes—him crying, her holding him, both drawing strength from the unexpected bond forming between them.

Andre's mind was chaos—grief over losing his grandmother, pain over losing another connection to his father, disbelief that this was happening now.

But beneath the chaos, a thought emerged: *Thank You, God. Thank You that I wasn't alone when I got this news. Thank You that I was here, with her, after just telling her she's my woman. Thank You that I don't have to go through this alone.*

Yes, he had his mother. Clarice would grieve with him, support him, love him through this loss.

But this was different. This was partnership. Someone who chose to walk through fire with him not out of obligation but out of commitment.

He looked at this beautiful, complicated, wounded, strong woman who held him like he was precious. This woman who'd just opened her private jet for him without hesitation. This woman who the church had tried to destroy, who had every reason to walk away from the mess that was his life right now.

And she was staying.

Thank You, God, he prayed silently, *for giving me this woman. For bringing her into my life right when I needed her most. Help me be worthy of this gift. Help me love her the way she deserves to be loved.*

Trange' felt his breathing even out slightly as the initial shock passed. She whispered into his ear, "We're going to get through this together. You hear me? Together."

"Together," he echoed, his voice hoarse but certain.

Outside Café Amelia, the sun continued its descent toward the horizon, painting the sky in shades of pink and gold. Inside, two broken people found wholeness in each other's arms, discovering that sometimes God's greatest gifts come wrapped in the most unexpected packages.

And somewhere—in Heaven or in the spiritual atmosphere or in whatever space exists between the divine and the earthly—Bishop Marcus Howard smiled, knowing his son had found exactly the partner he needed for the battles ahead.

Chapter 11: The Price of Prophecy

Three weeks had passed since the hellacious service shook Greater Mount Calvary to its foundation. Three weeks since revelation, confrontation, and the kind of spiritual warfare that left scorch marks on souls.

Andre and Trange', accompanying First Lady Clarice, had spent that time in Michigan—handling the burial arrangements and settling the affairs of the late Bishop's mother. The First Lady had returned the previous week, but she'd kept herself scarce, maintaining a profile so low it bordered on invisibility.

FaLessia remembered seeing Clarice pull into the church parking lot last Sunday morning. She'd watched from her office window as the older woman's Mercedes glided toward her designated spot—only to discover the painted letters "FIRST LADY" had been covered over with fresh black asphalt.

The joint board, operating within what they claimed was their discretionary authority, had decided that since Andre now held the pastoral position, it was "improper" for his mother to retain the title of First Lady. The preferential parking spot that had been hers for over two decades vanished overnight.

Clarice had sat in her car for five full minutes, staring at that blank space where her identity used to be painted. Then she'd put the vehicle in reverse and driven home.

She deemed the action petty and vindictive—a preview of the treatment awaiting her if she dared set foot inside that sanctuary. She'd decided to have fellowship at home instead, worshipping God in her living room rather than enduring the calculated cruelty of saints who'd forgotten how to love.

FaLessia had taken the last couple Sundays off herself. Church didn't feel the same anymore, not after all the revelations, the backbiting, the confusion, the mess that seemed to multiply rather than diminish. She eased back in her office chair at God's Healing Hands, her nonprofit, and tried to make sense of the divine purpose in all this chaos.

She believed God was the Master Builder, that He had a plan for every person. But at this juncture in her spiritual journey, she struggled to discern what that plan looked like—and more importantly, how she was supposed to align herself within it.

The rumors had intensified during Andre's absence. When word circulated that Trange' had accompanied him to Michigan, the gossip mill went into overdrive. Despite zero evidence, the narrative that "the pastor's fornicating with that fallen sister" gained traction, spreading like fire through dry grass. The drama escalated to the point where an emergency church meeting had been called for this afternoon.

FaLessia rubbed her temples, frustration and confusion warring in her spirit. Her phone vibrated a text from one of her friends with a link to an article. She clicked it and winced.

Trange' Moreau: Fashion's Fallen Angel read the headline of a regional fashion magazine's exposé. The article laid out every piece of gossip and scandal from her background, painting her as someone who'd seduced her way to success. Even in the fashion world—her world—the tide had turned against her.

FaLessia immediately texted Trange': **GIRL, DID YOU SEE THIS MESS IN FASHION FORWARD MAGAZINE?**

The response came quickly: **I'M AWARE. WITH EVERYTHING ELSE GOING ON, IT'S LOW PRIORITY. THEY ALWAYS LOOK TO TURN ON SOMEBODY WHEN THEY SMELL BLOOD IN THE WATER.**

FaLessia admired her strength. Andre would need that resilience—the combination of personal grief and church politics had to be overwhelming. Even while he grieved in Michigan, the plots to unseat him as pastor continued, gaining momentum in his absence.

A couple days ago, Clarice had received an official letter from the church secretary. The joint board formally announced she could no longer use the title "First Lady." That designation would be "reserved for the pastor's wife, whomever that may be."

FaLessia had raged when she heard about it. The hurt Clarice must be experiencing—at a church she'd spent decades helping build, from members who'd complimented her fashion every Sunday, who'd raved about her cooking and sensibility. But the second her husband died, everyone turned on her. Vultures circling a fresh corpse.

Nausea churned in FaLessia's stomach. She needed to hear from a good spirit. As if by divine timing, her phone rang. Moni Chen's name appeared on the screen.

She and Moni had become friends through Shaniece. Relatively quiet with a petite frame, Moni possessed a voice that rivaled Tamela Mann—a powerhouse that seemed impossible from someone so small. Every time Moni sang, FaLessia nearly leapt from her seat. And whenever they spoke, Moni had something inspirational to say, or she'd hum a hymn that brightened the darkest day.

"Well, look at God! He always got a ram in the bush," Moni's voice carried its characteristic warmth. "How's my sister doing today?"

FaLessia chuckled despite her mood. "I'm doing well. It was in my spirit to call you too. How else is my sister doing today?"

"I've been better," FaLessia admitted. "Just trying to navigate through all this mess."

"I've heard, and I've been praying. Seems like the adversary has set his eyes on Greater Mount Calvary and he's using any and everybody to try and tear that church down. Y'all must be on the verge of a great blessing—because the devil wouldn't attack this hard if he didn't know something good was coming."

The words struck FaLessia like revelation. Maybe something good would emerge from this chaos. Maybe her faith needed to increase so the power and presence of God could be truly realized.

"You know," Moni continued, "it's in my spirit to give you a song. You've heard 'For My Good' by Dottie Peoples?"

She started humming, vocalizing the beats, then singing. When she hit the note about being hurt while in church by church folks, emotion overwhelmed FaLessia. Tears streamed down her face as the lyrics ministered to wounds she'd been trying to ignore.

Serving God could be brutally difficult. As the late Bishop Howard used to say, "This walk ain't for the weak."

They ended the call with FaLessia thanking her for the unexpected ministry. She wiped her eyes, feeling slightly more fortified for the battle ahead.

The emergency meeting at Greater Mount Calvary was packed beyond capacity. FaLessia had never seen this many people show up for a church meeting. But deep in her spirit, she knew most of them had come for the drama, not the deliverance.

Faces she hadn't seen in months—some in years—filled every available seat. They'd elected not to hold the meeting in the sanctuary but in the church hall, as if even the building knew something unholy was about to unfold.

At the podium stood Deacon Jones, flanked by Mother Jones and Mother Williams. FaLessia thought to herself: *How fitting. The demons roll in packs.*

As she took her seat, gasps rippled through the congregation. She turned to see First Lady Clarice entering and sitting in the middle pews—not in her usual spot up front, but among the regular members.

"Here you go, First Lady," one of the ushers said warmly, approaching Clarice with a fan and bottled water. "Such a blessing to see you today."

Clarice looked up, smiled at the sister. "Thank you so much, I appreciate it. But I'm no longer a First Lady here. You can call me Clarice. Or Sister Clarice. Just not Mother Clarice." She laughed, trying to lighten the moment.

The usher's expression turned fierce with loyalty. "I will hear no such thing. You've been my First Lady for several years, since I joined this church. You are the kindest, sweetest person I've ever met in my life. You will *always* be my First Lady."

The comment touched Clarice deeply. She knew she'd walked into the lion's den. But like Daniel, she was going to pray that God would deliver her. And maybe—just maybe—God would send an angel to shut the mouths of these "lie-ons" like He did for Daniel.

Deacon Jones called the meeting to order, outlining that they'd convened this emergency session because of the "unrest" at the church. They were "concerned about the lack of leadership" since their pastor had been "absent with another member of the church" and "how that looks."

Comments immediately erupted from the congregation.

Mother Williams seized the microphone with practiced authority. "Now I know a lot of y'all are upset by the news that our pastor's shacking up with some woman over in Michigan or whatever. And all the dirty deeds that we've heard delivered to this church. But I know that God is better than that. And I know that we as a church are better than that. And if we come together, we can get all of this evil out of this church."

Roars of "Amen!" scattered throughout the congregation.

Minister Crystal Young looked around in shock, realizing the narrative being constructed wasn't remotely accurate. They were laying the foundation to manipulate the congregation without presenting facts.

Clarice sat in the back, clutching her Bible harder with each passing moment as they maligned her son.

One of the mothers jumped to her feet. "It's a sin and a shame what I'm hearing going on in my church—the church where I raised my children. I got married here. And to think I'm sitting here and all these demons are lurking around!"

Several "Amens" erupted from the congregation—a deacon from the third row shouted it so loud it echoed off the walls. Sister Perkins waved her fan frantically, like she was fanning flames instead of cooling herself. "That's right, tell it!" someone called from the back.

Then the floodgates opened.

"I got grandchildren in this church!" Another mother stood, her voice trembling with manufactured indignation. "And I will not have them exposed to this kind of behavior!" She clutched her chest like she might faint, and two women beside her grabbed her arms in support.

"Mmm-hmm, that's right!" The call-and-response was building momentum now.

A brother in a too-tight suit stood up, pointing toward the front. "We been faithful members for thirty years! Thirty years! Tithing, serving, supporting this ministry—and this is how we get repaid? With scandal and fornication?"

"Preach, brother!"

"Say that!"

"Tell the truth!"

An older woman stood, her voice breaking with theatrical emotion. "Bishop Howard is turning over in his grave right now! Turning over! This ain't what he built!"

"Oh Lord, have mercy," someone else shouted.

"The devil is busy!"

"He sho' is!"

FaLessia watched in horrified fascination as the orchestrated outrage spread like wildfire. Each voice seemed to feed the next, building upon fabricated grievances and half-truths until the room pulsed with manufactured righteous anger. They were performing for each other now—competing to see who could be the most scandalized, the most offended, the most dramatically appalled.

"And another thing—" A man near the middle stood, his voice cracking with passion that seemed more theatrical than genuine. "We got visitors coming to this church! What they gonna think when they hear about all this carrying on?"

"Lord help us!"

"We need to clean house!"

"Take back our church!"

The amens and hallelujahs bounced off the walls now, creating a cacophony of false piety. Some folks stood and sat repeatedly, like they couldn't contain their agitation. Others fanned themselves so vigorously it looked like they were trying to take flight. One sister dabbed at completely dry eyes with a tissue, performing grief she didn't feel.

FaLessia could see it clearly now—this wasn't spontaneous spiritual concern. This was choreographed chaos, designed to create the appearance of congregational uprising when it was really just a handful of manipulators pulling strings.

"I'm sick over what's happening here!" Another voice called out. "We need to take our church back!"

FaLessia stood, unable to remain silent any longer. "I can't believe what I'm hearing and witnessing here. The Bible says if it were possible, the very elect would be fooled. And I'm seeing so many of my brothers and sisters right now being fooled. These stories are not all true, and we need to have compassion and love and understanding before we make rash decisions. I know for a fact that the pastor is not shacked up with some woman. He is grieving the loss of his grandmother—"

"Girl, sit your tail down!" One of the mothers shouted from across the room.

"Excuse me?" FaLessia responded, shocked at the breach of decorum.

Mother Jones took the microphone. "This is a joint board meeting that we're hosting. This is not run by the trustees. You can have a seat."

Mother Jones returned the microphone to Mother Williams with a satisfied smirk.

207

FaLessia left her seat and walked toward the front, thinking, *I will not be silenced in my Father's House.*

"I'm not trying to take over the meeting," she said clearly, "but everyone else here is allowed to speak. Why can't I speak?"

They ignored her, continuing to address the crowd.

"What we have to do is take back our church," Mother Williams declared. "We have poor leadership here from this pastor that the trustees appointed. Church bylaws dictate that we can override the trustees with a majority vote from the church. And this is what we're calling for today."

A coup. That's what this was—a coordinated effort to seize control of the church from the trustees.

Several trustees shouted their disapproval. In response, the deacons verbally challenged them, voices rising, tension escalating.

Clarice sat back, praying harder, clutching her Bible tighter. *Lord do it, Lord do it,* she kept repeating in her spirit.

Patricia stepped to the front of the church. "What you're not going to do is disrespect my mother."

FaLessia started breathing prayers, exhausted by Patricia's antics. This direct affront, standing in her face, pushed the limits of her Christian restraint.

"Excuse me, Trustee Jones," FaLessia said evenly. "I was not trying to disrespect your mother. I am simply stating—"

Patricia interrupted, putting her finger in FaLessia's face. "What you're doing is trying to save your job. But you will not be disrespecting my mother in front of this church. Do you get me?"

FaLessia's blood boiled. *Lord, if this woman don't get her finger out of my face ...*

"Please remove your finger from my face," FaLessia said, not backing down. "I'm asking you nicely."

Patricia responded with mocking confidence. "Or what? What is Little Miss God's Healing Hands going to do?"

Chuckles erupted from sections of the congregation.

FaLessia stepped closer. "I'll ask you one more time to move—"

Patricia interrupted again. "Of course you would defend them. You probably come from the same stock that little Miss Trange' is from. We don't even know your background. You're probably just as loose as she is."

She laughed, and as she turned to face FaLessia fully, it happened.

Almost a reflex motion—FaLessia's hand connected with Patricia's face. The slap echoed through the church hall. Patricia's glasses flew across the room. She went down.

Deacons rushed to restrain FaLessia. The church erupted in chaotic energy—some horrified, others gleeful over the spectacle.

In that moment of weakness, FaLessia felt overwhelming shame. She'd allowed her emotions to overpower her. She started repenting immediately, apologizing profusely, not noticing Mother Jones advancing toward her with fury in her eyes.

"You hit my baby!" Mother Jones drew back her arm to return the gesture.

But in midair, Mother Heady appeared and grabbed her arm before the blow could land.

"You will release me!" Mother Jones turned toward Mother Heady with indignation.

"Enough," Heady said, her voice carrying authority that silenced the immediate area. "I've had about enough of you and your group of hellions in this church."

She turned toward the congregation and commanded that every believer put their heart and mind on God. Then she started praying—praying that the evil and wickedness of these people would be removed, that God would come in and clean out the church, remove the hellions, remove the confusion because God was not the author of confusion, and reveal to everyone who the true demons in this church were.

As she prayed, Mothers Williams and Jones and Deacon Jones stood frozen, unable to speak or move.

After her prayer, she addressed the church. "As the senior mother here at this church, I am sick of the foolishness. I'm sick of all the backbiting. I'm sick of everything that's going on. We as a body of believers need to come together and support our pastor, support each and every person that walks through this door and cut out all this foolishness."

Then she turned to face Mother Williams and Mother Jones directly. "And we need to start removing people from positions who are only designing to push their agendas and gain power at the church."

She also turned toward Mother Rose in the congregation, making deliberate eye contact.

"Of course you would take up for him," Rose called out. "Andre is your godson, isn't he? And you brought that gay boy Sage here! And aren't you messing around with Deacon Fry?"

Heady turned to face her, rage flashing in her eyes. "Now you hold on just one second here. Since my beloved husband died, the only man that's been in my bed is the Lord." She turned to Mother Jones "Now I tell you this, Mother Jones—this ain't a game you want to play with me. I know *all* about you. You want me to tell the whole church what I know about you? Trust and believe I will. So you need to back down, because I got one clip I've been waiting to release on you."

Mother Jones stood there, fully confident that Mother Heady—who'd stayed away from church drama—didn't know anything damaging about her past or present.

"Well, dear Mother Heady," she said with false sweetness, "there is nothing you can say that will embarrass me. I'm an open book."

"Oh really?" Mother Sandra Hearns rose to her feet, eyes bloodshot, body trembling. "Instead of being an open book, why don't you close your legs to other women's men?"

The church fell silent, every eye turning toward Sandra.

"Last night I couldn't sleep," Sandra continued, her voice breaking. "My spirit was chasing me, out of sorts. Something told me to look through Joel's phone. I've never done that in thirty years of marriage. But I did. And you know what I found?"

She looked directly at Mother Jones. "I found the exchanges between you and my husband. The late-night rendezvous. Him calling you 'baby.' Saying he loves you. And for you to sit in this pulpit acting all holier than thou, condemning another sister in

211

this church about her past—when your present is equally disgusting."

Mother Jones's face went pale, then flushed crimson. The church erupted in gasps and murmurs.

Mother Heady folded her arms in agreement. "Yeah, I heard about this a couple years ago. Just wasn't my place to say nothing. I'm sorry, Mother Hearns."

Patricia stood next to her mother, trying to console her. "I don't believe it. You're making this up about my mother. Mama, we don't gotta stay here and take this."

Mother Hearns stepped into the middle aisle. "Oh, you're gonna take it. You've been taking my man for the last thirty-plus years. If he loved you so much, why didn't he marry you? Clearly he was messing around with you at the same time as me, but he married *me*."

She looked at Patricia with something like pity. "And don't think you know your mother so well."

"Lady, get out of my face," Patricia said.

"Oh, I'm not 'lady.' Try stepmama."

Patricia froze. "What are you talking about? You're really losing it."

Mother Hearns gripped a stack of papers in her hand. "Here are the text messages where my husband pleads with your mother about leaving me and starting his life over with her. And finally, letting you know that he's your father."

The church exploded. Mother Williams stood stunned—she hadn't known.

Patricia snatched the papers, reading quickly, then looked at her mother's pale complexion. In Mother Jones's eyes, she could see the truth.

Patricia's world shattered. She grabbed her mother's arm and practically dragged her toward the exit, Mother Williams following in their wake. As they passed Clarice, Mother Jones made eye contact. No smile or glee on Clarice's face—just concern. And in her spirit, she started praying for them all.

Deacon Jones remained at the podium, lost. He looked over at FaLessia. "You gotta do something. I don't know what to do."

FaLessia reminded him that this was a joint meeting called by them—there was nothing she could do unless he adjourned the meeting, which would transfer power back to the trustees.

He adjourned the meeting.

Trustee Webb, sitting in the front row, quickly ended the livestream he'd been secretly running on his phone—with Andre on the other line, listening to everything.

He called the other trustees to the back room and put Andre on speakerphone.

"Pastor Howard, we're all here. I know you heard everything that's going on. We gotta do something."

Andre's voice came through, steady despite the chaos he'd just witnessed remotely. "I heard everything. And I've been praying hard. I will be returning next Sunday with a Word from God and the vision and purpose for the church."

He paused, and when he spoke again, there was authority in his voice.

"Next Sunday, I want you all to put forth a concerted effort to bring in everyone you can to church. The drug addicts, the prostitutes, the unsaved—I want everyone there for this Word from God. And FaLessia? Bring your friend Moni. I got a couple songs I want her to sing."

"Sometimes God allows a thing to be torn down so that He can build up a new thing. And as I sat here, the word that hit my spirit was: God is about to do a new great thing. And we're gonna believe Him for that. We will see the goodness of the Lord next Sunday."

"You all be blessed. And I will see you all next Sunday."

The phone went silent. The trustees looked at each other, exhausted but oddly hopeful.

Sunday was coming—and with it, a reckoning that would either destroy Greater Mount Calvary or resurrect it into something none of them could yet imagine.

Chapter 12: Consequences and Revelations

Above the Clouds

The Gulfstream G650 sliced through the atmosphere at forty-five thousand feet, its sleek white body cutting against a canvas of burnt orange and deep purple. The sun was setting somewhere over Tennessee, painting the clouds below in shades of coral and gold. From this altitude, the world looked clean—untouched by the mess of human drama, church politics, and buried secrets clawing their way to the surface.

Trange' sat in one of the cream leather seats, coffee cup warming her hands, watching the sky transform through the oval window. The jet's interior was all modern luxury—polished wood accents, soft ambient lighting, entertainment systems she never used, a galley stocked with gourmet everything. But right now, she wasn't thinking about the opulence surrounding her.

She was thinking about Andre.

Over the past several weeks in Michigan, she'd watched grief strip him down to something raw and authentic. His grandmother's death had devastated him in ways she hadn't fully anticipated. Prophetess Ada Pearle Howard—better known throughout Ann Arbor as the Third Eye Prophetess—hadn't just been his grandmother. She'd been his third parent, the woman who'd spoiled him ceaselessly, who'd taken him in when he left Louisiana for the University of Michigan, who'd doted on her only grandson with the kind of love that asked for nothing in return.

Andre had spent years of his life with her, flying back routinely to split time between his parents in New Orleans and his grandmother in Michigan. Prophetess Howard could read people with unsettling accuracy—whenever she talked to someone, she always saw something the Holy Spirit revealed to her. And she'd tell folks everything the Lord allowed her to see, even if they didn't want to hear it.

Her passing had caused an outpouring of grief across the Ann Arbor area. The funeral had been massive—hundreds of people whose lives she'd touched, whose futures she'd spoken into existence, whose destinies she'd helped shape through prophetic utterance.

And then there was the estate.

When her husband, Overseer Lavernas C. Howard—another great pastor—had passed years earlier, he'd left an estate valued in the millions of dollars. Properties, investments, accounts nobody had fully realized existed. Handling it all had consumed weeks of Andre's time. That, combined with the dozen churches wanting memorial services, had stretched their stay far longer than either of them anticipated.

Trange' watched him now, sleeping in the seat beside her, his head tilted against the window. His face carried exhaustion even in rest—the kind that came from carrying too much for too long.

Does he have the strength for what's waiting back home? she wondered.

Greater Mount Calvary and all its mess still brewed and burned back in New Orleans. The emergency meeting, the revelations, the chaos—it had all happened while they were in Michigan. Andre had listened remotely, heard every ugly word, every manipulation, every explosion of scandal. But hearing it through a phone wasn't the same as walking back into that sanctuary and facing it head-on.

Her mind drifted unexpectedly to her birth mother.

Time hadn't healed all wounds—some cuts went too deep for that. But part of her wondered about them. Worried, even. She glanced down at her phone and realized that since the ordeal at the church, neither her mother nor stepfather had reached out. Not once.

First Lady Clarice had given them her number, told them to call. They hadn't.

Trange' put on a front like it didn't bother her. But deep down, her heart hurt a little. Maybe more than a little.

Andre stirred beside her, blinking awake slowly.

"Did you enjoy your meal?" she asked, grateful for the distraction from her thoughts.

"One of the best meals I've had on a plane," he joked, his voice still rough with sleep.

He looked around, admiring the jet's interior—the way he'd been doing periodically since they'd boarded. It always brought him back to the same question, the one he'd been wondering about but hadn't quite known how to ask.

He looked into her eyes directly. "Based on what you told me about your background, how can you afford things like this?" He gestured around the jet.

She laughed at first, but then seriousness took hold of her expression.

"Well, silly, I bought it." She paused, her smile fading. "But it was with Delacroix money. Remember? He was my drag dad— or rather, the house mother when he took me in off the streets. He cared for me like I was one of his kids. Loved me so much."

Her eyes started to water.

"He contracted AIDS and was dying. And I stood by his side and took care of him. To pay me back—though I never asked for payment—he left his entire estate to me."

She looked out the window, composing herself. "Delacroix wasn't just a drag house diva. He was a real estate mogul who'd amassed a huge fortune. And although he had no biological children, he viewed me as his daughter. His estate was worth one hundred and fifteen million dollars, and he left it all to me."

Andre's eyebrows shot up, but he stayed quiet, letting her continue.

"He didn't trust me at first because he didn't really know me. He let me sleep in the storage room of the club. But then he saw something in me and brought me back to his chateau." She gestured around the jet. "This ain't even what I own today. I gave the girls back the club—they all jointly run it now. Have you heard of the Delacroix Foundation to help trafficked girls and displaced young women?"

Andre nodded slowly.

"Well, that was an organization I started in his memory. He was someone who took in a trafficked girl, someone off the street who had nowhere to go. I wanted to honor him by helping someone like me who needed a hand. Delacroix meant the world to me, and the least I could do was honor him the way he honored me when I had no one."

Andre grabbed her hand and looked into her eyes. "Thank you for sharing that with me."

She peered out through the jet's windows, and reality set in.

"Yeah, that's my past. But we need to discuss your future." Her voice turned serious. "We're approaching New Orleans where your church people are acting a fool. How are you gonna handle that?"

Andre's expression shifted—something hardened in his eyes, something resolute.

"With much prayer and supplication. That's all I can do—trust and believe that God's Will be done. There ain't a demon powerful enough to stop what God has put in place and ordained. I am approaching New Orleans with the full weight and power of the Holy Ghost and a commandment from God to the church. Let them demons be ready for a Word from God."

His words hit with such finality that all she could do was say, "Amen."

He laid his head on her shoulder and drifted back to sleep. She looked down at him and began thinking: *Look at my man.* She smiled, returned to her coffee cup, and looked out the window with wonder in her heart at how awesome God was.

She thought about Delacroix—a gay drag queen who God used to bring her out of darkness. First Lady Clarice, though grieving the death of her husband, still found it fit to be kind and compassionate to her in her time of need. Her group of friends who saw past her imperfections and recognized the true woman she was. And this man—who out of nowhere came and swept her right off her feet.

It had been over a month, and she almost felt like she loved him. Couldn't envision her life without him anymore.

She shook her head and smiled. *Scripture is right—God will take the foolish things to confound the wise.*

As she admired the skyline with the sun peeking over the clouds, she whispered, "Thank You, Lord."

The Breaking Point

First Lady Clarice and Mother Heady arrived at Mother Hearns' house just after noon. They'd wanted to check on her since the events of last Sunday—the revelation that her husband had carried on an extramarital affair with Mother Jones, spanning not just their entire marriage but their courtship as well, must have been a heavy weight on her shoulders, troubling to her spirit.

Sandra Hearns opened the door, and Mother Heady let out an audible gasp.

The once prudish, well-put-together mother seemed to have degraded into a shell of the woman she once knew. She stood there with hair disheveled, wearing a stained robe, eyes clearly beaten down from tears. An offensive odor emanated from her—the stale scent of unwashed skin and despair. The stench of depression hung in the air like humidity.

Her once rigid composure crumbled as she abruptly ran forward and bear-hugged Mother Heady.

First Lady Clarice stood there and silently prayed for strength.

They entered the house, and the interior matched Sandra's appearance. Dishes piled in the sink, mail scattered across the coffee table, curtains drawn against the sunlight. Empty tissue boxes littered the floor. A house that had always been immaculate now looked like grief had ransacked it.

Sandra led them to the living room, moving like someone who'd forgotten how to fully inhabit her own body. They sat on the couch while she collapsed into the armchair across from them.

"He's been having an affair with her our entire marriage," Sandra said without preamble, her voice flat. "Not only the marriage. Our courtship too. Before we even said 'I do,' he was already in her bed."

Mother Heady reached over and took her hand.

"I went through his phone while he was in the hospital having back surgery," Sandra continued, her words coming faster now, like a dam breaking. "I've never done that before—never felt the need. But something in my spirit wouldn't let me rest. And what I found..."

She trailed off, shaking her head.

"The messages go back years. Decades. 'Baby, I love you.' 'Can't wait to see you tonight.' 'She doesn't understand me like you do.' All the clichés you'd expect, but seeing them in black and white from your husband's phone..." Her voice cracked. "And then I found the paternity test results. Patricia isn't his goddaughter. She's his daughter. His *actual* daughter."

Clarice closed her eyes, grief washing over her for this woman's pain.

"Thirty-three years," Sandra whispered. "I gave that man thirty-three years of my life. Raised his child—correction, raised *their* child—thinking she was the goddaughter we were helping. Cooked his meals, washed his clothes, stood by his side at every church function. And the entire time..."

A creak came from the kitchen. All three women turned toward the sound.

"Oh, I'm sorry—is that Deacon Hearns in the kitchen?" Clarice asked carefully. "We didn't want to discuss this in front of him."

"No," Sandra said flatly. "That's the cat."

Both ladies looked at each other, confused.

Clarice ventured another question. "Well, where is Deacon Hearns?"

Mother Hearns sat back in her chair, her expression unreadable. "He ain't here. And he ain't gonna never be here again."

The ladies looked at each other again, fear and curiosity peaking inside them.

Mother Heady sat forward. "Well, where is he, baby?"

Sandra reached for a cigarette on the table—a shock since nobody had ever seen her smoke. She took a slow and deliberate pull, exhaling before speaking.

"As I said—he ain't here."

Silence sat over the room like a heavy blanket.

It had been several days since the revelation, and Mother Jones had become a recluse in her home. She hadn't been taking phone calls or visitors from anyone. Her phone blew up constantly with people wondering, seeking gossip about what happened. But she was not yet able to discuss it.

She'd been so careful over the years. Her secret had been well-kept, her background well-manicured. She was shocked and dismayed at how it all came crashing down. How had Sandra discovered everything? How had those text messages survived? She'd been meticulous about deleting things.

She'd fallen in love with Joel years ago. Decades ago, well before he knew Sandra Hearns. There was something that drew them to each other—a magnetism that her late husband had never been able to keep her from feeling.

During those days, Joel was a hot commodity among the women. People still raved about how he'd been a player back in the day, and how Sandra Hearns had supposedly "tamed" him.

Mother Jones had been no exception to his charm. His deep chocolate complexion, short-cut tapered hair, full lips, and deep voice were all that Southern girl needed to see and hear. She'd fallen victim to it—or maybe not victim, since she'd been a very willing participant.

In the final years of her late husband's life, he'd become impotent, which furthered her relationship with Joel. And when she became pregnant, she convinced her husband that this was their miracle baby. She knew deep in her heart he didn't believe her, but he was just happy to have a baby in his later life.

Before he died, she'd gotten a blood test to confirm that Joel was indeed the father. She'd shared that with Joel, and they'd both sworn secrecy—no one would ever know. Not even Patricia. Joel would always be there for her and the baby, even serving as her godfather—with heavy emphasis on the *father* part.

Although she hated the negative attention and hurt for her daughter, the overarching feeling consuming her was concern over Deacon Hearns. She hadn't seen him in over a week, though she'd heard he was in the hospital having back surgery.

She knew her daughter well enough—Patricia would be mad for a period, but she'd come around. And church folk, they eventually forgot because they always had bigger fish to fry. Her little sin was nothing in the grand scheme of church drama.

Out of nowhere, she heard footsteps angrily approaching. Her back was facing the unknown, unwelcome visitor. She tried to leap up, but her knees gave out and she fell to the ground.

She immediately started praying. "Lord! Somebody don' broke in my house! Protect me, Lord, keep me!"

She yelled out into the darkness: "Whoever you are, I'm a sanctified woman of God! You get out of here!"

The footsteps advanced.

She scuffled on the floor, searching for her glasses. Finally finding them, she put them on to reveal who was in her home.

"Sanctified woman of God?" The voice was bitter, familiar. "Is that right, Mama? Is that the same sanctified woman who cheated on the man I thought was my father? The same sanctified woman whose side dude is my real father? Is that the sanctified woman you're talking about?"

"Patricia, girl, you almost gave me a heart attack! Now help me up off this floor!"

Patricia stood there for a moment, staring.

"I said get over here and help me up off this floor! I don't care what happened—I'm still your mama!"

Patricia remained frozen.

Mother Jones gave her a look—the look that had made Patricia comply since childhood—and slowly, reluctantly, Patricia acquiesced. She helped her elderly mother off the floor and into the chair.

"Next time, don't take so long," Mother Jones snapped. "What's wrong with you?"

Patricia stood there in disbelief at her mother's audacity. *The gall of this woman,* she thought. *The nerve to ask me what's wrong after what she put me through.*

She sat on the couch adjacent to her mother and just looked at her. Her eyes told the whole story—the betrayal, the confusion, the shattered identity. But the pride and arrogance of Mother

Jones couldn't comprehend or allow what she perceived as disrespect in her own home.

"You lied to me my entire life," Patricia finally said, her voice trembling. "My whole life. Everything I thought I knew about who I am, where I come from—it's all been a lie."

"Now you watch your tone—"

"Watch my tone?" Patricia's voice rose. "You had an affair with a married man—a deacon in the church—for over thirty years! You let me believe Daddy was my father when he wasn't! You let me grow up thinking Joel Hearns was my godfather when he's my biological father! And you have the *nerve* to tell me to watch my tone?"

"Lower your voice in my house!"

"This is exactly why Daddy didn't trust you!" Patricia shot back. "He knew! He knew that baby wasn't his, but he loved you enough to pretend. And you repaid that love by continuing to sleep with Joel Hearns even after Daddy died!"

"You don't know what you're talking about—"

"I know *exactly* what I'm talking about! I read the messages, Mama! ALL OF THEM! 'Can't wait to see you tonight.' 'I wish Sandra didn't exist so we could be together.' 'Our daughter is beautiful.' Our daughter! He called me 'our daughter' in a text message to you!"

Mother Jones's face flushed. "You had no right going through my phone—"

"Your phone?" Patricia laughed bitterly. "I went through Deacon Hearns' phone! His wife showed me! She had every right to expose this mess, and you're worried about privacy?"

"That woman had no right—"

"That woman's husband has been sleeping with you for thirty-three years! She had EVERY right!"

The argument escalated, voices rising, accusations flying. Mother Jones defended herself with deflections and justifications—she'd been lonely, her husband couldn't satisfy her, Joel truly loved her, Sandra was cold and distant. Patricia fired back with the pain of a daughter whose entire identity had been built on lies.

Then, suddenly, Mother Jones clutched her chest.

"Oh... oh Lord..." She gasped, her face contorting. "My heart... Patricia, my heart..."

Shock flooded over Patricia. "Mama? Mama!"

"Look at you," Mother Jones wheezed. "Carrying on so much... almost giving your mother a heart attack. What you gonna do without me, girl?"

Patricia, completely disarmed, rushed forward. "I'm sorry, Mama! I'm so sorry! Just breathe, okay? Just breathe!"

She ran to the kitchen to get water.

Mother Jones watched her daughter disappear around the corner, then sat back in her chair with a satisfied expression. The heart palpitations mysteriously disappeared.

When Patricia returned with the water, Mother Jones took it calmly, sipping slowly.

"Now," she said, her voice suddenly steady, "you need to understand something. What happened between me and Joel—it's complicated. You can't possibly understand the intricacies of adult relationships."

Patricia sat down, still shaken. "Then explain it to me. Why did you do this? And why did you never tell me?"

Mother Jones launched into a story—a carefully crafted narrative of two star-crossed lovers yearning for each other but denied their love through the mysteries and intricacies of life. She painted herself as a romantic heroine, Patricia as the beautiful product of true love. She thanked God for her daughter with tears in her eyes.

Patricia stood up abruptly. "I need to go talk to him. I need to know what he was thinking. I need to hear his side of the story. Why did no one tell me?"

As Mother Jones opened her mouth to speak, the doorbell rang.

"I'm not taking any visitors," Mother Jones said firmly. "I already told you that."

Patricia brushed her off and went to the door. She opened it to find an ambulance, two EMTs, and a stretcher. Behind them, she could see someone lying on it.

She thought immediately that someone had heard their argument and called for help, or that her mother had actually called the ambulance during her "heart attack."

"Mom!" she called out. "The ambulance is here! Did you call them?"

Mother Jones leaped up and rushed to the door. "I didn't call anyone!"

The male EMT looked confused. "No one called us. We're here to set up respite care. Are you Eartha Jones?"

"I am," Mother Jones responded. "But I know nothing about any respite."

The male EMT looked further confused and reviewed his paperwork. "Yeah, it's all here. We're to set up respite at the home of Eartha Jones. It's on the order."

"What order?" She snatched the paperwork from him, scanning page after page.

The female nurse stepped forward. "We really need to get Mr. Hearns out of the weather. Where would you like us to set him up?"

"Set him up?" Mother Jones screamed. "What do you mean?"

She looked over their shoulders to see Joel Hearns lying on the stretcher, connected to multiple machines, his eyes closed, his body utterly still.

"Yeah, we have an order to bring him here for his post-surgical care and residency," the female nurse explained. "His wife provided the directives. She said she wants nothing more to do with him and that this is the place where he always wanted to be. She said you would be the perfect person to take care of him."

Mother Jones felt the world tilting.

"But don't worry," the nurse continued. "I'll be here four times throughout the week to take care of him. But we need to work out long-term care arrangements. It's such a blessing to have family around who can take care of him. His wife didn't seem too interested. She said you and his daughter would be taking care of him, and there was no need to put him in a home or send him back to her house. That this is the place where he deserves to be—a place he's been longing to be."

The male EMT interjected: "Now, if you two can't handle this, we need to get other resources lined up. Because he can't walk. He'll be bedridden for the rest of his life. We originally had everything set up at his house, but she changed everything early this week. Monday morning, actually. She said she got a revelation at church and was doing what's best."

He paused. "So where can we set him up?"

Mother Jones and Patricia reviewed the paperwork in stunned silence. The back injury had been far more severe than anyone originally thought. He'd suffered major damage to various vertebrae in his spine, rendering him permanently paralyzed from the waist down.

"Oh, she did leave a letter," the female nurse said, pulling an envelope from her bag.

Mother Jones snatched it and tore it open. Anger rolled over her as she read Sandra Hearns' words:

Since you two couldn't live without each other and have been running around all these years together, it's fitting that he spends the rest of his life with you. And since you couldn't stay off your back for all these years, you'll be perfectly fine in bed next to him—since he can't get off his back now.

I hope you enjoy the bed you both made. Don't even think about sending him back my way. If he shows up at my house, the next time you see him will be in a casket.

Mother Jones felt faint.

Patricia guided her to the living room and directed the EMTs to set Joel up in the empty bedroom upstairs.

They both sat there in silence as the sounds of medical equipment being assembled echoed from above.

Wondering what would be next. How they could possibly take care of this man. How his wife could be so cold and callous.

229

And Patricia wondered how her mother had allowed herself to get put in such a precarious situation.

Most of all, she wondered: *Where was God through all of this?*

Chapter 13: The Gathering Storm

Trange' sat in her Bentley outside Greater Mount Calvary, watching through the tinted windows as people gathered, fellowshipped, and filtered in and out of the church. The Sunday morning ritual looked peaceful from behind the protective glass—people dressed in their finest, exchanging greetings, moving with the easy confidence of belonging.

For the first time in her life, she was scared.

Not afraid—she'd been afraid plenty of times. Fear she could handle. Fear was that split-second decision on the streets, that calculation about which way to run, who to trust, how to survive. Fear was reactive, immediate, manageable.

This was different. This was scared—that deep, bone-level terror that came from being vulnerable, from caring too much, from having something precious to lose.

It had been several weeks since the spectacle that unfolded in front of this congregation. Several weeks since her past was weaponized against her, since she'd been publicly humiliated in God's House. She hadn't darkened these doors since that Sunday. Part of her never wanted to again.

She sat there, uncertain. Her hand rested on the door handle, but she couldn't make herself pull it. Normally, she would have driven away—put the car in gear, left this mess behind, protected herself the way she'd learned to do since she was twelve years old.

But she couldn't leave Andre.

He'd been meditating and fasting for the last three days, spending every moment before the Lord, not wanting to meet with anyone—including her. That had hurt more than she wanted to admit, but she understood. Some battles required solitude with God. Some preparation couldn't be shared.

She had to be there for him.

It was at that moment of crystalline clarity that she realized she loved him. Not the infatuation she'd felt initially, not the attraction or the excitement of new romance. Real love—the kind that made you show up even when everything in you screamed to run. The kind that made you vulnerable even when vulnerability felt like death.

It was her love for him forcing her to summon all her strength, all the regalness and class she'd cultivated over decades of self-construction, to get out of that car and face her foes and detractors. Possibly risk another incident. Maybe endure another public execution.

She closed her eyes and prayed—a simple, desperate prayer: *Lord, help me.*

As she reached for the handle, the door flung open.

Standing before her was one of her sisters: Coko Howard.

"Coko!" Trange' was utterly surprised. "What are you doing here?"

"I'm here to make sure my sister is supported," Coko said firmly, extending her hand. "And to rebuke any demon that gets in your way."

Trange' stepped out of the car, and to her surprise, she saw them all standing there: Sage, Renee, Shaniece, Moni, and Samantha—her entire squad, assembled like an army.

"Y'all came," Trange' whispered, emotion catching in her throat.

"Of course we came," Shaniece said, moving forward to embrace her. "You think we'd let you walk in there alone?"

"We're family," Moni added softly. "And family shows up."

Sage struck a pose. "Plus, honey, I heard your man is about to preach the house down. I'm not missing that for nothing."

They laughed, the sound breaking some of the tension.

Renee squeezed her hand. "We're here to support you and to hear this sermon from Andre. Word on the street is God gave him something heavy."

Samantha adjusted her designer handbag, her expression fierce. "And if anybody starts any mess, they're gonna have to deal with *all* of us."

As they stood outside in a huddle, several onlookers gave disapproving looks—eyes scanning their designer clothes, their confident postures, their obvious unity. Some of the stares carried judgment, others outright hostility.

Sage caught the looks and returned them with equal intensity, adding a little extra hand flourish for emphasis.

Shaniece wanted to chide him but found herself equally put off by the reception. The coldness was palpable, the rejection almost tangible in the air.

Coko gathered them together in a huddle. "Let's pray. Remember Scripture says, 'Though I walk through the valley of the shadow of death, I will fear no evil, for Thou art with me.'"

She launched into a rousing prayer right there on the church steps—her voice carrying authority and conviction, declaring protection, proclaiming God's presence, rebuking the spirit of division and judgment. Her words rang out clear and strong, unapologetic in their boldness.

Even some of the onlookers stopped and bowed their heads. Rumblings of "Amen" could be heard among some of the others, involuntary responses to the anointing in her words.

When she finished, Renee squeezed her shoulder. "Thank you for that prayer."

She paused, then added with characteristic bluntness: "Well, it's time for us to go in here. But I'm gonna say right now—I'm not here for any foolishness."

They chuckled, the sound masking the nervousness beneath.

Several of them locked arms—Trange' in the center, surrounded by her sisters. They provided not only a buffer and covering but a united front for whatever would come.

As they entered the church and made their way down the center aisle, they were immediately intercepted by a couple of ushers who attempted to direct them toward a section near the back of the church.

"Sisters, if you'll just—" one usher began.

Out of nowhere, Usher Terence Blackwell appeared. "Excuse me, my brothers," he said with polite firmness, "but I got direction from our pastor that these ladies and gentlemen are his special guests. I'll take it from here."

Without waiting for acknowledgment, he directed the entourage to the first row.

A couple of the ushers grumbled as the group made their way past them. Samantha pulled out her fan and popped it open with a loud *snap*, fanning herself while rolling her eyes at the ushers as she passed.

Sage walked next to her, admiring the display. "Girl, you gotta give me one of those. I want to be fancy and shady too."

They shared a laugh as they settled into their seats.

Minister Crystal Young approached them, her smile warm and genuine. "Good morning, saints! What a wonderful day to be in the House of the Lord."

She turned to Coko. "Minister Howard, I wanted to invite you to the pulpit with the other ministers. Pastor especially wanted to make sure that invitation was extended to you."

Then to Moni: "And Sister Moni, outside of your solo, Pastor wanted you to open up today's service with a song of your selection."

Shaniece smiled, knowing full well that Coko was very shy and that not being prepared beforehand was a stumbling block for her. She grabbed her friend's hand. "Just go and be led of the Lord. I know you got this."

Coko laughed nervously. "This is out of the blue, but... okay. Let God use me."

Shaniece grinned. "I can't wait to see how He does. Go on up there."

Coko shook her head and made her way to the pulpit.

People started flooding in as service time approached—and what a flood it was.

They came from all walks of life: men in worn jeans and faded t-shirts, women in simple dresses that had seen better days, teenagers in street clothes looking uncomfortable in a church setting. Some looked visibly drug-addicted—the telltale signs of addiction written on their bodies in track marks and sunken eyes. Others carried the hard edge of the streets—postures tense, eyes darting, ready to bolt at any moment.

They were the unsavory, the unwanted, the uncomfortable.

And they were exactly who Andre had invited.

A couple of parishioners couldn't hide their displeasure. Whispers rippled through the more reserved members—concerned murmurs about the "element" being brought into their sanctuary.

Mother Rose, sitting next to Mother Williams on the second row on the opposite side of the church, popped a mint into her mouth and leaned over. "Hey, what is going on today? Got a lot of unsavories in here."

Mother Williams responded, clutching her purse tighter. "Yeah. Today's the day to keep your purse close and unattended belongings accounted for."

Sitting on the opposite end of the pew within earshot, Mother Heady heard their mumblings. She started humming a hymn, then began thanking God—loudly enough to be heard—for all the people coming in.

"Thank You, Jesus, for bringing the lost into Your house!" she sang out.

A couple of other mothers joined in, their "Amens" punctuating Heady's praise.

Mother Rose and Williams looked down in disgust at the display, but Mother Heady remained unbothered, continuing to sing and glorify God.

The sanctuary had three entrances.

And almost simultaneously, three significant arrivals occurred.

Through the second entrance: First Lady Clarice and Mother Hearns appeared together, walking arm-in-arm.

Through the third entrance: Mother Jones and Patricia appeared, their postures stiff with tension.

A collective gasp and mumbling stirred through the congregation. It was as if the women were flanking each other—claiming opposite sides of an invisible battlefield.

First Lady Clarice and Mother Hearns took seats right behind Mother Heady, their positioning deliberate—surrounding themselves with allies.

The Joneses took seats in the back row on the opposite side of the church, as far from the front as possible while still being present.

Mother Rose leaned over to Mother Williams. "So she ain't gonna sit up here with us, huh? She got shame."

Williams, not knowing how to respond, offered weakly: "She just needs her own time."

She looked across the church, catching Mother Jones's eye, giving her friend a sympathetic look and waving her to come forward.

Something stirred inside Mother Jones. She'd promised Patricia she would keep a low profile today. But this was *her* church—she'd been a member for numerous decades. She wasn't going to let some harlot dressed in Versace keep her in the back of the church like she was the one who should be ashamed.

She rose and walked around the church, passing directly by Trange' and her friends with her nose turned up, not even acknowledging them, to take her seat with the other mothers—where the righteous dignitaries of the church were properly *supposed* to sit.

Mother Williams met her almost in front of Trange's group, giving her a big hug of solidarity.

Sage leaned over to Samantha and whispered loudly enough for several people to hear: "Isn't that one of your peoples right there? Williams, right? I think I see the resemblance."

He was joking, playing on the shared last name.

Samantha, nowhere near amused, elbowed him stiffly in his side.

"What?" he continued, laughing. "I'm just saying—that's your auntie right there, your friend."

He continued laughing, and even Shaniece had to chuckle despite herself.

Samantha hated the fact that the last name alone made people often think she and Mother Williams were related. It was the bane of her existence in this church.

Mother Williams, overhearing some of the snickers and comments, looked over at them and shook her head. "Lord, fix it," she muttered.

Renee leapt up quickly. "Oh, I'm gonna fix *you*—"

Shaniece quickly grabbed her arm to pull her back down, looking around to see if anybody noticed the near-confrontation.

Samantha started removing her earrings. "I'll fight an old woman. I knew something like this was going to happen today, but I'm ready."

Sage extended his hand to collect her earrings helpfully.

Shaniece looked over at them, her voice firm but quiet: "If you don't put your earrings back on, girl. You're in church."

Trange', instead of trying to calm the situation, whispered to Shaniece with a playful smirk: "You should have never introduced those two to each other. Sage is being a bad influence on Samantha. You're making her worse."

Shaniece had to suppress a laugh because it was true—since Sage and Samantha had become friends, they'd been feeding off each other's energy, encouraging each other's petty tendencies, becoming a dangerous duo of shade and sass.

Mother Jones and Mother Williams took their seats, settling in with visible satisfaction at having claimed their territory.

For a brief second, Mother Jones caught Mother Hearns' eye across the sanctuary.

The look that passed between them carried the weight of everything—betrayal, pain, knowledge, consequence. Mother Hearns' expression was unreadable, but her eyes held something cold and final.

First Lady Clarice, holding Mother Hearns' hand, sensed her anger and frustration building. Mother Heady extended her other hand back and grabbed Mother Hearns' free hand. They both started whispering encouragement to her, praying silently for peace to guard her heart.

Minister Young stepped to the podium and asked everyone to rise to their feet. "Let us welcome our pastor, Reverend Andre Howard."

He stepped out from the back room, flanked by a couple of deacons and ministers, and took his seat in the pulpit.

He immediately acknowledged Coko and Moni with a nod, then locked eyes with Trange' and gave her the slightest wink.

Lord, this man needs to stop. I keep trying to stay near the cross.

First Lady Clarice noticed the wink and the flirtatious energy between her son and his new beau. She smiled—a mother's knowing smile that said she approved, that she saw what was building between them, that she was grateful her son had found someone strong enough to stand beside him.

Minister Young thanked everyone for coming, then invited Minister Howard to the podium for the welcome.

Coko's stomach became a knot of nerves. She hadn't been prepared to speak, hadn't rehearsed anything. She gave a quick, silent prayer—*Lord, give me the words*—and rose to the podium.

She looked out over the congregation: the faithful members who'd been coming for decades, the newcomers from the streets still looking uncomfortable in folding chairs, the mothers watching with judgment, her friends in the front row silently cheering her on.

"Good morning, saints and visitors," she began, her voice steadier than she felt. "I want to acknowledge what many of you are probably thinking—we have a lot of different faces here today. People from different walks of life, different backgrounds, different... circumstances."

She paused, letting her words settle.

"But we serve the same God. The God who called the fishermen and the tax collectors. The God who touched the lepers and ate with sinners. The God who said, 'Come unto me, all ye that labor and are heavy laden, and I will give you rest.'"

Her voice grew stronger.

"So whether you came here in a Bentley or on the bus, whether you're wearing designer clothes or your only clean outfit, whether you've been saved for fifty years or you walked in off the street five minutes ago—you are welcome in this house.

Because this is God's house, and He doesn't turn anyone away who comes seeking Him."

"Amen!" several voices called out—some from the street folk, some from longtime members, even a couple from the mothers' section.

Coko smiled. "Now, to open our service, my sister Moni Chen is going to bless us with a song."

She stepped down, her heart pounding but her spirit soaring. Shaniece caught her eye and mouthed, *That was perfect.*

Moni rose and made her way to the front. She looked so small standing there—petite frame, simple dress, quiet demeanor. Nothing about her physical presence suggested the power she was about to unleash.

She closed her eyes, took a breath, and began: "Open My Heart" by Yolanda Adams.

Oh-oh, talk to me

Oh-oh-oh, oh-oh-oh

Oh-oh, talk to me…

The first notes that came out of her mouth stopped people mid-movement. It was a voice too big for her body, too powerful for her stature—a instrument that could only be divine in origin.

So show me how to do things Your way…

The congregation erupted as each note resonated more and more throughout the sanctuary. Her voice carried the weight of gospel conviction, reaching into hidden places, touching wounded spirits, calling forth tears and worship.

Church hadn't even officially begun, and several people were already caught up in the Spirit.

A woman from the streets fell to her knees, weeping—not the manufactured emotion of religious performance but the genuine breaking of someone encountering God for the first time in years.

One of the longtime deacons stood to his feet, hands raised, tears streaming down his face.

The nurses worked overtime, handing out tissues and helping those who were slain in the Spirit.

Moni sang like she was standing before the throne of God Himself—no performance, no showing off, just pure worship.

You're the lover of my soul

The Captain of my sea...

Andre sat in the pulpit watching, thanking God, praying harder that the Spirit of the Lord would come in and take hold of every person in the church. That a Pentecost would happen today. That Greater Mount Calvary would be changed for good.

When Moni hit the final note, the church was on its feet—half of them in tears, all of them undone.

The service hadn't even started yet.

And already, everyone could feel it: God was about to do something they'd never forget.

The Weight of Glory

Moni returned to her seat, still trembling from what had just moved through her. The congregation slowly settled, but the atmosphere remained charged—electric with expectation, heavy with the presence of something holy.

Minister Young approached the podium, her own eyes glistening. "Church, that was ... that was the Lord." She paused to compose herself. "And now, it's time to hear from our pastor. Saints, give God praise as Pastor Andre Howard brings us the Word!"

The congregation rose to their feet, applauding. Some were already shouting encouragement:

"Preach, Pastor!"

"Let him hear from God!"

"Feed us, man of God!"

Andre stood slowly, deliberately. He made his way from his seat to the podium, each step measured, each movement purposeful. He was dressed simply—a black suit, crisp white shirt, burgundy tie—but there was something different about him. Something in his bearing, in the set of his shoulders, in the way he carried himself.

He'd been in the wilderness with God for three days. Fasting. Praying. Wrestling. Listening.

And God had given him a Word.

He reached the podium and gripped its edges, his knuckles going white from the pressure. For a moment, he just stood there, head bowed, breathing deeply.

The congregation waited. The silence stretched—not uncomfortably, but pregnant with anticipation.

Trange' watched him from the front row, her heart pounding. She could see his hands trembling slightly on the podium. Could see his chest rising and falling with deep, measured breaths.

Lord, be with him, she prayed silently.

Then it happened.

An immense power overtook him—not gradually, but all at once, like being submerged in deep water. The weight of the Lord pressed down on his shoulders, filled his chest, coursed through his veins. It was so heavy, so overwhelming, that for a moment he thought his knees might buckle.

He gripped the podium tighter, anchoring himself, letting the presence of God fill every empty space inside him.

This was what Moses must have felt on the mountain.

What Isaiah experienced in the temple.

What the disciples knew in the Upper Room.

The presence of the Lord—undeniable, unmistakable, uncontainable.

Andre lifted his head slowly, and when he opened his eyes, they blazed with holy fire.

The congregation collectively inhaled. They could see it— whatever had touched him in that private place with God was now about to be released in this public place.

Mother Heady whispered to First Lady Clarice: "He's got the Word. The *real* Word."

Clarice nodded, tears already forming. She knew that look. She'd seen it on her husband's face a hundred times before he preached under the anointing. Her son was about to walk in his father's footsteps—but with his own divine assignment.

Andre opened his mouth, and when he spoke, the voice that came out carried an authority that didn't belong to a man in his thirties. It was ancient, prophetic, weighted with Heaven's mandate.

"Church," he began, and even that single word seemed to reverberate through the sanctuary. "God sent me here today with a message. And I'm not leaving this pulpit until every word He gave me is delivered."

The organ began to play softly underneath his words—not planned, but the musician felt the Spirit moving.

"Some of y'all ain't gonna like what I have to say," Andre continued, his voice rising. "Some of y'all are gonna get offended. Some of y'all are gonna want to leave."

He paused, his eyes sweeping across every section of the church.

"But I didn't come here to make you comfortable. I came here to deliver what thus saith the Lord!"

"Amen!" several voices called out.

Andre's grip on the podium remained firm, anchoring him as wave after wave of anointing crashed over him. The presence of the Lord was so thick now that several people in the congregation could feel it pressing against their chests, making it hard to breathe, impossible to look away.

"Turn with me in your Bibles," Andre commanded, "to the book of John, chapter three, verse sixteen."

The rustling of pages filled the sanctuary. Those who'd come from the streets without Bibles leaned over to share with neighbors who welcomed them into the Word.

"'For God so loved the world,'" Andre began reading, his voice resonant and clear, "'that He gave His only begotten Son, that whosoever believeth in Him should not perish, but have everlasting life.'"

He looked up from the Bible, his eyes scanning the congregation.

"My sermon today is simple," he said, his voice dropping low but carrying to every corner. "There is room at the cross."

He paused, letting the words sink in.

"There. Is. Room. At. The. Cross."

Several voices responded, "Amen!"

"See, somewhere along the way," Andre continued, his voice rising with righteous intensity, "the church forgot that the cross wasn't meant to be exclusive. It wasn't meant to be a members-only club. It wasn't meant to have gatekeepers standing at the door deciding who's worthy and who's not!"

The congregation stirred—some nodding in agreement, others shifting uncomfortably.

"We got folks in the church," Andre's voice grew stronger, "who think it's their job to guard the door. To check credentials. To inspect the past. To judge the present. To determine who's holy enough, sanctified enough, cleaned up enough to enter into the presence of God!"

"Preach, Pastor!" someone called out.

"But let me tell you something the Bible makes clear," Andre said, pointing his finger for emphasis. "Jesus didn't die for the clean folks. He died for the dirty ones! He didn't come for the righteous—He came for the sinners!"

Mother Jones's face flushed.

"The cross has room," Andre declared, his voice thundering now. "It has room for the prostitute and the tax collector. It has room for the thief and the liar. It has room for the addict and the broken. It has room for the woman caught in adultery and the man who denied Christ three times!"

The organ began to swell underneath his words.

"But see, we got gatekeepers in the church," Andre continued, pacing now behind the podium. "Folks who think because they've been saved for thirty years, because they've been members since the foundation was laid, because they can quote Scripture and shout on Sunday morning—that somehow gives them the right to decide who deserves grace and who doesn't!"

Several "Amens" erupted, but they were met with uncomfortable silence from certain sections.

"Let me ask you something," Andre stopped pacing and gripped the podium again. "Who made you God? Who gave you the authority to stand at the cross and turn people away? Who told you it was your job to measure someone's worthiness?"

Mother Williams and Mother Rose exchanged glances.

"The Scripture says in Matthew twenty-three," Andre's voice dropped to a dangerous quiet, "'But woe unto you, scribes and Pharisees, hypocrites! For ye shut up the kingdom of heaven against men: for ye neither go in yourselves, neither suffer ye them that are entering to go in.'"

The congregation held its collective breath.

"Gatekeepers," Andre said, his voice rising again. "That's what Jesus called them. Hypocrites who block the door. Who stand in the way of people trying to get to God. Who make the path to salvation harder instead of easier!"

He paused, his eyes sweeping across every face.

"And let me tell you something about gatekeepers in the church—they're more concerned with protecting their position than welcoming God's people. They're more worried about maintaining their power than extending God's grace. They use the Bible as a weapon instead of a welcome mat!"

"Tell it!" a voice from the street folks section called out.

"There is room at the cross for the woman in Versace," Andre declared, and Trange' felt every eye in the building turn toward her. "There is room at the cross for the man in rags. There is room at the cross for the millionaire and the homeless. There is room at the cross for the PhD and the dropout!"

The congregation erupted in praise.

"Because the cross doesn't care about your clothes!" Andre shouted. "It doesn't care about your bank account! It doesn't care about your past! The cross only asks one question: Do you believe?"

Tears streamed down faces throughout the sanctuary—street folk and longtime members alike.

"So to every gatekeeper in this building," Andre's voice became steel, "I got a message from God for you: GET OUT THE WAY!"

The church exploded.

"Stop blocking people from the cross! Stop judging who's worthy! Stop playing God with people's salvation! Because there is room—there is ALWAYS room—at the cross for anyone who comes!"

Andre stood there, still gripping the podium, still feeling the overwhelming weight and power of God's presence coursing through him.

And he knew—this wasn't going to be a sermon.

This was going to be a reckoning.

Chapter 14: Reckoning and Redemption

The church was still erupting in praise—hands raised, voices shouting agreement, bodies swaying with the weight of truth spoken. Andre stood at the podium, letting the energy build and crest before he raised his hand for silence.

The congregation slowly settled, though the atmosphere remained electric.

Andre's expression shifted—became more solemn, more weighty. He gripped the podium again, and when he spoke, his voice carried a gravity that made everyone lean forward.

"Church," he began, "God has a word for Greater Mount Calvary. And I need you to hear me clearly—He is not pleased."

The sanctuary went deathly quiet.

"Many things have been happening in this church that are outside of His Will. Gossip has become our currency. Backbiting has become our language. Division has become our doctrine. And today—*right now*—God is issuing a warning."

You could hear people breathing.

"No more," Andre declared, his voice rising with authority. "No more will He allow His Church to be a covenant of gossip. No more will this sanctuary be a den of thieves. No more will this congregation be a gathering of backbiters who destroy each other with their tongues!"

"Preach!" someone called out.

"What we need here," Andre continued, his eyes scanning every section of the church, "is a rededication ceremony. And it's happening right now."

Gasps rippled through the congregation.

"Effective immediately, I am dismantling all the boards in Greater Mount Calvary—with the exception of the trustees. Every auxiliary, every committee, every board—dismantled."

The mothers' section erupted in murmurs. Several deacons sat forward in their seats, shock written on their faces.

"And I'm issuing a call of rededication," Andre pressed forward, undeterred by the reaction. "If you want to stay on a particular board, you need to rededicate yourself to this church with a commitment to follow after God's Will under my leadership. This is a call to let go of the foolishness, the gossip, and the fodder that has been poisoning this body."

He paused, his expression deadly serious.

"Now I do issue one warning here—don't come up here and rededicate if you're not serious. Because God showed me something, and for those who do not take this calling seriously, there will be grave consequences."

The weight of his words hung in the air like thunder before lightning.

"I'm asking that Sister Moni sing 'There's Room at the Cross For You,'" Andre said. "And as she's singing, I want all the auxiliary boards—with the exception of the deacons and the mothers—all your members who want to remain on these boards to come up now."

Moni stood, took the microphone, and began to sing. Her voice filled the sanctuary with that same anointing that had opened the service, but now it carried a different quality—invitation mixed with warning, grace mixed with accountability.

The cross upon which Jesus died,

Is a shelter in which we can hide

For a moment, no one moved. The congregation sat frozen, uncertain, processing the magnitude of what was happening.

Then one usher stood—Brother Terence Blackwell, who'd escorted Trange' and her friends to the front row. He walked down the aisle with purposeful steps, his face set with determination.

That broke the dam.

One by one, they came. The nurses in their crisp white uniforms. The ushers in their dignified suits. The choir members in their robes. The youth ministry leaders. The hospitality committee. Wave after wave of people flooded to the front of the church.

Some came with tears streaming down their faces. Others walked with heads bowed in shame. A few came defiantly, as if daring God to challenge their commitment. But they came.

Andre directed Minister Young to anoint each person. She moved down the line with oil and prayer, touching foreheads, speaking blessings, calling forth genuine transformation.

"Do you rededicate yourself to this church?" Andre asked each person who came forward. "Do you commit to laying down gossip, laying down division, laying down everything that has grieved the Spirit of God in this house?"

"Yes, Pastor."

"I do."

"Yes, sir."

One by one, they affirmed their commitment. Andre prayed over each group—his hands raised, his voice carrying authority and compassion. He declared freedom from bondage to negativity, released them from the spirit of gossip, and called forth a new commitment to unity and love.

The auxiliary boards filled the altar area—dozens of people on their knees, being prayed over, being commissioned for genuine service rather than political maneuvering.

When the last person had been anointed, Andre's voice rang out again.

"Next, I want all the deacons and the mothers to stand. Don't come up yet—just stand."

Slowly, reluctantly, the deacons and mothers rose to their feet throughout the sanctuary. Mother Heady stood immediately, her posture straight and unashamed. Mother Hearns stood beside her, gripping the pew in front of her for support. Mother Williams started to rise, but Mother Jones grabbed her arm and pulled her back down.

Williams looked at her friend in confusion but sat back down.

Several deacons stood throughout the congregation—some with confidence, others with visible trepidation.

"Sister Moni, keep singing," Andre said.

There's room at the cross for you...

"I want you to examine yourself," Andre's voice carried across the sanctuary. "Really examine yourself. Pray silently and ask: Is this the walk for you? Is this truly the calling God has placed on your life? Or have you been operating in a position for your own glory, your own power, your own agenda?"

The silence was profound—broken only by Moni's voice and the occasional sniffle as people wrestled with conviction.

"If you believe this is truly your calling," Andre continued, "if you're ready to serve with a pure heart and clean hands—then come forward."

Mother Heady moved immediately, walking down the aisle with the authority of someone who'd never had anything to hide. Mother Hearns followed close behind her, each step seeming to lighten her burden. Several other mothers made their way forward—genuine women of God who'd been outnumbered by the political operators but had maintained their integrity.

The deacons came too—men who'd served faithfully despite the drama, who'd prayed when others plotted, who'd sought God's face when others sought their own advancement.

Mother Williams tried to stand again, but Mother Jones's grip on her arm tightened. *"Don't you do it,"* Jones hissed. *"Don't you dare leave me sitting here alone."*

Williams sat back down, torn between loyalty to her friend and the conviction burning in her chest.

Andre began to pray over those who'd come forward—a powerful, Spirit-filled prayer that called them to a higher standard, commissioned them for genuine ministry, and released them from the bondage of religious politics.

As he prayed, something shifted in the atmosphere. The presence of God grew heavier, more tangible. People who'd come forward out of obligation suddenly found themselves genuinely touched by the Spirit. Tears flowed freely. Hands raised in surrender rather than performance.

And in that moment, an overwhelming sense came over Mother Williams—a conviction so strong it felt like physical hands pushing her forward.

She shot up out of her seat and headed toward the front of the church, breaking free from Mother Jones's grip.

"Bernice!" Jones hissed, but Williams didn't look back.

Mother Rose watched Williams go and felt obligated to follow. She rose slowly, not out of conviction but out of calculation. She knew God—and this young pastor—wasn't going to take her position away. She'd been a mother too long, served too many years, given too much to this church. They needed her.

She walked to the front with her head high, her expression defiant rather than repentant.

Mother Jones remained unmoved. She felt conviction stirring in her heart—all the events of the past weeks flooding her mind like a movie reel. The affair. The lies. The manipulation. The cruelty toward Trange'. The public humiliation. Joel lying paralyzed in her spare bedroom.

But pride prevented her from standing. Pride kept her rooted to that pew while everyone else moved forward. Pride convinced her she'd done nothing requiring rededication, nothing demanding repentance.

She sat alone in her section, arms crossed, jaw set.

Andre prayed over the new deacon and mother board—a powerful prayer of commissioning and warning. He introduced them to the congregation as the newly sanctioned leadership and gave them a holy charge: to serve with integrity, to lead with compassion, to guard the flock rather than control it.

"I want you to step back but not sit yet," Andre instructed them. They formed a line behind him, creating a visual representation of the new order being established.

Andre's voice rose again, filled with urgency and passion.

"There is room at the cross!" he declared. "And now I'm calling everyone who is lost. Every adulterer, every drug and sex addict, every thief, every liar—come to this altar and give your life to God! Come back home!"

Moni began singing "Change Me" by Tamela Mann, and her voice seemed to shake the very foundations of the building.

Change me, oh God

Make me more like you...

They came in waves—a flood of humanity pouring down the aisles.

The woman who'd walked in with track marks on her arms came running, sobbing, falling at the altar. Three teenage boys in saggy jeans and oversized shirts stumbled forward, tears streaming down their faces. A man in a business suit who'd been sitting in the back, looking sophisticated and put-together, broke down crying as he made his way to the front—decades of secret sin finally being brought to light.

Dozens of people flooded the altar—some from the streets, some who'd been members for years, all of them desperate for the real thing, tired of pretending, ready for genuine transformation.

And then it happened.

Coko caught the Holy Ghost.

One moment, she was sitting in the pulpit, watching the altar call with tears in her eyes. The next moment, she was on her feet, shouting, running, dancing in the Spirit with an abandon she'd never experienced. The shy, reserved Minister Howard was gone—in her place was a woman completely overtaken by the power of God.

The church erupted.

More people caught the Spirit than there were people to help them. Several ushers who'd been standing ready to assist fell under the power themselves. Nurses who'd been prepared to hand out tissues found themselves on the floor, overcome by the presence of God.

The sanctuary became holy chaos—beautiful, messy, authentic chaos. People were crying, shouting, praising, repenting, being transformed. The carefully constructed religious order dissolved into genuine spiritual encounter.

Mother Jones remained seated, stolid and unmoved. Her face was a mask—no emotion, no reaction, no acknowledgment of the move of God happening all around her.

Patricia came up to sit with her mother, sliding into the pew beside her. She watched the scene unfolding with something like longing in her eyes, but she remained unchanged, mirroring her mother's posture of resistance.

After what felt like hours but was probably thirty minutes, the intensity began to settle. People slowly found their way back to coherence, though the atmosphere remained charged with the afterglow of God's presence.

Coko returned to her seat in the pulpit, her hair disheveled, makeup smeared with tears, completely undone in the best possible way.

Crystal Young and Andre moved through the crowd at the altar, anointing and praying for each person who'd come forward. They laid hands on the addicts, the prostitutes, the broken, the lost—declaring freedom, speaking life, releasing them into their new identity as children of God.

As the crowd began to disperse back to their seats, faces glowing with newfound hope, Andre returned to the podium.

"I have two more things before the benediction," he announced.

The congregation, already emotionally exhausted, settled in to hear what could possibly be left.

"Would my mother and Sister Trange' Moreau please come to the front?"

A collective gasp went through the sanctuary. Trange' froze in her seat, her heart hammering. Clarice stood immediately, her face serene, and made her way to the pulpit. She turned and extended her hand toward Trange'.

Shaniece gave her a gentle push. "Go on, girl."

Trange' stood on shaking legs and made her way to the front, hyperaware of every eye following her movement. She climbed the steps to the pulpit and stood beside Clarice, who squeezed her hand reassuringly.

Andre looked out over the congregation, then at his mother with love and respect in his eyes.

"The joint board was correct in one thing," he began. "My mother can no longer hold the title of First Lady—not because she's unworthy, but because that title should belong to the pastor's wife."

Clarice nodded, her eyes glistening but her smile genuine.

"However," Andre continued, "it was in my spirit from the Lord to honor my mother's decades of service and her genuine heart for God's people. Therefore, I am appointing her as the Head Mother of the Mother's Board."

The newly rededicated mothers applauded, genuine joy on their faces. Even some of the congregation who'd been skeptical found themselves clapping—it was the right decision, and everyone could feel it.

"The title of First Lady," Andre said, his voice dropping lower, more intimate, "will go to my future wife."

He turned to look directly at Trange'.

The sanctuary held its collective breath.

"And God has already told me who she is."

In one smooth motion, Andre dropped to his knees in front of Trange', pulling a small box from his pocket.

The church exploded in gasps and shouts.

Trange' stood there, completely overwhelmed. Her hands flew to her mouth. Tears sprang into her eyes. This couldn't be happening. It was too sudden, too public, *too much*.

But a still, small voice in her spirit whispered: *Yes.*

She looked over at her friends in the front row—her sisters who'd walked this journey with her.

Shaniece had tears streaming down her face, giving her an enthusiastic thumbs up.

Renee was smiling wide, mouthing, "Yes! Yes!"

Samantha gave her a look that clearly said, *Girl, get your man.*

Sage was mouthing dramatically, *"How many carats?"*

She turned back to Andre, who was still on his knees, looking up at her with such love and vulnerability that her doubts melted away.

"Yes," she whispered.

"What was that?" Andre asked, smiling through his tears. "I didn't hear you."

"Yes!" she said louder. "Yes, I'll marry you!"

Before Andre could even stand to embrace her, Clarice grabbed Trange' and pulled her into a fierce hug, tears flowing freely. "Welcome to the family, baby. Welcome home."

Andre laughed. "Ma! That's my job to hug her first!"

The congregation erupted in laughter and applause. Even some of the skeptics found themselves smiling—there was something undeniably genuine about this moment, something that transcended the drama and politics.

In the back of the church, Mother Jones stood abruptly and walked out, her heels clicking sharply against the floor. Patricia hesitated for a moment, then followed her mother into the parking lot.

No one noticed or cared. They were too caught up in the joy of the moment.

Andre finally got his embrace, pulling Trange' close and kissing her forehead. Then he turned her to face the congregation, keeping one arm around her waist.

Before he could speak, FaLessia rose from her seat and made her way to the podium. Andre stepped aside, giving her the floor, curious about what she had to say.

"Church," FaLessia began, her voice steady and clear, "as a trustee of Greater Mount Calvary, I have a statement from the Trustee Board that needs to be read at this time."

She pulled out a folded paper from her Bible and unfolded it carefully.

"The Trustee Board of Greater Mount Calvary Cathedral wishes to make the following declaration: We have full and complete confidence in Pastor Andre Howard's leadership and vision for this church. The events of recent weeks have been orchestrated by a spirit of division and gossip that has no place in the house of God."

Her voice grew stronger as she continued.

"We ask this congregation to dismiss the gossip, to release the bitterness, and to give these newly rededicated boards and our pastor a chance to lead us into what God has for Greater Mount Calvary. Just as God gave each and every one of us another chance when we didn't deserve it, we must extend that same grace to one another."

"Amen!" voices called out throughout the sanctuary.

"The old order has passed away," FaLessia declared, her eyes scanning the congregation. "Behold, all things are becoming new. And we, as trustees, stand unified behind our pastor and the leadership he has established today. This is not a suggestion—this is a mandate from the governing body of this church."

She folded the paper and looked directly at the congregation with an intensity that made several people shift in their seats.

"So if you came here today thinking you were going to continue operating in gossip and division, you need to make a choice right now: either get with God's program or get out. Because Greater Mount Calvary is moving forward, with or without you."

The church erupted in applause and shouts of agreement.

FaLessia handed the microphone back to Andre and returned to her seat, satisfied that the trustees' position had been made crystal clear.

Andre nodded his appreciation, then turned to the congregation with Trange' still beside him.

"Church," he said, his voice thick with emotion, "meet your new First Lady."

He looked at Trange', giving her the floor. "How do you feel?"

Moni, reading the moment perfectly, appeared beside them and handed Trange' the microphone.

Trange' stood there, looking out over the congregation—at the newly rededicated leaders, at the street folk who'd just given their lives to Christ, at her friends who'd stood by her, at the mothers who'd judged her, at all of them.

When she spoke, her voice was clear and strong.

"I didn't see this coming," she began, a nervous laugh escaping. "To be honest, I wasn't even sure I'd be welcome back in this church after everything that happened."

She paused, composing herself.

"But I want to make something clear right now. I am not going to be an ordinary First Lady."

The sanctuary went silent, everyone leaning in to hear what she'd say next.

"I will be an *Extraordinary Only Lady*," she declared, emphasizing each word with conviction. "Not because I'm perfect—Lord knows I'm not. Not because I have a spotless past—we all know I don't. But because I serve an extraordinary God who specializes in taking broken things and making them beautiful.

Who takes the rejected and calls them chosen. Who takes the condemned and declares them redeemed!"

"Amen!" voices called out.

"So, to everyone who thought my past disqualified me," Trange' continued, her eyes sweeping across the sanctuary with grace rather than bitterness, "thank you. Because God used your rejection to push me into my destiny. Thank you for reminding me that I don't need your approval—I only need His."

The church erupted in praise.

"And to everyone who stood by me," her voice softened as she looked at her friends, at Clarice, at Mother Heady, "thank you for showing me what real love looks like. Thank you for being the hands and feet of Jesus when religious spirits tried to destroy me."

Andre looked at her with such pride and love that several women in the congregation sighed audibly.

"I don't know what kind of First Lady I'm going to be," Trange' admitted with refreshing honesty. "I'm going to make mistakes. I'm going to stumble. I'm going to need grace—a lot of grace. But I promise you this: I will love God's people with everything in me. I will serve this church with my whole heart. And I will stand beside this man of God as we follow wherever the Lord leads us."

She turned to Andre. "Even if it means walking through fire."

"Especially through fire," he said, and kissed her—a real kiss, not a church peck, right there in front of God and everybody.

The sanctuary went wild—shouting, clapping, praising, celebrating. The musicians kicked in, the organ swelled, and spontaneous worship broke out throughout the building.

It had been a morning of reckoning and redemption. Of tearing down and building up. Of endings and new beginnings.

Greater Mount Calvary would never be the same.

And as Trange' stood there in Andre's arms, surrounded by the family God had given her, she thought about the cross—and how there really was room for everyone.

Even for a foster kid from the streets who'd become a fashion mogul.

Even for a woman with a past that tried to define her future.

Even for someone the church had tried to reject.

There was room at the cross.

And she'd finally found her place there.

Chapter 15: At Last

Several Weeks Later

Greater Mount Calvary buzzed with controlled chaos. People rushed through corridors carrying last-minute arrangements—adjusting ribbons, straightening chairs, testing the sound system one more time. The sanctuary had been transformed into something ethereal, almost dreamlike.

Victorian elegance met modern sophistication in the color scheme: soft lilac and creamy vanilla creating an atmosphere of timeless romance. Cascading arrangements of white roses, lilac hydrangeas, and delicate baby's breath adorned every pew. Ivory tulle wrapped each column, secured with oversized satin bows in pale purple. Hundreds of pillar candles at varying heights lined the aisles, their flames flickering like captured stars. The altar stood draped in vintage lace, with an arch overhead woven through with white roses and trailing ivy that seemed to float in the soft lighting.

At the altar, the groom stood fidgeting with his boutonniere. His hands trembled slightly—not with doubt, but with the weight of anticipation.

Minister Coko leaned over from her position as officiant, her voice gentle. "Are you going to be okay?"

He nodded, his throat tight with emotion. It wasn't doubt causing his nervousness—it was the suddenness of this wedding, the reality that in mere moments his life would change forever. And beneath that, a question that kept circling his mind: *Am I man enough to handle this bride?*

In the back room that served as a makeshift bridal suite, controlled pandemonium reigned.

Samantha worked with focused intensity on the veil, her fingers moving with practiced precision despite the time pressure. "We have to hurry! We are late! Where is Shaniece?"

As if summoned, Shaniece burst through the door, slightly breathless, carrying an elaborate bouquet. "Here are the flowers! And don't even ask about getting Imani ready—it was a complete nightmare."

The flower girl, Imani, rushed in behind her aunt, her little face scrunched in concentration as she tried not to wrinkle her lilac dress.

Samantha looked around frantically. "Where is Israel?"

"He's already up there with the groomsmen," Shaniece assured her, smoothing down her daughter's dress. "He's been ready for an hour. You know how he is—always early."

Renee swept in like a force of nature, triumph written across her face. "I pulled off a miracle. The reception hall is completely set up, everything is perfect, and—" She pointed at the bride with mock severity. "—you and Andre owe me. Big time."

Shaniece chimed in, a playful smile tugging at her lips. "Yeah, all of us, actually."

Samantha opened her mouth to add her own commentary when the opening strains of music drifted through the door.

Her eyes went wide. "How are we starting and the bride isn't even there yet?"

FaLessia burst through the door with the energy of a stage manager on opening night. "Showtime, ladies! Let's move!"

Like a well-drilled military unit, they all fell into line.

The Processional

Moni stood at the front of the sanctuary, microphone in hand, her voice filling every corner of the sacred space. She began singing "This Will Be (An Everlasting Love)" by Natalie Cole—but with her signature gospel inflection that transformed the already joyful song into something transcendent.

You brought a lot of a sunshine into my life

You filled me with happiness I never knew...

The doors opened, and Shaniece appeared first, gliding down the aisle in a stunning lilac gown that caught the candlelight with every step. Her smile was radiant, genuine—she'd helped orchestrate so much of this day and watching it come together filled her with satisfaction.

Samantha followed, her own lilac gown cut slightly different but equally elegant. She moved with the confidence of someone who knew she looked amazing, her natural flair for drama contained just enough for the solemnity of the occasion. Her smile radiated joy—this was family, this was celebration, this was everything she'd fought to protect coming to fruition.

Renee came next, her expression softer, almost vulnerable. She'd been through her own valley of shadows recently, and witnessing this moment of pure happiness touched something deep within her that she'd thought was permanently hardened.

Then came the flower girl, carefully scattering rose petals with exaggerated concentration. Imani's little face was serious with the weight of her responsibility, her lilac dress floating around her like a cloud. Israel walked beside her as ring bearer, carrying the pillow with utmost dignity, his little suit making him look like a miniature businessman.

Moni's voice swelled as the back doors opened wider.

Rev. Dr. Mario DeSean Booker

To you I'll be serving

'Cause you're so deserving

Hey, you're so deserving,

You're so deserving...

The bride appeared.

The entire congregation rose to their feet, a collective intake of breath rippling through the sanctuary.

She was breathtaking.

The vintage-inspired gown—ivory lace over champagne satin— hugged her frame before flowing into a cathedral train that seemed to float behind her. The sweetheart neckline showed just enough cleavage to maintain its elegance. Her veil, secured by a delicate tiara that caught the candlelight, cascaded down her back like a waterfall of tulle and lace. She carried a bouquet of white roses and lilac freesias, their fragrance trailing behind her as she moved.

But it wasn't the dress that captured everyone's attention—it was her face. Pure joy radiated from her, vulnerable and unguarded in a way that few had ever seen. This woman who'd built walls for protection, who'd constructed personas for survival, who'd learned to armor herself against the world—she walked down that aisle with her heart completely exposed.

Every eye followed her journey to the altar. Longtime members who'd judged her most harshly found themselves smiling despite themselves—there was something undeniably holy about this moment. The street folk who'd come to faith on that powerful Sunday morning watched with tears streaming down their faces, seeing tangible evidence that God really did redeem and restore.

She reached the altar and locked eyes with Mother Clarice, seated in the front row.

Clarice was almost overcome with emotion, tears streaming freely down her face. She leaned over to the woman beside her—and whispered with barely controlled joy: "I am so happy for her. Your love story inspired her to let go and be loved."

"Indeed," came the whispered response, eyes glistening with shared emotion.

At the altar, the bride took her place beside the groom, their hands finding each other instinctively.

The Ceremony

Minister Moni stepped forward, her Bible open, her expression carrying both solemnity and joy. When she spoke, her voice rang with authority tempered by love.

"Dearly beloved, we are gathered here today in the sight of God and these witnesses to join this couple together in holy matrimony. What a blessing it is—what an absolute gift from the Lord—that Mother Heady Mitchell and Deacon Samuel Fry are exchanging vows and becoming one before Christ!"

The congregation erupted in joyful agreement—"Amen!" and "Praise God!" ringing throughout the sanctuary. Everyone had known this was coming, had helped prepare for this moment, had celebrated the unlikely but beautiful romance between the church's senior mother and the faithful deacon.

Clarice grabbed the hand of Trange' beside her and squeezed. "She's so happy!"

Trange' squeezed back, her voice thick with emotion. "I am so happy for her."

269

Andre leaned forward from his position as best man, unable to resist. "Do I have to separate you two?"

Soft laughter rippled through their section.

Since the engagement announcement at Greater Mount Calvary, the story had spread throughout the community. Deacon Samuel Fry—known affectionately as "Sammy" to his friends—had decided to take a chance. At one of their regular dinner gatherings over a plate of his favorite smothered pork chops and rice, he'd asked Mother Heady Mitchell to marry him.

In typical Heady fashion, she hadn't dissolved into tears or gasped in surprise. She'd thought for a second, chewed her pork chop thoroughly, and considered the proposal with the same practical wisdom she brought to every major life decision.

After she'd rededicated herself at the church during that powerful Sunday service, after watching the transformation happening throughout Greater Mount Calvary, she'd realized something profound: even as an old woman, she still had more life in her body. And Sammy Fry was someone she couldn't imagine not having in that life.

Her response had been characteristically direct: "Well, what the heck. Let's do it."

They'd originally planned to go down to the courthouse and get married—simple, practical, no fuss. But Andre and Clarice had talked them out of it, insisting they belonged in the church, that their union deserved to be celebrated properly.

"We'll throw together a wedding for you," Clarice had promised. "The church will take care of everything."

They'd protested, not wanting the stress, but the entire congregation had rallied. Everyone pitched in with such enthusiasm that resistance became impossible.

Trange' had offered to get Mother Heady a designer dress—which Heady had initially refused before Trange' showed up with three options and wouldn't take no for an answer. Samantha had helped with planning and coordination, her organizational skills finally being used for something positive rather than schemes. Shaniece had offered the twins as ring bearer and flower girl, giving the ceremony that family feeling that both bride and groom craved. Renee was handling all the catering through her restaurant, creating a menu that would make this reception legendary. Moni sang, her voice providing the soundtrack for their sacred moment. And Coko officiated, honored to preside over such a meaningful union.

Andre had wanted to marry them himself, but he'd made the choice to be a participant instead—standing as Deacon Fry's best man, honoring his godmother on her special day.

Now, Moni continued the ceremony with beautiful solemnity.

"Marriage is not to be entered into lightly, but reverently, deliberately, and in accordance with the purposes for which it was instituted by God."

She looked at Deacon Fry. "Samuel, do you take Heady to be your lawfully wedded wife? Do you promise to love her, honor her, comfort her, and keep her in sickness and in health, forsaking all others, for as long as you both shall live?"

Deacon Fry's voice was steady, his eyes never leaving Heady's face. "I do."

Moni turned to Mother Heady. "Heady, do you take Samuel to be your lawfully wedded husband? Do you promise to love him, honor him, comfort him, and keep him in sickness and in health, forsaking all others, for as long as you both shall live?"

271

Mother Heady's response came without hesitation, her voice strong despite the emotion shining in her eyes. "I do."

"The rings, please."

Israel stepped forward solemnly, presenting the pillow with the two simple gold bands.

Deacon Fry took Heady's ring, his hands surprisingly steady as he slipped it onto her finger. "With this ring, I thee wed. All that I am, I give to you. All that I have, I share with you."

Mother Heady took Sammy's ring, her own hands trembling slightly as decades of walls came down. "With this ring, I thee wed. All that I am, I give to you. All that I have, I share with you."

Moni's smile could have lit the entire sanctuary. "By the power vested in me by God and the state of Louisiana, I now pronounce you husband and wife. Deacon Fry—you may kiss your bride."

Sammy Fry cupped Heady's face in his hands with such tenderness that several people in the congregation openly wept. The kiss was soft, reverent, the kiss of two people who'd waited decades to find each other and refused to waste another moment.

The sanctuary erupted with applause and cheers.

Moni's voice rose above the celebration as the couple turned to face the congregation: "Ladies and gentlemen, I present to you Mr. and Mrs. Samuel and Heady Fry!"

She began singing "At Last" by Etta James, her voice wrapping around the classic like silk.

At last, my love has come along...

The newly married couple proceeded down the aisle, their faces glowing with joy that transcended age, circumstance, and everything they'd both survived to reach this moment. Congregants reached out to touch their hands, to offer congratulations, to witness up close the miracle of two people brave enough to choose love even in the autumn of their lives.

The Reception

Outside the sanctuary, people buzzed with excitement, gathering around the new couple. "The Frys!"—the name rang out with celebration and a touch of humor. Who would have thought Mother Heady Mitchell would ever be anyone's Mrs. Fry?

Clarice approached Heady, who extended her hand with genuine joy. "I's married now! Can you believe it?"

Heady took her hand, squeezing it firmly, her eyes dancing with mischief and happiness. "Not at first. But God is showing up around here, so all things are possible."

They embraced—two women who'd weathered storms, who'd stood together through chaos, who'd chosen grace over bitterness.

Heady pulled back, her expression turning serious for a moment. "Thank you, Clarice. For being there for me. And for what you did for this church. You could have left, could have walked away after everything they put you through. But you stayed. You fought. And look at what God has done."

Clarice's eyes filled with tears. "We fought together, sister. And we're going to keep fighting—for this church, for these people, for the Kingdom."

Patricia approached hesitantly, her expression guarded but genuine. "Mother Heady—I mean, Mrs. Fry—congratulations."

Heady embraced her warmly, feeling the tension in the younger woman's body. "Thank you, baby. That means a lot coming from you."

Patricia's smile didn't quite reach her eyes. "I need to head home soon. To take care of... things."

Understanding passed between them—the unspoken weight of what Patricia was carrying.

"Give her my love," Heady said softly. "And tell her she's always got a home here when she's ready."

Patricia nodded, not trusting herself to speak, and headed toward the exit.

As she disappeared through the doors, sadness drifted over Clarice and Heady like a shadow crossing the sun.

"It's a shame what happened to Mother Jones," Heady said quietly.

Clarice nodded, her expression troubled. "A shame and a warning."

Out of protest after the rededication Sunday, Mother Jones stopped coming to church. Two weeks passed without her darkening the doors—two weeks of stubborn pride refusing to yield to conviction.

Then one day, as she headed up the stairs to check on Joel, she tripped.

The fall down those stairs wasn't life-threatening, but the sheer irony was almost biblical in its precision: she was now paralyzed, just like Joel. Different location—her injuries affected her lower spine—but paralyzed nonetheless.

Patricia had become caretaker to both her biological father and her mother. She'd tried to get Mother Hearns to take Joel back, but Sandra had refused with finality. "That bed he's in? That's exactly where he belongs."

Patricia had put her mother and Joel in the same room—both paralyzed, in beds next to each other, forced into the proximity they'd craved in sin but now experienced as judgment.

"I don't know if it was God or not," Clarice said slowly, choosing her words carefully. "But the Bible does say 'Touch not my anointed and do my prophets no harm.' I just hope during this time that His Will be done. Maybe this is her time—where she can't run from God anymore. Now He has her in a perfect spot where all she can do is sit, or rather lay, and totally depend on Him."

Heady was quiet for a moment, then squared her shoulders with determination. "Well, enough of all this heavy talk. I'm ready to get to the reception hall and cut a rug. These old bones can still move!"

Clarice laughed—genuine, joyful laughter that released the tension. "Then let's go celebrate, Mrs. Fry. You've earned it."

The Reception Hall

The reception venue was nothing short of spectacular. Renee had outdone herself, transforming the hall into something that belonged in a luxury magazine spread.

Crystal chandeliers cast warm light across round tables draped in ivory linen with lilac overlays. Each centerpiece featured towering arrangements of white roses, purple orchids, and cascading greenery that seemed to float above vintage silver candelabras. Gold chargers anchored place settings of fine china and crystal stemware. A massive head table sat on a raised platform, decorated with an abundance of flowers and twinkling fairy lights that created an almost magical atmosphere.

The food was extraordinary—a fusion of Southern comfort and upscale dining that had guests going back for seconds and thirds. Stations offered everything from Renee's famous jambalaya to elegantly carved prime rib, from fresh seafood displays to a dessert table that looked like an art installation.

But the real centerpiece was the joy.

Mother Heady—Mrs. Fry now—danced with her new husband, their movements slow and deliberate but filled with such happiness that it was impossible not to smile watching them. Deacon Fry held her like she was precious, and Heady's face glowed with a contentment she'd never allowed herself to feel before.

Other couples joined them on the dance floor. Andre spun Trange' around, both laughing as they practiced for their upcoming wedding. Shaniece danced with her husband, while the twins ran around the edges of the dance floor playing their own games. Even Samantha, who claimed she didn't dance, found herself swaying to the music, pulled onto the floor by Sage who refused to let her sit out.

The older saints sat at tables, fanning themselves and commenting on how beautiful everything was, how happy they were to see Mother Heady finally get her blessing. The newer members—those who'd come from the streets on that powerful Sunday—sat slightly awkward in their Sunday best, but welcomed and included, experiencing what church celebration looked like when it was genuine.

The Balcony

Trange' and Andre slipped away from the reception area, finding a quiet balcony that overlooked the city. The night air was cool and refreshing after the warmth of the crowded hall.

The moon hung full and bright above them, casting silver light across everything.

They stood close together, champagne glasses in hand, looking out over the twinkling lights of New Orleans.

"Our wedding is next," Trange' said softly, leaning into Andre's side. "Three weeks."

"Three weeks," Andre repeated, his voice carrying wonder and anticipation. "And then we get to do this forever."

"Forever," Trange' echoed, testing the word, and finding it didn't scare her the way it once would have. "You know, I never thought I'd have this. Never thought I'd be standing here planning a wedding, engaged to a pastor, about to become a First Lady."

Andre turned to face her, his hand cupping her cheek. "Extraordinary Only Lady," he corrected with a smile.

She laughed. "That too."

"You know what I keep thinking about?" Andre's expression turned serious, his eyes searching hers in the moonlight. "That Sunday when everything fell apart. When your past got exposed and the church tried to destroy you. I keep thinking about how close I came to losing you before I ever really had you."

Trange's eyes glistened. "But you didn't lose me."

"No," he agreed. "Because God had other plans. Better plans. Plans that included watching my godmother get married at seventy-three. Plans that included dismantling every toxic system in that church and rebuilding it the right way. Plans that included you standing beside me as we do this work together."

"Plans that included me learning what real love looks like," Trange' added quietly. "Not the transactional relationships I'd known before. Not the survival-based connections. But real love—the kind that shows up, that stays, that chooses you even when choosing you is hard."

Andre pulled her closer. "I'm going to spend the rest of my life showing you that kind of love. Every single day."

"And I'm going to spend the rest of mine showing you that a woman with a past can have a future," Trange' countered. "That redemption is real. That God really does make all things new."

They stood in comfortable silence for a moment, being present with each other under the vast Louisiana sky.

"Three weeks," Andre finally said, lifting his champagne glass.

Trange' lifted hers to meet his. "Three weeks until forever."

The glasses clinked together with a delicate chime that seemed to echo in the night air. They sipped, their eyes locked on each other, and then Andre leaned in and kissed her—soft and sweet and full of promise.

Below them, the reception continued. Music and laughter drifted up to where they stood. Mrs. Fry was probably still on the dance floor, celebrating the love she'd finally allowed herself to receive. The church family was gathered, genuinely unified for the first time in years. And tomorrow, they'd all wake up and continue the work of being the body of Christ—messy, imperfect, but genuinely trying.

But for this moment, on this balcony under this moon, two people who'd both survived impossible things stood together and looked toward a future that finally, miraculously, felt full of hope instead of fear.

Trange' rested her head on Andre's shoulder, and he wrapped his arm around her waist, and they stayed like that—watching the moon, listening to the music, holding onto each other and the promise of all the tomorrows they'd face together.

At last, their love had come along.

And this time, it was real.

Rev. Dr. Mario DeSean Booker

Epilogue: No Ordinary Beginning

VOGUE Magazine: *"Fashion Icon Trange' Moreau Weds Prominent Pastor in Stunning Santorini Ceremony - A Masterclass in Elegance Meets Faith"*

People Magazine: *"When High Fashion Meets High Faith: The Trange' Moreau and Pastor Andre Howard Wedding Spectacular"*

Essence: *"A Love Redeemed: Pastor Andre Howard and Designer Trange' Moreau Say 'I Do' in Greece - Two Weddings, One Epic Love Story"*

New York Times Style Section: *"Trange' Moreau's Dual Wedding Celebrations: From New Orleans Sanctuary to Santorini Sunset"*

W Magazine: *"The Wedding of the Year: Trange' Moreau's Exclusive Santorini Estate Celebration Draws Fashion Elite, Hollywood A-List, and Proves Redemption Never Goes Out of Style"*

InStyle: *"Inside the Greek Island Nuptials That Had Everyone Talking: Trange' Moreau Marries Pastor Andre Howard"*

Four weeks later, the stretch Cadillac Escalade glided through the streets of New Orleans, its black exterior gleaming under the late afternoon sun. Inside the luxurious interior, Trange' held her husband's hand, her wedding rings catching the light—a stunning set that combined classic elegance with modern design, much like their love story itself.

She leaned against Andre's shoulder, her mind drifting back over the whirlwind of the past month, hardly believing any of it was real.

The local wedding at Greater Mount Calvary had been everything she'd dreamed and nothing she'd expected all at once. The sanctuary had been transformed into a garden paradise—thousands of white roses imported from Ecuador, cascading purple orchids, and trailing ivy creating an atmosphere that felt both sacred and enchanted. She'd worn a custom gown that took three of her most talented designers six weeks to create—vintage French lace over champagne silk, with a cathedral train that seemed to float behind her like a cloud of dreams.

The congregation had been packed—standing room only, with people she'd never met standing outside the church just to witness the moment when the Extraordinary Only Lady became Mrs. Andre Howard. Members from the streets who'd given their lives to Christ on that powerful Sunday stood shoulder to shoulder with longtime saints, all united in celebration. The newly rededicated mothers and deacons had served with genuine joy, toxic politics replaced with authentic ministry.

Andre had cried when she walked down the aisle—genuine tears streaming down his face that he didn't try to hide, his love written across his features for everyone to see. Their vows had been traditional but deeply personal, each word carrying the weight of everything they'd survived to reach that altar. When Minister Coko pronounced them husband and wife and Andre kissed his bride, the church had erupted in celebration that lasted a full ten minutes—shouting, praising, rejoicing in a love that had overcome every attack against it.

But the Santorini wedding—that had been something else entirely, something out of a fairy tale.

They'd flown their closest friends and family to Greece for an intimate ceremony at an exclusive private estate perched on the dramatic cliffs overlooking the Aegean Sea. The setting was breathtaking—pristine white-washed buildings with blue domed roofs against impossibly blue water that seemed to stretch into eternity. The sun had set in shades of coral, orange, and deep pink that looked painted by the Lord across the endless sky.

Her high fashion clients had attended—designers, models, magazine editors she'd worked with for years. Celebrities she'd dressed graced the guest list alongside church members who'd never left Louisiana before. The blend of worlds that once seemed impossible to merge had come together beautifully, proving that when God orchestrates something, He doesn't see the divisions humans create.

She'd worn a different gown for the Greek ceremony— something more ethereal, more free. Flowing white silk that moved with the Aegean breeze, Grecian-inspired with delicate gold threading that caught the sunset. No train this time, just movement and lightness, like she was floating. They'd exchanged vows as the sun kissed the horizon, with only the sound of waves crashing against ancient rocks and the soft strains of a string quartet filling the air. It had been intimate despite the star-studded guest list, deeply personal despite the cameras from major fashion magazines capturing every moment for their glossy pages.

Two weddings. Two celebrations. One love story that had defied every odd stacked against it.

Her mind turned to her friends—her sisters who'd stood by her through fire.

Shaniece had been her matron of honor at both ceremonies, and the support she'd shown throughout the entire journey had been unwavering, unshakeable. Even more meaningful, Shaniece and her family officially joined Greater Mount Calvary as members. Watching her friend worship alongside her every Sunday, seeing their children playing together after service, laughing over brunch and prayer meetings—it felt like family in the truest, deepest sense.

Samantha had caught the bouquet at the Greek wedding—literally dove for it with the same competitive energy she brought to everything in life. But more importantly, she'd met someone. Nico, a gorgeous English-Greek man with Mediterranean charm and unexpected depth, had swept her completely off her feet. He'd already made a trip to the States to see her, flying across an ocean for a woman who'd built walls higher than most. Samantha needed this—needed someone who saw past her defensive mechanisms and loved her anyway.

Renee was opening a new restaurant called Chateau L'Assiette, and Trange' couldn't wait to eat there. After everything Renee had been through, watching her channel pain into purpose through culinary artistry was beautiful to witness.

Coko had accepted a ministerial position at the church, preaching on third Sundays while her husband David served as deacon. Watching shy, reserved Coko step into her calling with power and authority reminded everyone that God doesn't call the equipped—He equips the called.

And Moni—sweet, powerful-voiced Moni—had gotten a record deal and was working on her debut album. The voice that had opened so many services, that had ministered to so many souls, would soon reach the world.

God had truly blessed them all beyond measure.

Her mind drifted to the church itself, to the transformation that continued to unfold. Mother Heady Fry radiated joy every Sunday, sitting beside her husband who adored her completely, proving it's never too late for love. Mother Clarice had fully embraced her role as Head Mother, starting mentorship classes which paired older women with younger members, and creating outreach programs that reached people instead of judging them.

The church was becoming what it was always meant to be—a hospital for sinners, not a museum for saints.

As they passed Greater Mount Calvary Cathedral, brief sadness washed over Trange' like a shadow crossing the sun. Mother Jones had gotten an infection and, in stubborn pride, refused to go to the hospital. It had spread rapidly through her weakened body, and she'd died in her bed at home—holding Joel's hand. He'd passed less than forty-eight hours later. The doctors said congestive heart failure; others whispered it was a broken heart. Either way, the two who'd loved in secret for decades had left this world together, their story ending in tragedy rather than triumph.

Trange' had texted and called Patricia repeatedly, offering condolences, extending grace, trying to build a bridge. No response. Patricia hadn't shown up to either wedding ceremony. But when Andre texted her, she'd responded immediately— paragraphs of conversation, questions about his day, remembering inside jokes from their childhood.

Go figure, Trange' thought with a mixture of irritation and wariness, making a mental note to watch Patricia very closely around her husband. Some people never changed, and jealousy had deep roots.

The Escalade turned onto a tree-lined street in the Garden District, pulling up to the estate they'd purchased for their new marital home. They'd barely lived in it yet—it was waiting for them to make it theirs, to fill it with memories and laughter and the life they'd build together.

As they pulled into the circular driveway, the driver's voice carried pride and warmth: "We made it to your new estate, Mr. and Mrs. Howard."

They stepped out into the golden afternoon light, staring up at their beautiful new residence—a stunning Victorian mansion with wraparound porches and gardens that needed tending.

A figure approached from the shadows near the side of the house, moving hesitantly, almost desperately. A hand reached out and touched Trange's shoulder.

"'Tavia."

Trange' let out a startled scream. The driver responded with military precision, pulling his weapon and training it on the woman. Andre moved into full protective mode, pushing Trange' behind him, his body becoming a shield.

He stared at the disheveled woman before them—dirty, torn clothes, matted hair, wild eyes that held something between fear and resignation. Recognition settled in slowly, like puzzle pieces clicking into place.

Trange' moved from behind Andre, her voice barely above a whisper. "Lee Lee? Is that you?"

"Yup," the woman responded, her voice hoarse and flat.

Utter shock coursed through Trange's body. Her sister. Leanne Marie Burns. The one person from her blood family she'd actually loved, actually tried to protect before everything fell apart.

"How? Why?" Trange's mind raced. "Wait—is that blood on your shirt? Are you hurt?"

"Nope," Leanne said with eerie calm. "Ain't mine."

"Lee, what's going on? What are you doing here?"

Leanne's voice remained emotionless, detached, like she was reporting weather. "Maw and Paw are gone. Drug deal went bad. Real bad. Had nowhere else to go. That pretty fancy lady Pat brought me here when I showed up at the church looking for you. Said you'd love to take me in, that family was everything to you now." She looked up at the mansion, letting out a low whistle. "Pretty fancy house you got here, 'Tavia. Long way from that foster home, huh?"

Mental note: thank Patricia for her eagerness to insert herself into her business. Again.

"Call me Trange'," she said automatically, the correction coming from years of practice.

"T," Leanne's voice cracked, the facade breaking for just a moment. "Who's gonna take care of me now? I got nobody. Nobody left."

Concern, fear, and confusion plastered across Lee Lee's face— the little sister she remembered breaking through the hardened exterior.

Andre stepped forward, his pastor's heart overriding any hesitation. His voice was gentle but firm. "We can make room for you. You're family."

Trange' stood bewildered and worried, her mind spinning. She just couldn't escape her past. Couldn't outrun it, couldn't hide from it, couldn't pretend it didn't exist. And she knew her sister was just as much trouble as their mother had been—maybe more, because Lee Lee had never learned to channel her survival instincts into anything productive.

She looked up to the sky, past the mansion's roof, past the trees, searching. *Lord, I know there's a purpose in this. I know You don't do anything by accident. But I don't see it right now. I don't understand. Please reveal it to me and prepare me for whatever's coming.*

What a way to start her first night in her new home, with her new husband—with old drama and an unwelcome visitor from a past she'd tried so desperately hard to leave behind.

But as Andre's hand found hers, squeezing gently with reassurance and unspoken promise, she remembered something Mother Heady had told her just weeks ago while helping her pack for Greece: "God don't waste nothing, baby. Not your pain, not your past, not even the people who hurt you. He recycles it all into purpose. Especially the pain. Always the pain."

Maybe this wasn't an ending to her redemption story.

Maybe it was just the beginning of someone else's.

Maybe being the Extraordinary Only Lady meant extending the same grace she'd received to the people who needed it most—even when they showed up covered in blood on your doorstep.

The three of them stood frozen in tableau—the successful designer and her pastor husband facing the broken sister who represented everything they'd overcome. The driver still had his weapon drawn. The mansion stood behind them, symbol of everything Trange' had built. And ahead of them lay a choice: close the door on the past or open it wide and trust God with whatever walked through.

Trange' took a deep breath and squeezed Andre's hand back.

"Come inside, Lee Lee," she finally said. "Let's get you cleaned up."

www.ingramcontent.com/pod-product-compliance
Lightning Source LLC
Chambersburg PA
CBHW080742250626
47162CB00010B/2999